I Wanted To Murder For My Own Satisfaction

Published by Long Midnight Publishing, 2024

copyright © 2024 Douglas Lindsay

All rights reserved. No part of this publication may be reproduced or transmitted in any form or by any means without permission of the author.
Douglas Lindsay has asserted his right under the Copyright, Designs and Patents Act 1988 to be identified as the author of this work.
All the characters in this book are fictitious and any resemblance to actual persons, living or dead, is purely coincidental.

ISBN: 979-8300040284

www.douglaslindsay.com

By Douglas Lindsay

The DI Buchan Series:

Buchan
Painted In Blood
The Lonely And The Dead
A Long Day's Journey Into Death
We Were Not Innocent
The Last Great Detective
I Wanted To Murder For My Own Satisfaction

The DS Hutton Series

The Vikström Papers

The Barney Thomson Series

DCI Jericho

The DI Westphall Trilogy

Pereira & Bain

Others:

Lost in Juarez
Being For The Benefit Of Mr Kite!
A Room With No Natural Light
Ballad In Blue
These Are The Stories We Tell
Alice On The Shore

I WANTED TO MURDER FOR MY OWN SATISFACTION

DOUGLAS LINDSAY

LMP

For Kathryn

1

A Thursday morning in early October. Weather grey, no sign of rain. Something of autumn in the air, but it was the centre of the city, and the feeling was quickly evaporating.

Daylight not long upon the land, DI Alexander Buchan sitting in the Jigsaw Man's café. An Americano with hot milk, a pain aux raisin, a glass of orange juice, a glass of water.

No thoughts of the day ahead. There were a few cases passing across his desk, but it had been quiet enough in the last month that every member of his team had managed to catch up on training and courses. It was one of the bugbears of DCI Gilmour, the new head of Glasgow's Serious Crime Unit. Training and development was there for a reason. Everyone had to do it, and as head of a team, it was Buchan's job to be on top of his section.

Dull, they all thought it, yet in its way preferable to an abundance of major crime.

What had there been since the summer ended? The double-rapist McGinn. The continuing spiral of knife crime, some of which fell under their remit, much of which was dealt with at a local level. A squalid tax avoidance case, that had ended up including sex and bribery and extortion, all of it conducted behind the cover of a shirt and tie and a respectable place in the community.

He popped the last of the pastry into his mouth, and washed it down with coffee. Tapped his phone to check the time. Contemplated another coffee, then decided he would have it at the office, while standing at the window watching the river. Eventually work would begin, and perhaps a determination to get on with the day would come with it.

His phone pinged. Agnes Roth, in St. Andrews.

Morning! How's your day looking? East coast wind here. It's FREEZING! Got Christopher Marlowe at nine. xx

There was a picture attached, Agnes smiling over a cup of coffee.

Buchan replied, though as usual he did not reciprocate with

a photo.

*

'It's like the quiet part of an action movie,' said Sgt Kane.

She and Buchan were standing at the office window, looking down on the city, the rush hour on Clyde Street and the Broomielaw in full swing. The river was flat and dull, the tide full and edging towards the turn.

'Everyone hates those bits in action movies,' said Buchan after a few moments.

Kane nodded along, then took another drink.

'Depends on the script, I guess. Sometimes they work.'

'Really? Can you think of an example?'

'No, but I'm sure it must've happened at some point. Nevertheless, you kind of need them all the same. When you're full-on, non-stop action for two hours, there's something of an imbalance. Oh, I know, like when Gerard Butler and the US President are taking a break from killing bad guys in *London Has Fallen*, and they drink bottled water, and Butler says, 'I'm thirsty as fuck.'' She smiled. 'Now that's scriptwriting.'

'I missed that one,' said Buchan. He smiled a little more than he used to.

'Well, I just told you the best bit, so you can probably skip it. How's Agnes getting on?'

'Seems to be enjoying it so far. Currently reading Hemingway, Marlowe and Nabokov.'

'There's a combo.'

'I suppose it is.'

'She still coming home every weekend, or has she found someone her own age yet?' asked Kane, and she gave him a quick sideways glance just to make sure the joke had landed safely.

'Weirdly she keeps coming back to me,' said Buchan, drily. 'Must be my vivacious wit and good humour.'

'That'll be it,' said Kane.

They stood in silence, watching the morning come alive, the sound of car horns carrying across the river.

'Morning!' said Detective Constable Dawkins walking in behind them, and they turned and acknowledged her. 'You've got mail,' she added, placing a letter on Buchan's desk.

'Mail? Was it posted in the last century?' he said, and Kane laughed and said, 'Probably fan mail from someone who's seen you on TV, what with your natural vivaciousness and humour.'

The women shared the joke, and Buchan turned back to his view out over the river. Another drink, the coffee starting to get a little too cold, and then he nodded to himself, and accepted that it was time for the day to start.

'Let's get to it,' he said, although it wasn't really aimed at anyone other than himself.

'Boss,' said Kane.

*

He didn't pay much heed to the letter, not opening it until almost ten o'clock in the morning. Once opened, however, it got his attention, and after checking up on a few things, he walked up the stairs to speak to DCI Gilmour on the seventh floor.

2

Gilmour read the letter aloud, as though there was an audience there to hear it, or one watching on television. Her way of processing the information, making sure it stuck, Buchan assumed.

'I awoke one morning to unexpected omnipotence, though I did not know what to do with it. I thought it a strange burden. Did it now fall upon me to change society for the better? To save the Earth? Should I be a benevolent, or a vengeful Christ? I will admit I am yet to decide.

'I thought, nevertheless, that I would stick my toe in the water. A few well-chosen victims. That is, after all, what omnipotence truly means, is it not? Control over life and death. And so, you will find them scattered through the pages of the news these last few weeks.

'Did the teacher in Perth who died of a heart attack, deserve her fate? Some might say. Was her death an act of good or evil? As with most things, it depends upon to whom one listens. And we will find the same applies to the drug dealer in Dundee, the social care officer in Methil, the businessman in Oban.

'And so it has begun, and the world waits to see on which side of the wall it will fall. I feel something coming, though. I feel it in my bones, as sure as I feel this all-encompassing power that courses through my veins, a weight on my shoulders though it may prove to be.

'I will be in touch, inspector.'

She read it through again, this time silently, and then lifted her eyes.

Gilmour had been part of the team conducting an internal audit of the SCU earlier in the year. When the dust had settled, and Chief Inspector Liddell had been removed, Gilmour had been offered the opportunity to replace her, and had surprised everyone – those at SCU, her husband, herself – by accepting.

'You've looked into the deaths mentioned here?'

'Work in progress,' said Buchan. 'Some of it's pretty vague. Dead dealer aside, they weren't police matters. The teacher in Perth we know. She'd been accused of bullying and harassment. Two of her pupils had committed suicide in the past three years. She'd always protested her innocence, there'd been a couple of internal inquiries, she'd been cleared. And she died of an apparent heart attack. A post mortem was done, she fit the demographic in terms of age and health, there was nothing to suggest anything untoward.'

'And the others?'

'The businessman in Oban we're still trying to identify. The Dundee drug dealer's also a little vague. There are three options in the last two months. We're trying to pin it down. There was a social care officer in Methil who was killed in a car accident a couple of weeks ago. We're assuming this is who he's talking about. Still looking into it, but doesn't look like there's going to be a fatal accident inquiry. The driver of the car called the police, never left the scene. Said the woman had stepped out in front of his car, looking at her phone.' Buchan punched his left palm.

'That'll do it,' said Gilmour.

She looked at the letter again. Buchan waited, taking a glance over his shoulder at the window and the view across the river. He'd used to automatically stand there while talking to Liddell, but he hadn't yet reached that kind of familiarity with Gilmour.

'You said 'he' about the letter writer?'

'Just a matter of speech,' replied Buchan. 'There's nothing to suggest anything either way.'

'And no one else received one of these letters?'

'We made some calls. So far, it would appear not.'

She puffed out her cheeks, then let out a long breath.

'I'm guessing you won't like this any more than I do.'

'No,' he said. 'I have no idea who this is. Presumably someone who's seen me on the news at some point, although it must've been a while ago.'

She was reading the letter again, and she tapped a line near the end.

'This is bad,' she said. '*I feel something coming.*'

'Aye,' said Buchan. 'That's the warning shot.'

Her eyes ran over the letter one final time, then she held it forward for Buchan to take back.

'Nine hundred and ninety-nine times out of a thousand when you get these things,' she said, and didn't bother completing the sentence, as Buchan nodded along.

There was a good chance it was a joke. A very good chance. Nevertheless, Buchan's gut reaction was that it was authentic. They just had to hope that this was the skill of the person who'd sent it. That they could write a convincing, joke letter to the police.

'What else have you got on at the moment?'

'A few things. Mostly McGinn, and the Hardie case.'

She scowled at the mention of them.

'Neither of these are going anywhere right now. Give this whatever time you think it needs. Or deserves. Perhaps have Danny work with you, see if you can make any inroads. Keep me posted.'

'Ma'am.'

'Fingers crossed it comes to nothing.'

Buchan nodded and turned away.

3

Buchan stood beside the coffee machine for a moment, stared at it in contemplation, and then turned away without making anything for himself. He pulled a chair up beside Constable Cherry, who was typing on his laptop. Cherry finished a sentence, closed the laptop, and turned.

'How are we doing?' asked Buchan.

'Had a long chat with Sergeant Edelman in Whitfield. Think we've managed to narrow down our Dundee dealer. So, there've been no arrests for any of the three deaths. One of them, they're pretty sure was an in-house job. She said it'd been coming. There's some bullshit omertà crap going on – her words – like everyone's a suspect, and everyone knows who did it, but the guy's dead, and everyone's happy. No one's talking.'

'They have a particular suspect?'

'Seven or eight of them. Next guy, I'd seen that one on the news already. Bar fight. Guy was a veteran of nineteen arrests, seventeen convictions and not much prison time. He liked a fight, as did the guy who punched him and put him in hospital. Once in hospital, the victim had an aneurism, and,' and he ran a finger across his throat. 'This one's still with the procurator. Since the victim was the instigator, there's self defence to be thrown into the mix.' He glanced at his laptop as though it was still open and showing the information, then continued, 'Which leaves Marti McCulloch. Died of an overdose. Lived on his own, died on his own. He'd been on their radar of course, but they'd never had enough to absolutely pin anything on him.'

'I bet they hadn't,' muttered Buchan.

'He mainly dealt in cocaine. Toxicology says he'd been an infrequent user up until that point, he'd tried a new batch, and it had been bad. Really bad. If it had got out,' and he let out a low whistle.

'Maybe it was never going to get out,' said Buchan.

'Possibly.'

'He was the main guy?'

'Yep.'

'There's no way he was trialling every batch they got in to make sure it was OK.'

'Nope.'

'So why'd he do it this time?'

'I'm going to venture that that question hasn't even been asked. It's being viewed as a win. Drug dealer dead, a couple of hundred thousand worth of bad shit stopped before it hit the streets. Tick, tick.'

'How come whoever discovered the body didn't clear the place of drugs before they called the cops?'

'It was phoned in anonymously. The guy lived alone, feds went round there, there was nothing to suggest anyone else's involvement.'

'Seriously? And they haven't, I don't know, asked people? Done some sort of an investigation?'

'Well, I'd say they've certainly done some sort of an investigation, it just doesn't appear to have been particularly in-depth. Like I say, it's being seen as a win.'

They looked at each other for a moment, and then Buchan turned away, and stared out of the window.

Where was there for this to go at the moment? Was it worth his trouble driving to Dundee? Where else? Perth and Methil? That was a reasonable round-trip from Glasgow. The death in Oban was something of an outlier in terms of location.

First of all, however, he would get the letter checked out, for what that was worth. If the writer was playing a game, a throwaway attempt to mess with the police on a dull afternoon, then perhaps they would find something quickly. However, if it was as he suspected, and the letter was true to its evil intent, nothing would be revealed.

'Damn it,' he muttered. 'Send over what you've got on the Dundee case, then I'm going to head over there. I should stop in at Perth first. Give me those details as well. And dig up what you can on the Methil case, send it on, and I'll swing down there on the way home. And you're on this today, Danny. So any ideas, any leads, just run with them, give me a call if anything leaps out at you.'

'You want me to get the letter over to forensics?'

'I'm going to do that now. I'll speak to Ruth, and I'll get her to copy you in on anything that comes up.'

'Cool,' said Cherry. 'Thunderbirds are go.'

And he turned away from Buchan, and opened the

computer.

Buchan felt the burn of the letter in his pocket, wishing he'd been more careful when he'd opened it.

'You on top of today?' he asked Kane.

Kane took a moment to realise he was speaking to her, then turned away from her computer screen. She stared at him while she plucked his words out of the air, and then nodded.

'We're all good,' she said.

'Danny's with me on this letter. Just going to speak to Ruth.'

'K.'

Buchan turned away. The bad feeling in his gut wasn't going anywhere.

4

Meyers was sitting in her small office, leaning on her desk, reading the letter, a cup of coffee held in her right hand, though she hadn't lifted it in a while. Buchan was standing at the window waiting for her to finish. The forensics team was based on the other side of the building from Buchan, and the view here was a nothing view looking south, away from the river, where the tourists didn't come. Office buildings, and to their left, the Sheriff Court.

As frequently happened these days, he was thinking about Roth. She was always home by the time he got in on a Friday evening. Those evenings had become the best night of the week. The one he really looked forward to. A bottle of wine, the weekly download, the pleasure, the relief, the fun of seeing each other after four days. It had been so long since he'd felt like this, it still felt vaguely unnatural. His was a life of grim melancholy. Of assault and murder, wheeler-dealers and con artists, rapists and thugs. He was the gruff, middle-aged, joyless, seemingly soulless curmudgeon. And here he was, in love with a young woman, and his soul had been unearthed. And, despite everything, she appeared to be in love with him in return. Indeed, as she'd pointed out to him the one time they'd really talked about it, she'd started it.

And so he walked the thin line between succumbing to the pleasure, and the feeling that came with the world he inhabited, that something, at some point, would go wrong, because that's what happened.

'Interesting,' said Meyers, and Buchan immediately snapped from his reverie and turned.

'The letter, or the fact that I'm giving it my attention?' he said.

'The latter,' she said, smiling at Buchan's self-awareness.

She lifted her coffee and took a drink.

'Sure I can't get you one?' she said.

'It's OK,' said Buchan. 'What d'you think?'

'I think you get fifty of these a day.'

'Not in letter form, anymore,' he said, 'but that's fair.'

'So, what's the story?'

'It feels like something,' said Buchan.

Meyers held his gaze for a moment. She was not, of course, in a position to tell the inspector she wasn't interested, but there was more than enough respect between them for her to be able to let him know what she was thinking.

'This says someone with too much time on their hands, reads the local news from everywhere, and makes up a story.'

'Possibly,' said Buchan.

'You don't have much on at the moment,' she said.

'As you're aware.'

'What'd the chief think?'

'She's okayed me and Danny spending a day or two on it.'

'She doesn't want the bad press in case it comes to something.'

'Possibly.'

'But that doesn't really explain it, because we can't apply that logic to everything.'

'This is where the gut instinct comes in,' said Buchan.

'And the chief has the same thing?'

'Yep.'

'Hmm.'

She took another drink, then put her elbows on the table, clasped her hands and rested her chin, while she continued to look over the letter.

'I like how, when you came in, you handed me the letter without wearing gloves, holding it with a pair of tweezers, or you know, wearing an NBC suit. Any of the usual procedures.'

She looked at him, smiling, and he impassively stared back. Impassive on the verge of sheepish.

'I opened the letter without due regard,' he said. 'And not at a rush, either.'

'You didn't sense its importance from the outside, then?'

'You mock me, sergeant.'

'Yes,' said Meyers. 'You're right, inspector, I'll take a look, of course. You've got the envelope?'

Buchan reached into his pocket and, holding the envelope with the ends of his fingers, placed it on the desk.

'Anyone else touched either of them?'

'The envelope, likely many people. Ellie handed it to me, no one else since then. The letter, myself, Sam and the chief.'

'Sure you don't want to keep it to use as a napkin at lunch before you give it to me?' she asked drily, and Buchan nodded an acceptance of the mildly comic rebuke, and then turned away.

'Thanks, Ruth,' he said.

'I'll get to it now, let you know what we find,' said Meyers, and Buchan was gone.

5

'Got our man in Oban,' said Cherry, as Buchan returned to the office.

Something in Cherry's voice, and Kane gave him a curious look.

'Kristo Kivisaar,' said Cherry. 'Estonian. Had a small tech company, covering a multitude of apps. Hairdressing, plant swap, cleaning, massage. An app bundle for every need in life.'

'In Oban?' said Buchan.

'They're apps,' said Cherry, 'they operate in fifty-seven different countries. He just lived in Oban.'

'I just showed my age again, didn't I?' said Buchan, and Cherry laughed and said, 'Yes, you did, boss.'

'What was the thing?' asked Kane.

'What thing?'

'There was a thing in your voice when you said we'd got our man.'

'Right. Died of autoerotic asphyxiation,' said Cherry.

Buchan couldn't help the small eye roll.

'Haven't seen one of them in a while,' said Kane, letting out a low whistle.

'That's because you work in the Serious Crime Unit,' said Buchan. 'I can get you a transfer to the Idiot Unit if you'd prefer.'

'Ha.'

'Are they sure?' asked Buchan. 'I mean, are the local police sure? It wouldn't be the hardest thing to fake.'

'As sure as they can be,' said Cherry. 'I guess, like some of the others, a solution presents itself, and they've got no reason to make anything more of it. They're no less able to spend time on something that might be nothing in Oban, than anywhere else. He was unmarried, seemed to be a bit of a tech genius loner, but he had a couple of friends, and they both verified that it was a known sexual practice of his.'

'And I thought all you men talked about was sport,' said Kane.

13

'The friends were both women,' said Cherry, with a low-key gotcha tone, as though proving that yes, indeed, men do in fact only talk about sport, was a win.

'Sounds like over-sharing,' said Buchan.

'Whatever it is, there really doesn't sound like there's anything there for us,' said Cherry. 'The guy did the thing, messed up, and he died.'

'What was it about him that would've made our letter writer include him in a list of people who deserved what they had coming?' asked Buchan.

'A couple of the apps are very controversial. Suggestions that they're used by groomers. Haven't established yet if Tech is looking into them. Shall I take a look at it?'

'Sure, but as with all of this, don't dig too unnecessarily far down. Was his death reported in the media?'

'Yes, but not the details. Local businessman died, no suspicious circumstances,' said Cherry. 'That was about it.'

'Anything online?' asked Kane. 'There's bound to be a community for that kind of thing, isn't there?'

'Didn't check,' said Cherry. 'Would you like me to?'

Buchan thought about it for a moment, and then nodded.

'Give it a go, but really, again, don't go disappearing down endless rabbit holes of niche sex kinks. Give it half an hour, and if there's nothing doing, pull the plug.'

Cherry seemed to be considering something, but was in reality just trying to think of something funny to say, and when nothing came, he nodded and turned away.

'Right,' said Buchan to Kane, taking his car keys from the drawer. 'I'm hitting the road. We all good?'

'Boss,' said Kane, nodding, and Buchan said, 'Give me a shout if you find anything useful, Danny,' and Cherry said, 'Sir,' and Buchan headed for the door.

6

Sergeant Williams in Letham station in Perth had been dismissive. He'd been wary to start with, with the arrival of a senior detective inspector from Glasgow, and as the conversation had progressed, the wariness had given way to indifference, bordering on contempt. Buchan had elected not to disclose the reason for his suspicions about the death of Mary Logan. His vagueness hadn't helped.

Logan had been overweight, and had been on blood pressure medication for over ten years. She'd been everyone's definition of a heart attack waiting to happen. And then it had happened. There was no story.

She'd died alone in her house, and there was nothing to indicate there'd been anyone else present. Buchan had asked if they'd done any kind of investigation, and that had not helped the tone of the discussion. Scenes of crime officers had not been deployed to her house. On asking if he'd be able to see the house, Buchan had been informed that, as far as Williams knew, the place had already been cleared, as Logan's daughter readied it for sale.

'Way I hear it, daughter's as unpleasant as the mum,' he'd said.

And that was as far as Buchan had got.

*

Stuck in traffic, having left the A90 to come into Dundee, Buchan sent a short text to Roth asking if she was free for a quick chat. The phone rang a few seconds later.

'Hey,' she said. 'How are things?'

'I've got something on in Dundee,' he said. 'Just about there now. Cutting down to Methil straight after. You got time for coffee in a couple of hours maybe?'

'Oh, cool. I'm free all afternoon,' she said. 'Call by on your way to Methil if you can, no point going down there, then having to come back up.'

'Perfect,' said Buchan. 'I'll give you a shout when I'm crossing the river.'

'Oakie doakie!'

They ended the call. Buchan put the car in first, and crawled towards the traffic lights.

*

Buchan had arranged to meet Sergeant Beth Edelman at Marti McCulloch's house. They were standing in the front room, where McCulloch's body had been found on the sofa. The room, like the house, displayed all the hallmarks of someone with money, and no concept of how to usefully, or tastefully, spend it.

The room still smelled of death, which was strange, because the body had been removed eight days previously. Perhaps the room had smelled of death for years.

'My cat's called Edelman,' said Buchan, to break a short silence.

The sergeant looked at him a little curiously, and then smiled.

'That's nice,' she said.

'Just felt I had to get it out there,' said Buchan.

'You had to move past the fact I've got the same name as your cat,' she said.

He nodded. He didn't look at her. He'd felt a little stupid saying it. Should've kept his mouth shut.

'You must like American football,' said Edelman.

'My ex-wife,' he says.

'Nice you got to keep the cat.'

'There's always a bright side,' said Buchan, then he indicated the last resting place of McCulloch the drug dealer and said, 'Tell me.'

'It's out of hand around here, as you can imagine,' Edelman began. 'Drugs, dealers, import, distribution, users, deaths. It's all off the scale. With current staffing levels, if we had nineteen-seventies levels of drug crime, maybe we'd be able to cope. But this has spiralled and spiralled and we are so far behind. I won't say you wouldn't believe, because of course you'd believe.'

She glanced at him. He nodded, not looking at her, his eyes travelling around the room, getting the measure of the victim.

'This was obviously unusual. You get a feel for when these kinds of clowns might do this to themselves, and he was never one of them. If he'd been stabbed, no one would've been surprised. But it's not like we're dealing with intellectual giants here, so this is the kind of thing that can happen. A quiet night in, sitting on what he was sitting on, it's not like the guy's reading Steinbeck or Carl Sagan, contemplating the great issues of humanity. He's watching football, he's drinking, and he thinks, wonder whether this stuff is any good. Why not? He tries it, turns out it's not so good.'

'He's really that trusting of his supplier?'

She answered with a small shrug.

'What can I say? He'll have been getting the same shit from the same place for fifteen years. I'll bet he was exactly that trusting of his supplier.'

'This must've caused some ructions.'

'Not so's we've heard yet. We're still seeing the local aftermath play out.'

'The power vacuum.'

'Exactly. Once that's run its course, another couple of folk have had their throats slit, and a natural order has been established, then we'll see how it plays with the supplier. But let's not forget, these guys are East Fife, the suppliers are Real Madrid and Bayern. The new big shot in town ain't going to start complaining.'

'And the batch that killed McCulloch, it's been tested?'

'Sure. Heavy on the strychnine. Not unusual to find some of it in there, of course, but this was heavy with a capital H.'

'He took a big hit?'

'He did. Look, I know how it looks. It was odd. Definitely odd. There's a possibility the whole thing was planned, and it seems strange that, drunk or not, McCulloch decided to go for this. But this is where we are. There are no witnesses. There's no sign of anyone breaking in, no mention from McCulloch to any of his friends that he was seeing someone or expecting someone. No witnesses to anyone being in the vicinity of the house. No CCTV footage from hereabouts of anyone looking suspicious, or of them heading in McCulloch's direction. Nothing at all to indicate contact between McCulloch and *anyone*. There's also no reason to think the supplier would know McCulloch would even try the drug, so it really wasn't a hit job. We think one of his people came round to see him because he wasn't answering his calls, found him dead and panicked.

'It's a thing that happened, and that's just about all you can say of it with any certainty. There's nothing to suggest it was a murder attempt from anyone in-house or elsewhere, and I know DI Grainger looked into that. The drugs came in through the usual route, from the usual sources. Sure, it's not like we're getting statements from the people involved, but there's just nothing untoward here. From our perspective, it happened, a bad man is dead, let's enjoy the moment and wait and see who we have to deal with next, because in the grand scheme of things, ultimately it means nothing.'

'Hmm,' said Buchan.

What else had he been expecting? He'd read the report, after all.

He turned away, and walked to the window. A lace curtain, outside a grey street on a grey day, cars lining the road on both sides, turning it into a single lane.

'It feels like you have new information,' said Edelman to his back, and Buchan nodded without turning. 'Your constable was fishing a little, but didn't give me any detail.'

'I got a letter from someone potentially claiming responsibility,' and then he turned to see the look of slight surprise on her face.

'Was it signed?' she asked, and Buchan smiled.

'No, and it was so flimsy, so devoid of rationale or intent, so whimsical almost, that you'll think me foolish for even having travelled over here to ask questions.'

Her brow creased a little.

'But it mentioned McCulloch by name?'

'Not even that. It said a Dundee drug dealer.'

'Doesn't entirely narrow it down. We've had a few on our hands die recently.'

'My constable narrowed it down, decided McCulloch was the most likely. And here we are.'

'You have a copy of the letter with you?' asked Edelman.

Buchan had already thought it through, and he'd been prepared to lie. He had done, after all, in Perth. Edelman, however, instilled a feeling of trust in him. He lifted the photocopy from his pocket and passed it across.

Edelman took it, and read it quickly. Halfway through she shivered. Shook it off. Got to the end, handed the letter back to Buchan.

'Right,' she said.

'Gut instinct,' said Buchan.

'I get that. *I woke this morning with unexpected omnipotence*. Shit.'

'I know,' said Buchan. 'I mean, there's just something about it that hits in the right place.'

'You've shown it to CSI?'

'My forensics sergeant thought I was over-reacting. She'd have put it straight in the bin if I'd left it up to her.'

'Right. So you said you came through Perth, and you're on your way to Methil?' she asked, and Buchan nodded. 'How'd it go in Perth?'

'Let's just say I didn't feel able to share the contents of the letter,' said Buchan, and she laughed.

'Not sure I'll share it with DI Grainger either. To be honest, he really wouldn't want me to. He loves the phrase *half a thing*. He got it from some old TV show. *Don't come in here with half a thing*. That's his catchphrase.'

'This is less than half a thing,' said Buchan, and she nodded again. 'And now that you've read the less than half a thing, does it say anything to you? Remind you of anyone involved in the on-going drama around here?'

'No,' she said. 'Sorry. I mean, that opening line, it's part psychotic, part poetic, and I admit, poetry's pretty much a crime 'n all, but unfortunately not one we're able to prosecute.'

Buchan laughed.

'Right,' he said. 'You been around here a long time?'

'Used to be in Anstruther and then, well you know how it is, cutbacks and belt-tightening, and there went the sergeant position, and it was here or Kirkcaldy and I chose here.'

'Devil or the deep blue sea,' said Buchan, and he thought of the old Cab Calloway song as he said it, and she smiled and said, 'Pretty much.'

'You mind if I take a look around?' he asked.

'Yeah, sure,' said Edelman. 'Come on. You've got to see this guy's bedroom. Dear God.'

7

Roth read the letter a couple of times, the coffee cup moving to and from her lips. Outside, beyond the golf courses, the cold wind still blew in from the North Sea, the grey water choppy, the sky grim. There had been glorious sunshine for the Dunhill Masters the previous weekend, as though the good weather had managed to hang on at the whim of the golfing gods, but it had now given way to autumn. Still there was a typical buzz about the place, a town of students and tourists and golfers, as there usually was.

'Well, that's something,' she said, as she passed it back to him.

He shouldn't have been showing her the letter, but he continued to act as though she remained one of his staff, and he trusted her completely.

'What d'you think?'

'I get it,' she said. 'It's worth a look. If you were still chasing it this time next week, I might think you were practising work avoidance, but that's not really you, is it? How'd you get on with complete randoms in other stations who aren't as attuned to this kind of thing as you?'

'Short shrift in Perth, a helpful sergeant in Whitfield.'

'I guess that's how it's going to go.'

'You got any insight now that you're studying literature?' he asked, lifting his coffee as he said it.

'Oh, nice,' said Roth with a smile. 'Am I an expert witness?'

'That's exactly who you are,' said Buchan.

'OK, I'll take that. There might be literature professors questioning your use of a first-year student, barely one month into her course, as an expert, but let's run with it.' She took another drink, giving Buchan time to say, 'You read books, that's enough for me,' and she nodded and said, 'Right. Well, it's a nice bit of writing, so there's that. *I woke this morning with unexpected omnipotence.* I mean, that's striking. Has something of an old-fashioned feel. You can imagine it in Bulgakov or

20

some such, and I'm saying that, but to be honest, I've never actually read Bulgakov.'

'Wait, I thought you were an expert?'

'I am. Just not in Bulgakov. So, that grabs you from the off. And the style of course, the casual treatment of death. Also striking. The whole thing does kind of get the hairs standing on the back of your neck, you know? But what does it amount to? That, I'm not sure. There are so many options.'

'Which d'you think the most likely?'

'The guy's nuts, and I mean, like genuinely nuts,' and she made a circle at the side of her head, 'he reads the local news around the country, he finds out about all these deaths, he makes a list, he checks it twice, he writes a letter to the nice police officer he saw on TV once, telling him he's responsible because he's got *powers*. Thereafter, well, it depends how nuts he really is. Does he start adding to the death toll through his own actions? Does he continue to send letters based around random deaths occurring throughout the country? Has he ticked the box of low key-wasting-police-time, and off he goes to the next item on his list, and we never hear from him again?'

'Any possibility he actually killed these people?'

'I don't have enough information to make that call,' she said. 'Think you're going to have to answer that one. From what you said, all of the victims you know about so far might have had it coming. Or, at least, someone somewhere might've thought they had it coming. In which case, we're in a classic vigilante situation.'

'Hmm,' said Buchan.

He took another drink, lifted his apricot Danish pastry and took a bite, turning to look out of the window as he did so. She followed his gaze. Golfers, golfers everywhere, the grey October weather be damned.

'There is the other option,' said Roth, and Buchan raised his eyebrow a little at the smile on her face.

'No,' he said.

'Well, you never know. There's a hell of a lot of strange shit in the world.'

'Someone waking up a God transcends the strange shit,' said Buchan.

'I'm not sure it does. In fact, I think it might be the very essence of strange shit.'

'Let's hope if it ever happens,' said Buchan, 'the god in

question turns out to be benevolent.'

'Hey, you ain't read the Old Testament, or anything about the Greek and Roman gods. They were all assholes. No such thing as a benevolent god. And talking of which, how's Edelman?'

'He misses you. Mopes around the apartment all week, waiting for you to come home.'

Roth laughed, and they drank their coffee and finished their pastries, and outside the window the October day passed by on the east coast, bleak and grey and even.

8

There had been roadworks on the M80, so he'd sought to avoid them by crossing the Forth and coming home along the M8. The M8 was in gridlock around Bathgate, and so by the time he walked into his apartment it was nearly eight in the evening, and he was tired and grim and feeling like he'd wasted his day.

The sitting room was almost dark, illuminated by the last light of the day out west and the lights on the buildings across the river. Edelman was in position, curled up on the seat by the window. He lifted his head at Buchan's arrival, yawned, and then settled back into position. Buchan stood in silence for a moment, contemplated pouring himself a drink, and then walked through to the bedroom, got undressed, went into the en suite and set the shower running.

*

'So, I'm standing in the office of a detective constable in Methil. And the detective constable is reading the letter, and I realise I'd got this guy completely wrong.'

Buchan was by the window with a glass of white wine. He'd catch a slice of toast, a few pieces of cheddar, a couple of tomatoes. Two glasses of wine.

Edelman was sitting on the arm of the chair looking out on the river at night. He wasn't really listening. Behind them, the room illuminated by the lights beneath the kitchen cabinets, so they could see themselves in the window if they chose. Both Edelman and Buchan were looking through that, at the lights of the buildings across the river reflected in the water.

'The constable says, I'm sorry, sir, but seriously, what the fuck? Really? I mean, really?' He paused, took a sip of wine. 'And I'm standing there, and I'm the senior officer, I'm the grown-up in the room, and I'm the one showing off the spurious note from some time-wasting nutjob somewhere, and this kid – who makes Agnes look ancient – is looking at me like I'm a time-wasting idiot, and I didn't say anything because…' and the words momentarily ran out, and he waved them away, then he continued, 'And he says, really, sir, things must be quiet in Glasgow, but seriously, they are not quiet in Fife, and we don't have the time for this kind of, and he stopped himself saying *shit*, and I was going to get into an argument with him, or a discussion at least, then I thought, it doesn't matter, it's not going to go any different from anything else that's happened, and so I thanked him for his time and left.'

He took another drink. Outside the cold October night was still, the river a flat calm for the display of muted colours cast across it from the other side. In the air the sounds of the city, the low rumble, the quiet hum occasionally pierced by the sound of a siren or a distant car horn.

'And, you know what?' he said, and still Edelman paid him no attention. 'I left there and I thought, with absolute certainty, that the writer of this letter is going to be back. And he's going to write more, and at some point he's going to follow through. And Agnes was right. The first thing she said, the first possibility she gave. He's trawled the news, he's claiming deaths that would have happened anyway, but soon enough, he's going to add to the list. And that kid… he's never going to hear from me again, but he's going to realise he was wrong, and he's going to be waiting for the call. But we're going to have so much more to do.'

He lifted the glass again, hesitated, and then put it to his lips and finished it off. Finally Edelman gave him a glance, seemed just for a moment to nod in agreement, and then he turned back to the night, and the slow, unchanging drama outside the window.

9

A week had passed. Another Friday morning. Buchan sat in the Stand Alone café with his coffee and his pastry, and a small bircher from the chiller cabinet, something he'd taken to eating when he and Roth had travelled to Switzerland earlier in the year.

He'd looked at the news on his phone, but not for long. The never-ending wars were spreading, and the statesmen of the world were either helpless or hapless or profiteering, and so those wars were going nowhere, and it depressed him.

His own patch was quiet. There'd been a widely-reported gangland murder that previous Monday, but it had been an internal feud, and they'd had the suspect in custody before dawn on Tuesday. There remained plenty of work to be done to make sure the case was airtight, but they had their guy, and more than likely when the dust had settled, and his lawyer had managed to inflict the accused with common sense, a guilty plea would be made, and it would be relatively straightforward.

The Jigsaw Man was behind the counter chatting to the two baristas on duty, which was unusual. 'Keeping my hand in,' he'd said to Buchan, with a smile.

He took the last of the bircher, then pushed the small pot away, laying the spoon down beside it. Had another drink, pulled the Danish a little closer to him, staring out of the window while he gave himself another few moments. Raindrops ran down the glass, collecting in streams, racing to the bottom. He remembered sitting in the back of his parents' car, watching the rain on the window, creating races, making small bets with himself.

He shook away the reminiscence, lifted the Danish, took a bite.

His phone rang.

'Sam,' he said, putting the phone to his ear, dabbing the corners of his mouth with a napkin.

'Body in Tollcross Park,' said Kane, her voice with a familiar sense of urgency. 'You on your way already, or are you still in the café?'

'Still here, just leaving,' said Buchan, getting to his feet, forgetting the food, lifting the coffee. 'Wait for me, I'll cross the bridge. Two minutes.'

'Boss.'

She hung up. Buchan stopped at the door, glancing back into the shop. The Jigsaw Man recognised the sudden departure. They nodded, Buchan left at a pace.

*

Kane was driving one of the unmarked Polos. Screeched to a halt, blue light already going. Buchan got in quickly, coffee balanced between his legs, seat belt on, waited until Kane had accelerated into the busy early-morning traffic, blue light and siren going in the grey light of dawn, before taking another drink.

'Taking the motorway?' said Buchan, as Kane headed off in the wrong direction.

'It's brutal around the Green this morning,' she said.

Buchan drank his coffee, waiting for Kane to thread her way through the traffic before engaging. She would know little at this stage in any case.

'The day starts with a cliché,' said Kane, her voice more relaxed, a few minutes later, outside lane, lights and siren still going, ninety-five miles per hour.

'Male violence, leading to the death of a young woman,' said Buchan.

'Yes. From the report that came in, sexual assault, battery, murder.'

Buchan's face hardened, a low, unintelligible mutter beneath his breath.

'Are we so in the world of detective fiction that the corpse was found by a guy walking his dog?' asked Buchan, and the line felt cheap and stupid as he said it, though he knew Kane wouldn't care.

'Called in by a guy who's still on the scene. Don't know his story,' she said. Then a moment or two later she added, 'Don't know if there's a dog.'

'Whereabouts in the park?'

'Trees behind the swimming pool. Sounds like it's easy enough to block off, and we might be able to do it without actually closing the pool.'

'We'll decide when we get there,' said Buchan, and Kane nodded.

They drove on in silence, bar the loud swirl of the siren.

10

Buchan and Kane and Dr Donoghue, the pathologist, were standing together over the corpse. The morning had fully dawned, grey and damp. The rain had stopped, though it was still in the air, and would not be long in returning. In amongst the trees, where the murder had been committed, it remained dark. The park, bar the carpark and the swimming pool, had been cordoned off, the police presence large. The public were interested, but there was no view from anywhere of the action.

They were yet to identify the body. The woman had had short green hair. The way the body was lying they could see seven tattoos, though there were potentially more. Random, casual designs. A goat. A telephone. An umbrella. Many piercings on both ears. She still wore a short black skirt. Branches, inserted into either her anus or vagina, protruded. Her left cheek was pressed against the damp soil, showing the dark bruising on the right side of her face. Her throat had been slit. Both hands had been amputated and cast aside. There were marks on her wrists and ankles where she'd been harshly bound. The plastic ties the killer had used, now cut with a knife, had also been left behind, although only one of them was visible. The knife, too, had been left at the scene.

'I think I might have had enough,' said Donoghue out of nowhere, and both Buchan and Kane glanced at her. That had been unexpected.

'How d'you mean?' asked Buchan, though there was some sympathy in his voice. Seeing this kind of thing once in your career was enough, and this was not the first for any of them.

'Enough death,' said Donoghue. 'Enough of... *this*.'

'Would you like me to call someone else?' said Buchan, and she turned to him, her brow creased, surprised at the speed of the offer.

'No, of course not,' she said. 'But I think... I think I might be done soon. Really, I'm just... exhausted.'

She turned back to the corpse, took a long breath, and said, 'Come on, doctor, no point standing around,' then nodded vaguely in the direction of Buchan and Kane, pulled on the pair of gloves, and bent low over the corpse.

They watched her for a moment, they looked upon the body of the victim, and then they took a couple of paces away, and looked around. There was a man standing on the other side of the trees, head bowed, looking at his phone. Buchan could see the vacant expression, the bored flick of the thumb as he scrolled through social media.

'She was left where she was killed,' said Kane, and Buchan nodded without turning to face her. 'The killer's happy for us to find the scene of the murder, the bonds, the murder weapon. Everything. Here it all is, on a plate.'

'Stupid, or supremely confident,' said Buchan. 'Let's hope it's the former.'

'I know what you're thinking,' said Kane.

'We've been waiting for something from our phantom letter writer,' said Buchan, and Kane nodded.

'Except, of course, all we might get is another letter taking credit for something he didn't do.'

'If it happens,' said Buchan, 'we'll see how specific he is, though there was a general lack of specificity last time. It would be easy enough for him to prove his involvement if he wanted to.'

'If he's able to,' added Kane.

'Yep. Long way to go. You speak to the guys around here, I'm going to have a word with,' and he made a gesture towards the man on his phone, Kane nodded and turned away, and Buchan walked through the trees.

'Morning,' he said, approaching the guy.

A moment before he realised he'd been spoken to, then his head lifted, he looked a little surprised, and he slipped the phone into his pocket.

'Hey.'

Buchan smelled the alcohol from a couple of yards. He chose not to get any closer.

'Didn't catch your name,' said Buchan.

'Liam.'

'Just Liam?'

'Docherty. Liam Docherty.'

'What's the story, Mr Docherty?'

Docherty seemed a little disconcerted by Buchan's manner, then he finally pointed vaguely behind himself and said, 'Live over there. Top-floor flat, out on Tollcross Road, you know. Had to drive to work, and I'm like that, just don't be a muppet, man. At the pub last night, watching the Rangers. Hey, wanting them to get gubbed, before you get the wrong idea, you know. I was fucking hammered, man. Don't know what time I got in. Alarm goes off, ding-a-fucking-ling, and I'm lying there like that, you know. Like, you are fucking kidding me, man, I've been asleep for about five seconds. So I gets up and I stand in the shower, and then I makes myself a cup of coffee. You know, that really expensive Nescafe shit. Fuck man, it was on offer in Tesco, I cannae usually afford that. Like four spoonfuls of the stuff, man, coffee was thick as a bastard. So I drink that, and I'm thinking, I'm still steaming man. But I've got to drive to work, right? So, I'm thinking, I cannae be losing my licence, man, just cannae. So, I Google it, right? Fastest way to sober up. Have a shower. Drink coffee. Go for a walk in the fresh air. Fuck man, that was a' that was left. I comes out here, finds her dead 'n that, and I don't mean to be callous or nothing, but see that lassie in there, biggest stroke of luck you can imagine. Don't have to pull a sickie, don't even have to lie a little. I calls my boss and I says, police business, I'll be in when I can. So, now, by the time I've spoken to youse lot, chances are, you know, everything's gonnae be cool. I can drive to work 'n that. Had a bacon butty a wee while ago, that's gonnae help, right?'

'So, you were walking through the park, and what? She's pretty far inside those trees.'

'I was on my second lap, no, wait, third, third lap, had to take a pish. No one else around, but you know, I still wasn't going to stand in the middle of the path, right? I steps into the trees, and fuck me, she was right there. I mean, I wasn't about to pish on her or nuthin', but fuck me man, never seen anything like that in my life.'

'Did you still go?' asked Buchan, drily.

'Called the polis first, then stepped over there. I'd be careful if you walk into those trees looking for clues. Fuck it, man, everything's soaking anyway.'

'What time was this?'

''Bout half-seven.'

'And there was no one else around? Seems unlikely.'

'Aye, there were a few cunts in the park, but no one around here, you know.'

'Anyone suspicious?'

He stared at Buchan, and then laughed humourlessly.

'You mean, like they'd just murdered her? I mean, cunt's been dead way longer than this morning.'

'They would be returning to the scene of the crime. Hanging around, waiting to see when the police are notified. Wanting to appreciate the spectacle they've created. Perhaps even waiting to be interviewed by the police, so they can throw them off the scent or, more likely, just because they're going to enjoy it. Being this close, revelling in it, while the police have no reason to suspect them.'

'Ha. I suppose. Look at you, been watching the cop shows.'

Buchan stared blankly at him, but Liam Docherty's general good humour at being interviewed in a murder case wasn't going to be diminished by a harsh look from a detective.

'Nah, just the usual, you know. Guy walking his dog, another guy walking his dog, a woman walking her dog, some twenty-five-year-old dickhead out running.'

'You come into the park a lot?'

'First time this year, but I live right over there, man. See the fucking thing every day whether I like it or not.'

'So, you don't know what time you got home last night?'

He scratched his ear.

'One, maybe. Wasn't really paying attention, man.'

'You hear anything from the park, were you aware of anything?'

'Like someone getting murdered?' asked Docherty, amused again.

'Yes, like someone getting murdered,' said Buchan sharply.

'Aye, all right, man, keep your hair on,' said Docherty, taking a step back. 'Fine, OK. But like I says, I was pished. Fucking Stalingrad could've been going on in here I wouldnae a' noticed, man. Some wee snowflake lassie like that getting stabbed tae fuck? She could've been the bird out of *Psycho*, screaming her head aff.'

'Why'd you say snowflake? You know her?'

'Fuck no, but you see these wee cunts all over the place, right? Fucking Palestine that, and trans the next thing, and my pronouns are complete/twat. Fucking hate the lot of them.'

'You're basing that entirely on her having green hair?'

'Aye.'

'You don't know her?'

'Never seen her before in my life.'

That'll do, thought Buchan.

'Thanks,' he said. 'Don't go anywhere, we'll need to get a written statement.'

'Really? You mean, I cannae go to work?'

'Just using common sense, rather than a breathalyser, I can tell you're still about twenty times over the limit. Call your boss, tell him you won't be in…'

'Her.'

'Tell her you won't be in. Stick around, someone'll come to take a statement and get all your details shortly.'

'Fuck me, man, re-sult.'

Buchan gave Docherty's good humour another dismissive look, and then turned away and walked back towards Kane.

11

Buchan parked the Facel Vega on the street outside a row of new-build terraced houses in Shettleston. Turned off the engine, and sat for a moment, staring straight ahead.

'We all good?' asked Kane.

'Maybe just been infected with the doc's feeling of disillusionment.'

'I know,' said Kane. 'This life. You want something to happen to make it interesting, then you get what you asked for…'

'And we have to do this,' said Buchan, and he glanced at her, added, 'Come on,' they got out of the car, walked up the short path, and rang the doorbell.

*

Alan Conway was staring at the piece of furniture in the middle of the sitting room that might've been described as a coffee table. It was covered in stuff. A closed pizza box – the aroma in the air suggested it wasn't empty – a cereal bowl, a few sodden Rice Krispies in the bottom, three mugs, one glass, one crushed McEwan's can, a book of Sudoku puzzles. Buchan thought of Duncan the Pakistani priest, sitting at the bar in the Winter Moon, drinking beer.

It had been several weeks since Buchan had been to the bar. Now when he went, through habit or duty or something he didn't quite understand, it was as though he was out of synch, like a glitch in time meant he was half a second ahead of everyone else. The Winter Moon spoke of melancholy and loneliness, and Buchan no longer felt either.

He would go some evening the following week, he thought. See how Janey was doing, although she didn't seem particularly interested in him caring.

Conway was pale, though he'd been pale before they'd told him his girlfriend had been murdered. Kane had offered to make tea and he'd refused. And now they were in his sitting room, and he was on the sofa, staring at the pizza box, and Kane was in the chair across from him, and Buchan was standing at the window, watching two young guys outside who were eyeing up the Facel. Possibly admiring, possibly contemplating whether they could steal it.

'You didn't see her yesterday?' asked Kane, repeating the question she'd asked thirty seconds previously.

Conway lifted his head at last.

'Them,' he said.

'You didn't see Fin yesterday?' said Kane, without missing a beat.

'No. I was working all day, they were working all evening. Sometimes...' He swallowed. Kane realised he was likely to be sick at some point. Perhaps it would be better if he just got it over with. 'Sometimes I met them after work to walk them home.' Another long pause, and then, his voice small, he said, 'I didn't last night.'

'Why was that?'

He stared off into nothing. The two guys outside had wandered off, and Buchan turned back to the room. He had the same thought about the lad being sick that Kane had just had.

'They said not to bother,' said Conway, the words creeping reluctantly out into the world. There was grief to be faced, there were tears to be shed, there were people to tell, social media profiles to be updated, there was horror to be addressed, but first this. The awfulness of the police interview. And didn't the police always suspect those closest to the victim?

'Why?'

'They were working 'til eleven, maybe a bit later. I was knackered, and they said, really, it's fine, the way home's perfectly fine, don't worry about it.'

His voice started to break.

'What was the last contact you had?' asked Buchan from the window.

Conway didn't look at him, giving Kane the answer as though she'd asked the question.

'Text about half-ten. Just, you know, the usual.'

'What did they say?'

Something in his eyes, a realisation, and then he shook his head.

'You don't have to see it, do you?'

'What's the problem?'

He swallowed. Now he looked at Buchan, as though preferring to speak to a man on this matter.

'It was intimate,' he said.

'That's OK,' said Buchan. 'We don't need to see it. Intimacy aside, did they say anything about when they were leaving, what they were doing after work?'

'A little later than usual, going home, going to bed. Their shift starts at two this afternoon.'

His voice broke, and he couldn't hold back the tears. An ugly sound, loud, then his head twitched and he grimaced, and he quickly brought it under control.

'Sorry,' he said, his voice angry.

'That's OK,' said Kane. She gave him another few moments then said, 'Are you all right for us to continue? You're sure I can't get you something to drink?'

'It's fine,' he said, his lips set firm, eyes down, forcing himself through it. 'Tell me what they did to them.'

Kane didn't immediately answer, and he looked at her.

'Tell me.'

'We'll need you to come and identify the –'

'I know. Tell me.'

'Fin's throat had been slit.'

A loud swallow, he fought the contortions on his face.

'Is that all? Had they… had they been raped?'

'We don't know yet,' said Kane.

'How can you not know?'

'The body hasn't been examined,' she said, her voice as neutral as possible. 'That will be taking place at the moment. The inspector and I were at the scene of the crime, Fin's identification was made, we went to the supermarket, you were listed as Fin's next of kin, and here we are.'

'Their work knows?'

'The head of HR knows, and we asked that she tell no one else for the moment. Having spoken to you, we'll now go and speak to the night manager about Fin's shift yesterday evening.'

'You met Heather, then?'

'If you mean the head of HR, then yes.'

'You know her?' he asked.

'Well, no, we've never met her before.'

'Can't keep her mouth shut. If she knows, the entire store knows.'

Another tear blurted, and he sniffed and rubbed the back of

35

his hand across his face.

'Did she ever leave work with anyone from the store?' asked Buchan, and Conway turned to him, his face riddled with a thousand emotions.

'Can you not show some respect?' he said.

Buchan stared curiously at him, not understanding.

'They're dead,' snapped Conway. 'Is respect too much to ask of you lot?'

Buchan had an apology on his lips, but chose not to make it.

'Did they ever leave work with anyone from the store?' he asked instead, his voice level.

Another heavy breath, a straightening of his shoulders, then quick breaths through his nose.

Finally, 'I don't think so. They didn't really... they didn't, you know, they didn't have too many friends there. It was just work. Turn up, stock shelves, come home. Tell me what else.'

'What else?' asked Buchan. 'How d'you mean?'

'What else had they done to them? Tell me.' A pause, and then when he got nothing in reply he repeated, his voice raised, 'Tell me!'

Buchan felt hollow standing here, and didn't recognise the feeling. One of not wanting to be there. Maybe this was why he found Donoghue's words so affecting. She'd voiced exactly what he'd already been thinking.

'Far as we can tell they'd been sexually brutalised, but as the sergeant said, we don't have the results of the examination. They'd been bound, then their hands had been severed.'

The loud swallow from Conway, the look of horror on his face, and then he was up out of the sofa, his hand going to his mouth.

He didn't make it anywhere near the bathroom, the vomit exploding from him as he ran out of the sitting room.

They watched him as he stumbled over his own sick, and disappeared from view, the door to the toilet slamming shut a moment later, then they slowly turned and looked at each other.

A few moments of silence, during which Buchan sensed her rebuke.

'That went well,' said Kane, after another few moments.

12

A familiar scene, thought Buchan. You've seen it in the movies, you've seen it on TV.

The cadaver on the plinth. On one side, the pathologist, on the other, the detective. They were staring at the corpse.

Buchan and Kane had been to the supermarket. The night manager had come in. It was apparent that he'd hardly known Fin Markham. No one at the supermarket had been aware they were non-binary. Kane had felt the need to ask. The head of HR had looked confused. 'We have three non-binary members of staff, there's no stigma, there's no, you know, no *thing* here. Be who you want to be as long as you do your job. If Fin had been non-binary, this was a comfortable space for her to do that.'

'One of my staff identifies as a rabbit,' said the night manager, his voice flat. 'We have to call her Bunny.'

It was only the grim circumstances of their discussion that let them know he hadn't been joking.

They had accompanied Alan Conway to see Fin Markham's corpse. He had broken down in tears the instant the sheet had been pulled back from her face.

Kane was now taking him back to his house, while Buchan had remained in the examination room. They'd been standing in silence for a couple of minutes.

'You're not listening to the Beatles,' said Buchan out of nowhere, the realisation only just occurring to him.

'I stopped,' she said.

He raised his eyes, but Donoghue was still staring at the corpse. He wasn't sure how far she'd got with her examination, but she certainly wasn't doing it at that moment.

'You stopped?'

'Yes…'

Her voice trailed off, but there was more coming. He looked at her, then let his eyes drop.

'A few weeks ago. A young child had climbed onto the top of her parents' car. She was playing on the roof, her mum had told her to get down, but wasn't really paying attention. The

37

kid fell off. Landed on her head, on tarmac, died on the spot.'

'I saw the report,' said Buchan.

'The mum... the parents had been looking at their phones. At first the mum said she was getting directions, so there was *cause*. There was a reason she'd been ignoring her daughter climbing on the roof of the car. Ultimately she admitted she'd got distracted, looking at Twitter. X, whatever it is now. The dad was reading football updates.

'I had to examine the kid for signs of neglect, since there were no witnesses to confirm the parents' story, which was bad enough as it was. And I did confirm their story. Healthy kid, no sign of abuse. Parents fucked up, now they've got the rest of their lives to think about it.'

Buchan had a question or two about the case, but he didn't ask. It wasn't about the case anyway. It wasn't as though Donoghue hadn't previously had to examine corpses of the young.

'I was at home a few nights later. Nothing special. Some Chinese thing I threw in the microwave. I was eating dinner, reading a short Japanese novel one of my friends passed on, Sir Paul was playing in the background, and there was something niggling at the back of my head. A discomfort that had been there for a few days. Didn't know what it was. Then... you won't know *The Song We Were Singing*. McCartney, sometime in the nineties. Nice song. And it started playing, and the dead kid came into my head, like she was sitting at the table with me, because it'd been playing when I'd been carrying out the post mortem.' She swallowed. She still didn't look up. 'So I stopped listening to the Beatles in here. I think maybe I'll stop altogether for a while. I listened to Jean Sibelius last night while I ate dinner. You know Sibelius?'

'Agnes plays him sometimes.'

'I like Sibelius. I like the Finns, though I'm not sure why.' Another pause, but she wasn't done. 'And that was the niggle at the back of my head, and it really coalesced, sitting there, eating a Chinese thing, listening to Paul McCartney. I just don't want to be here anymore. I don't want...,' and she sighed and gestured along the naked corpse of Fin Markham. 'I don't want this. I've had enough.'

'Have you handed in your notice?'

She didn't immediately answer, then finally met his eyes for the first time since he'd re-entered the room.

'I did it while I was waiting for the cadaver to arrive. Apparently I have to give three months' notice in my grade. I thought about speaking to Heidi to see if that could be expedited, and I found out that Heidi left last month. The person to whom I now answer in this behemoth of a public service, doesn't even know who I am. I doubt they would look favourably on my request for exceptional circumstances, particularly since the circumstances are hardly exceptional. Pathologist tires of death. No one saw that coming.'

'What will you do?' asked Buchan.

Donoghue wasn't much older than he was. Far too early to retire, whether one could afford it or not, he thought.

'God,' she said, with familiar exasperation. 'I really don't know. Not this. Maybe I'll go and be a volunteer gardener at a National Trust property. Can you imagine? No responsibilities other than keeping the hedge in order and watering the pelargonia.'

'That's a plant?' said Buchan.

'Heathen,' she muttered. 'Come on, let's do the girl.'

'Careful, you might offend someone.'

He got another glance from her, and then Donoghue looked back at the corpse, a scowl on her face.

'Non-binary, was she?'

'Apparently. Far as anyone at the supermarket could tell, she was a woman.'

'Pathology concurs,' said Donoghue, then she made a small gesture, indicating the side of the head. 'Here, there's a nasty contusion. Blow from behind and the side. That would've been the start of it.' She mimicked the chopping movement of the attack. 'Didn't necessarily knock her out, but she's on her knees. Gag quickly wrapped around her head, you can see the marks here at the side of her mouth, and then knee in the back to hold her down, ties around her wrist, then her ankles, and then it was just going to have been a matter of time.'

'How much time?'

'Yet to make a full examination, but there was penetration. Whether that was post mortem or not, I don't yet know.'

'Did he ejaculate?'

'Yes. We got his semen, for what it's worth. Given how easy he's made it for us to gather all the evidence we usually need – DNA, murder weapon, crime scene – he's either an idiot or he knows, somehow, that he's immune.'

'The sergeant and I were saying the same thing.'

'I've already sent the sample off, and I'll take more in case this turns out to be the work of more than one man. I have a feeling, nevertheless, that it won't.'

'Vicious psychopaths tend to work alone,' observed Buchan quietly. Donoghue did not respond.

Silence returned, and began to deepen. What was it that was still holding him here?

'I should let you get on,' said Buchan, forcing the words out, although not immediately moving.

'Roger that, inspector. I'll be in touch, but seriously, whatever your expectations are, set them lower.'

Buchan nodded, kind of grimaced, and then turned away.

13

Mid-afternoon, the team assembled in the ops room. Buchan and Kane, constables Cherry and Dawkins, and Detective Constable Isobel Marks, who'd arrived, eventually, to replace Roth. Late twenties, private school educated, a confidence about her, but Buchan admired her clear thinking, her drive. Ambitious, it was apparent, but with a determination that nothing would be handed to her. She would get where she was going on merit.

'How are we all doing?' asked Buchan, taking a seat, looking around the table.

Nobody had anything particular to say, a few nods aside.

'OK,' said Buchan, 'so far we have, the victim is Fin Markham, aged twenty-two. Assigned female at birth. Declared herself non-binary two years ago. She was, as we've come to realise, quite selective with this. I'm not going to get into she, they, her, them whatever over this, and I don't want you to either. She called herself what she liked, so we'll do the same for now. Obviously, when speaking to friends and family, we must take care not to cause offence. In here, in this room, I don't care.' A pause, and then he added, 'Unless anyone else does,' and he looked around the table. A couple of definite no's, a couple of nods. 'OK. So, far as I know, she hadn't said to her parents about being non-binary, and she hadn't said to anyone at her place of work. She had said to her boyfriend, and a couple of her friends. Any others?'

'She was a member of the Democratic Green Party,' said Cherry. 'Served on their committee on non-binary and asexual rights.'

'It's not the regular Greens?'

'Nope, a splinter group. Broke away a couple of years ago, apparently. Don't have too many members, but they exist, and they claim to be getting bigger. Feels a little Peoples' Front of Judea to me, but I doubt they'll have a sense of humour about that.'

'You've spoken to them?' asked Buchan.

'Yes. And they are, I suspect, going to weaponize the hell

41

out of this. A member of the Democratic Green Party has been murdered. A non-binary person has been murdered. There's political capital to be had.'

Buchan had already known this would be coming. Virtually everything that arrived at the door of the police in the Internet age would become a political issue in someone's hands.

'So far,' said Buchan, 'I've got nothing that's actually going to do them any good on this front. Anyone else?'

No one had.

'They'll reach,' said Cherry. 'They're already doing it online.'

'Thanks for the heads up. Can you put together something for me on the kinds of things they're saying.'

'Boss,' said Cherry, nodding.

'Thanks.'

Buchan tapped the table, scanning his notes.

'Isobel, how's the friendship group looking?'

'It's been exhausting so far, but people are going to be who they're going to be. Everyone's crying. More than half of the people I spoke to are clearly already calculating their part in the drama of their friend being dead. What will they say on social media? How exactly will they signal their sadness to the world? How will they let the peoples of the earth know that they are also a victim?'

'Any genuine reactions amongst all that?' he asked, not wanting to linger on the whims of the youth of the world. They'd been there before, after all.

'One boy in particular. Has known her since school, works in a small bookshop on Ingram Street. Nice kid, but he was genuine. Raw. No phones, no calling anyone else, no questions about anyone else, or who knew, or whatever. By far the most interesting.'

'Any possibility he already knew she was dead?' asked Buchan, and Marks nodded at the roundabout way of asking the question.

'I don't know, but his reaction was far more of a tell than any of this fake emotional bullshit from people who you later find out hadn't spoken to her in six months, and would've struggled to remember her second name until ten minutes previously.'

'OK, that's good,' said Buchan. 'You'll put something together for me on everyone you've spoken to.'

'Will do, sir, and I'll keep at it. Still got a few to go.'

'What was the interesting kid's name?'

'Ben Holloway.'

'K, thanks. Ellie, you've been going through her social media?'

'Yep. I'm afraid we have a panoply. X, Insta, TikTok, Snapchat.'

'They all said she was a phone addict,' Marks chipped in, and everyone else nodded.

'And it shows,' said Dawkins. 'If we ever get hold of her phone, God, I hate to see the number of hours daily usage we're talking about. Ten, twelve, maybe more.'

Buchan snapped his fingers, and looked at Kane.

'We tracked the phone yet?'

'Nothing. Conway said he'd noticed this morning when he was trying to get hold of her, that her location wasn't showing on Snapchat. I'm going to guess the phone was dropped in the river or put in a fire or something.'

'The killer would've tried to crack it, if they'd had the skill,' said Dawkins. 'If they failed, they'd've got rid of it, and if they managed to get in – and maybe they extorted the code from her, or used facial recognition – they'd've searched it for anything they might find useful, and then they'd've got rid of it.'

'Any action on her bank accounts, credit cards?' asked Buchan, and Kane shook her head, then added, 'All quiet on the western front,' for good measure.

'Ellie,' he said, indicating for her to continue. 'You were saying about social media.'

'Of her time,' she said. 'A million comments on everything. Very outspoken. Abortion, winter fuel payments, renationalising the rail network, scrapping HS2, child benefit cap, non-doms, trans rights, Trump, independence, nuclear power, Just Stop Oil, Gaza, Lebanon, on and on. There wasn't a modern day leftist cause célèbre she hadn't picked up and used to beat someone over the head.'

'Oh, I love the sound of her,' said Kane, grimly, and Buchan gently tapped the table.

'And mixed in with all that, of course, were the selfies at dinner and the selfies with the boyfriend, and the selfies on the West Highland Way, and in Kelvingrove, and on the Falkirk Wheel and on the beach at Troon that one day the sun shone in August. We've seen this girl a thousand times. If I can be blunt, she thinks she's amazing, and insightful, and brilliant, and funny, and maybe she is, but if she is, she's one of a million who are doing the exact same thing.'

'Well, that's the modern way,' said Buchan.

'The trouble with it is,' said Kane, 'it extends the people who might've been interested in her, and who might have contacted her privately, to a huge number. In fact, in terms of police resources, it might as well be infinite.'

'She had favourites on these sites?' asked Buchan, and Dawkins nodded.

'She did. I'll put a list together of people we're going to need to talk to,' and Buchan nodded, and said, 'Thanks, Ellie,' and then he turned to Kane.

'Sergeant?'

'I've spent most of the day at the supermarket. This is a girl who lived much of her life online. She had no friends at work. She didn't ignore people, but she made no effort. One guy said he'd asked her out a few months ago, and she'd said no, and hadn't spoken to him since. He observed this as classic human behaviour. They'd been getting to know each other, he made a move, he was rejected, then she put the barriers up. Should've kept my mouth shut, he said.'

'Smart kid,' said Buchan.

'The guy was like fifty,' said Kane.

'Right. Anything off about him?'

'I don't think so. In fact, I'm going to rule him out right now. Very straightforward. Rueful, and more than a little upset she's been murdered.'

'You've got a write-up?'

'Nearly done.'

'K, thanks.'

Buchan looked through his notes, nodding to himself as he went.

'OK, people,' he said after a few moments. 'We're about on top of this as we can be at the moment. I'm afraid no one's leaping off the page, though I do want to pursue the boyfriend a little further. Speak to some of his friends, colleagues, et cetera.'

'I wasn't really getting the vibe,' said Kane.

'No, me neither.'

'But, you're right, start closest to home.'

Buchan let out a long sigh, then looked around the team.

'Ultimately,' he said, then he let the sentence go for a

moment.

'She could've been a warm body,' said Kane.

'Yes,' said Buchan, 'exactly. A warm body. Our perpetrator wanted to kill someone, and she was in the right place at the right time. For him, if not her. In which case, everything we do here, talking to the boyfriend and the work colleagues and the family and the political people, whoever else, it's all for nought, because this was entirely random.'

'And you're wondering if it's the guy who wrote the letter,' said Cherry.

'Yes, I am. I mean, ugly though that might be, whatever the situation is here, we have a brutal murderer on our hands, and if he's going to be sending us letters, that gives us a leg up. It's better than him not sending letters.'

He tapped the table again, deciding that they'd had enough introspection.

'Anyone got anything else at this stage?' he asked, and was greeted by negatives, and so he pushed his chair back and quickly got to his feet. 'Let's go then, folks. Another couple of hours, then leave it for the day.'

And the first of what they presumed would be many ops room meetings on the death of Fin Markham was done.

14

'She infected you?' asked Roth, watching him curiously across the table.

Buchan had just told her about Donoghue hitting the wall, struggling with it, and then handing in her notice. He hadn't included the detail about the McCartney song. Partly because he couldn't remember the name of it, but mostly because he didn't really think it was relevant. Her decision to leave wasn't about the Beatles, that had just been a way into the conversation.

'Maybe she did,' he said. 'Maybe it's just been the last couple of years. This job's not supposed to be about us, but there've been too many times when we've become part of the drama.'

'It's been all right the last few months though, right?'

Friday evening dinner. Saffron tagliatelle with spiced butter, accompanied by a Pouilly-Fumé. Bud Powell was playing, the volume low. Edelman was on the couch, having stirred briefly upon Buchan's arrival.

Edelman was very comfortable with the new living arrangements.

'It has, but I think we're probably all a little more worn out than we'd like to admit.'

'You're not all secret morning drinkers, are you?'

Buchan lifted his glass of wine and took a longer than usual drink.

'There's no secret. We take it in turns to provide vodka and doughnuts for breakfast.'

She smiled with him, silence briefly entered the conversation, and Bud Powell seemed to get a little louder.

'You can see it in Isobel,' said Buchan after a while. 'Only a few years on the force, newly qualified as a detective, there's just an indefinable something about her. Freshness, maybe. If you didn't know us, and you were to spend ten minutes with the group in the ops room, you'd easily guess she was the newbie, and she's older than Ellie and Danny, so it ain't age-related.'

'Yeah, I know. I still feel guilty sometimes.'

'Don't,' said Buchan, a little more forcefulness in his voice. 'You did the right thing, and the same goes for, well, anyone in the police, to be honest. It can be a lousy job. I mean, it's been slow the last couple of months, and then this comes along, and it's traumatising, and awful, and dehumanising, rips your guts out, and this is why we're here. To have this kind of thing happen.'

'Someone has to do it.'

'They do, but no one owes anyone the time. You do it for however long it suits you. And let's talk about something else, I feel like I'm talking myself into handing in my resignation.'

She smiled, she leaned across and squeezed his arm, a quick movement, retreated back across the table, lifted her wine.

'You were doing Hemingway today?' said Buchan, to abruptly change the subject.

'Could he write a love scene?' she said. 'That was the thrust of today's lecture.'

'Could he?'

'Dr Grey, for reasons unexplained, decided to sit on the fence. I guess he wants us to make up our own minds.'

'What d'you think?'

Roth put her hand to her chest, affecting an accent of pre-war drama.

'I love you, darling. Do you, darling? Yes, yes, I do, darling, you're so terribly important to me. But do you really, truly love me darling, the way I love you? Yes, darling, I do, I love you terribly.

'And repeat…'

He smiled along with her.

'Oh my God, he was so bad. I mean, don't get me wrong. The guy was writing in the nineteen-twenties, if you consider he wasn't so long after stuffy Victorian era whatever. His language is incredibly modern. His ideas, his directness, his brutality. It's magnificent. The guy is a thing for a reason. But he sucked at romantic dialogue.'

'I'll make sure not to read any of his love stories,' said Buchan.

'You never read anything by anyone ever,' said Roth, with a laugh.

'I'm on page seven of that Polish book you said I should read.'

'I gave you that a year and a half ago!'

47

'And so I'll be finished by the time I'm a hundred and ten. I'm still reading.'

'Funny.'

They shared the moment. Silence returned, the music filled the space. Dinner was eaten, the wine was drunk, the evening passed into night.

15

It was the first Saturday Buchan had worked in five weeks. Coffee and toast at home with Roth, Radio 3 playing Philip Glass and Hadda Brookes, Hans Zimmer and a Bach Oratorio – Roth observed that since the only Bach she ever listened to was the Christmas Oratorio, *all* his oratorios sounded like it was Christmas – and now he was walking along the Clyde, still to cross the river, on the way to the office.

A regular Saturday in October. The sound of the city quieter than during the week, the river dull, no traffic upon it, no home Old Firm game until the following day.

His thoughts were of Roth, as they regularly were at the moment. It would pass, he told himself. His brain would get used to it, get used to having this funny and wonderful woman in his life, and he wouldn't have to think about her so much. But for now, as he walked along the promenade, the sound of the city around him, he thought of her lying naked in bed. The curve of her hips, the way her breasts lay when she raised her arms above her head. The look in her eyes, the touch of her fingers on his skin.

He shivered.

His phone pinged loudly in his pocket, and he absent-mindedly took a look. It was from Eric on the front desk. **Unsure if you're in today. You wanted me to let you know when another letter arrived.**

He stopped, read it again, thought about replying then decided there was no need, Eric was hardly going to expect politeness, and then he walked on the short distance to the office building of SCU, thoughts of Roth gone, a new tension settling upon his shoulders.

*

Buchan stood at the window, a cup of coffee he didn't need in his hand, looking down on the river. Thinking through the implications, thinking through how the rest of the day would look. Kane was behind him, reading the letter, a third, then a fourth time. Hoping to find something Buchan might have missed, to have some useful insight that Buchan would absolutely not be expecting from her. No one was reading this and extracting anything from it, he thought. This was just a killer taunting the police, nothing more.

Indeed, not just taunting the police, but taunting him specifically. It was his name on the envelope, he who'd been selected for frontline mockery. He'd thought it the previous evening, though hadn't voiced it, when saying to Roth about how he and the team had too often been part of the narrative, when they really ought just to be on the outside looking in, keeping things in order and bringing people to justice when required. And now here he was again, once more brought into the story on the whim of a killer.

I confess, I did this without reason. I wanted to murder for my own satisfaction.

Knowing that I could kill people, knowing that I could fool the police, knowing that I could come after the self-righteous, the pious and the cruel, knowing that I could bring justice, felt good. It was not, however, enough.

What is the point of control over space/time and the peoples of the earth, control over life and death, if one is not to have a little fun. To experience joy. To feel the spill of warm blood across the fingers. To truly know the moment of dominion.

Perhaps the branches were too much? We fine-tune as we go.

The experiment continues.

Kane came and stood beside Buchan at the window, following his gaze down onto the river.

'It's something,' she said.

'What does that mean?'

'Twenty minutes ago we had nothing. Now we know that this, in the killer's mind, has been coming. We've already got an investigation open on him from last week, and now we've confirmed that, as we thought, the previous letter came from a man. Again, there's nothing obviously given up to us from this letter, but he's written to us twice now, and he won't stop. We have a channel of communication. It may be one-way, but this kind of guy will be watching the news, and we can make it two-way. We need to see if he's going to play. I'd say he seems keen. So, does it actually move us any closer to identifying him?

Not yet. But…'

'It's something,' said Buchan coldly, and Kane nodded.

'It is, and we need to start thinking about how we're going to use it.'

Buchan rubbed his chin, then the coffee cup drifted to his lips.

'I'll speak to Ruth again,' said Buchan. 'She was going to be –'

'She's in her office already,' said Kane. 'You think this nullifies everything we were doing on the life and times of Fin Markham?'

'I do. But just because we now have a connection between this murder, and some random deaths around Scotland in the last few weeks, it doesn't mean there's actually a connection, and it doesn't mean the person who killed Fin wasn't setting up the play, so we'd assume it's someone who didn't know her.'

'Agreed. We'll stay on it. I'll fill the others in as they arrive, but we'll stick to what we had planned for the day.'

Buchan drained the cup, nodded at Kane, nothing else to say, and walked quickly from the office.

16

He found Sgt Meyers in the canteen, a bacon roll and a cup of tea.

'I should go back to my desk,' she said on his arrival, already starting to get up, and Buchan said, 'It's fine. Eat. And read,' and he laid the letter, in a clear plastic envelope, on the table in front of her.

The bacon roll looked perfect, and he wondered why he didn't have them more often. A well-fired roll, the pieces of bacon protruding, dark and crispy.

He swallowed, and watched her face as she read the letter. A couple of involuntary twitches of her mouth, he saw her eyes go back to the start and reread it, and then she looked up.

'Dammit. Sorry I was so dismissive.'

'You did as you were asked in any case.'

'I'll take this away now, get it back to you asap. You already made copies?'

'Yes,' said Buchan, then he indicated the letter and said, 'What d'you think?'

'Seems even the gods aren't great with punctuation anymore,' she said glibly, and Buchan looked at the letter, upside down, with curiosity, and now that it had been pointed out to him, it leapt off the page.

'No question mark at the end of the *what is the point of control* sentence,' he said.

'Obviously he didn't get it proofread. And you never said anything public about the branches, so this confirms at least he's the killer.'

'Yes,' said Buchan. 'When that letter arrived last week, we thought there might be something coming, and now it's here. We're going to run with it,' and he tapped the letter as he said it.

'Roger that,' said Meyers, and then Buchan got to his feet and said, 'Eat, drink, don't rush. Give me a call when you've had a look,' then he was walking away as she took a large bite from the roll.

17

Not long after ten, in a butcher's shop on Tollcross Road. Buchan had asked Rachel Randall to step outside with him, to go somewhere away from her work, to have the conversation. Randall had insisted she didn't have time. She had half a pig to butcher in the next hour. Buchan could wait, or the conversation could be conducted in the cold back of the shop, while Randall took to the pale meat with a large cleaver.

There was something visceral about the setting that appealed to Buchan, and he'd agreed. A little hesitation when she'd asked him to put plastic covers on his shoes and head, but he was here now.

A raising of the blade, the loud crack as it struck the wood, cutting through the ribs in the process. In the air, the smell of raw meat.

'Talk me through it,' said Buchan, as Randall continued to work.

'Talk you through this?'

'No,' said Buchan, annoyance in his voice out of nowhere. 'Thursday night. Tell me what you saw.'

Another crack of the knife, and then she held a section of the ribs down, and began to make smaller, less forceful cuts between the bones.

'I was outside the King's Head. Had gone for a vape. Blueberry. God, if fourteen-year-old me could see me smoking blueberry, I'd've topped myself.'

'Just you?'

'Me and Janice and Kim.'

'How long had you been at the pub?'

'Kim wanted to watch the football. Janice and I were there for the gin cocktails. Maybe four hours. Maybe four and a half.'

She continued to vigorously separate the ribs.

'So, you, Janice and Kim were standing outside after four hours in the pub,' said Buchan. 'Go on.'

Randall paused, recognising something in Buchan's voice when he'd said *four hours in the pub*, then she cut round the edges of the ribs, suddenly her movements more careful and delicate.

'It was cold. They two bailed after about a minute, and I was going to join them, but it was quiet out there, you know. A few cars about, but otherwise, nice. Sky was clear. I mean, you ever been in the Highlands on a clear night? That is a lot of stars. Standing on a street in Glasgow, looking up between two tenements, with all that light pollution... not so much. But still, kind of beautiful, you know.

'And I'm just standing there, neck craning a bit, starting to hurt a little, I won't lie, and I hear the click-click-click of a girl in a pair of fuck-me shoes. I look round, and there's this wee stoater with green hair, and I'm like, wow, where did she come from?'

Buchan thought to himself how Randall might be stretching the definition of fuck-me shoes, but he wasn't going to interrupt.

'So, she's passing by, and I look back up at the sky, I don't look at her, and I say, see that bright star, blueish tinge, just to the left of the plough? She stops, but I still don't look at her, because I know she's looking. And I say, that's the Eurypides galaxy, more than seventy times the size of the Milky Way. Scientists think there could be as many as ten million habitable planets in that galaxy alone. *Ten million*. Makes you realise the chances of us being the only life in the universe are infinitesimally small.

'I still didn't look at her, but she's not walking off.'

'You're an amateur astronomer?' said Buchan, and Randall laughed.

'Professional bullshitter, as my dad says. See the stars, I have absolutely no clue. I've got trouble identifying the moon. There wasn't even a bluish planet next to the Plough. There might not even have been the Plough, I just made it all up. But you just look at the sky and say, look at that reddish star, that's a brown dwarf called M-74, and people think you're a genius.'

Buchan was of a mind to express some appreciation – this is Glasgow, he thought – but it wasn't the place.

Randall hauled another large, unidentifiable piece of the pig onto the table, it was set in position, the cleaver was raised, and then brought down with another loud crack into the wood.

'She spoke to you?' asked Buchan.

'I finally had a wee look, and she's looking at me. I thought for a minute she might've seen through me – though, I'll let you in on a wee secret, when they know you're making it up, that works just as well, they appreciate the effort – then she says, it's beautiful. That was it. It's beautiful. And we look at each other, and you know what I realised?'

Buchan stared at her as she continued to butcher the haunch, waiting for the answer, until he accepted he was going to have to ask.

'What?'

'I didn't fancy her. Something about her, you know? I just thought, maybe the sex'll be decent, but she's probably going to want to read me poetry when we're done, and that's not worth it. I mean, to be honest, I'd let Margot Robbie read me the complete Shakespeare for a shag, but this lassie? I just thought, let it go.'

She stopped the movement of the cleaver, her head dipped, a slender strand of dark hair that had come loose from her headcap fell across her forehead, she stood in a pose that could have been captured in art and called *Introspection*, and then she turned to Buchan.

'I know I'm full of it, but this is going to live with me, like it or not. If I'd actually made a move, and she'd actually fallen for it…'

'You don't need to think like that,' said Buchan.

'How can I not?'

'She had a boyfriend, they were pretty serious. Green hair notwithstanding, going off for sex with a woman outside a pub was not who she was.'

'Oh. I mean, really?'

She didn't look like that had given her any relief.

'How'd it play out?' asked Buchan.

'We stood there for a moment, and I dried up. I'm just looking at her thinking, if I say one more word, she's about to start reciting *The Rime of the Ancient Mariner*, and it was low-key awkward for a second, because whether she was going to sleep with me or not, she knew fine well I'd been hitting on her, and now I wasn't, then she just kind of shrugged and walked on.'

She stared at Buchan, glanced at the meat, and then got back to work.

'You watched her walk away?'

'A bit wary at first, in case she looked round and saw me looking at her, but yeah, after she was like fifty yards away, something like that.'

'She went along Tollcross Road?'

'Yeah. Crossed the road at Wellshot, and then into the park. Then I went back inside as she was cutting to the left of the swimming pool.'

'So, the last you saw her, she was in the park, walking between the flowerbeds to the left of the swimming pool.'

'Yeah.'

'And she was still walking as you turned away, you didn't watch her until she was out of sight?'

'Nah, that was it. It was Baltic out there.'

She glanced up. Buchan was still looking at her expectantly.

'What?' she said.

'You know what's coming next, Rachel,' said Buchan.

'I'm not sure I do.'

'Was there anyone else around? Were there cars going by? Did anyone else pay any attention to her? A curtain twitched in a window, a car slowed on its way past.'

Randall was nodding.

'Yeah, fair enough, I see that. Reasonable question.'

'You hadn't thought about it before you called us?'

'Just thought I should tell you I'd seen her.'

'So, think about it now.'

'Yeah.'

She was still holding the cleaver, though her hands were now inactive. She scratched her chin with the top of her forearm.

'Couple of cars went by. Maybe, I don't know, four or five the entire time she was there. I mean, it's Tollcross Road, it's literally the New York of roads.'

'Never sleeps.'

'Exactly. Always something going on. Wait.'

She looked up again, something different in her eyes. A small awakening.

'Damn,' she said.

'Tell me.'

'There was a guy, you know. I mean, I just hadn't been thinking about it, and now that I say this, it seems super-obvious. Like, *super-obvious*, and you're going to start with your whole police spiel, you know. What height was he, and what did he look like, and what age was he, and who would play the guy in a movie? But really, it was just some guy in the distance, like a figure in the night, walking along. And the trouble with me saying this, is that it's more than likely it was just some guy out for a walk, and the next thing you know youse've got me in the witness box and I'm testifying that some bloke sitting there in handcuffs is the killer, and this guy could be completely innocent, and then ten years down the line I'm being sued for twenty-five million for my part in this guy's wrongful imprisonment, and that's if I haven't been murdered by one of his mates.'

'That escalated quickly,' Buchan couldn't stop himself saying.

'Sometimes you've got to think strategically.'

'Tell me about the guy.'

'There we go. That's what I'm talking about. I contact the police to try and be helpful, and boom, you come in here and basically ask me to make things up.'

'Dammit,' snapped Buchan. 'I'm not going to ask you to create a damned photofit. Just the basics. How far away was he? Where was he in relation to the girl? Anything at all remarkable about him? If you have no way to describe him other than as a shadowy, dark figure, then fine. Don't reach, don't make anything up. Just tell me what you saw.'

'OK, OK, keep your hair on.'

Buchan stared harshly, waited.

'He was over there, you know, other side of the road. Just a guy. Tallish, I guess, but that's all I've got. I mean, tall people are allowed to walk along the road, right?'

'Did he go into the park?'

Randall stared at him, and Buchan recognised that at last she was trying to recapture the moment.

'I'm going to say I don't know. I saw her in the park, he was heading in that direction, and I don't know if he went in after her.'

'It didn't occur to you he might be following her?'

Randall laughed ruefully.

'See? Five minutes ago you were saying, you don't need to feel bad, she was never going to sleep with you, and now you're like, you could've saved her if you'd gone after the guy.'

'No one's saying that. Just tell me what you remember.'

'I'm trying to!'

Deep breath.

'There was a guy, just a guy. I wasn't thinking anyone's

getting murdered. He was a guy walking along the street in the same direction as the girl.'

'Could he have been following her?'

'How do I know?'

'Had you noticed him before you started speaking to her?'

Randall stared hopelessly across the remains of the butchered pig, but Buchan could see she was thinking about it again.

'I don't... I don't think so. I was just out there, cold, thinking about my life choices. The green-haired girl comes along, we chatted, like hardly at all, then she walked off into the park. There was a guy coming along Tollcross Road. Just an average guy. Cold night, maybe he was wearing a beanie, but I can't think what colour it would've been. At that distance, those crappy streetlights, couldn't tell anyway. He was wearing a coat, but that's as much as I've got. Tallish, wearing a coat. Just some random grey, blue, green, nothing colour, you know? And then, last I looked... I don't know, I was looking at the girl. Maybe the guy was in the park by then, maybe he wasn't.' There was a pause, and then she made a small gesture and said, 'You mind letting me do my job now,' and Buchan stared across the pig and wondered if it was worth the effort to try and push her a little more.

'We'll need to get a statement,' he said.

'Why?'

'You're the last person known to have talked to her, and there's a fair shout that was only a few minutes before she was murdered. We're going to need a statement.'

Put so bluntly, it appeared to hit Randall once again, and the knife was stilled, and she stared at the table, leaning forward a little, her weight running through her arms.

'You need it *now*?' she said.

'I can take it if you've got the time to suspend what you're doing, or else you can go into your local station later, or come into town and one of my staff'll take care of it.'

Randall swallowed, then finally lifted her gaze.

'I don't have time now,' she said.

Whatever fight had been driving her before, had vanished with a snap of the fingers.

'You can go into the station along the road, or come into Carlton Court. What'll it be?'

'Wait, is this you getting me to hand myself in, then you'll arrest me?'

Buchan looked curiously at her, then accepted that people had every right to be suspicious of the police. He backed off, tried to remove the harshness from his voice.

'There'd be nothing to stop me doing that now if I thought it remotely appropriate. It's just a statement, that's all. Would appreciate it if you could do it this afternoon.'

'I can go along to the local at three.'

'Thanks,' said Buchan, 'I'll let them know you're coming.'

18

Buchan stood at the Facel for a moment, and then decided to take the short walk to the park before heading back to the station.

The day was classically Scottish, mid-October in all its bleakness. He came along the road, and stopped outside the King's Head, standing where he imagined Randall would've stood. Along to the right, out of sight and around the corner, the supermarket where Markham had worked. Away to the left, the park across the road.

He fitted Randall's narrative to the scene, and then he walked along the road, and turned into the park. It was fully open again, apart from the wooded area behind the swimming pool, which remained heavily taped off, with one officer on duty to ensure the integrity of the crime scene.

They were waiting for the final word from Meyers, and then the officer would be removed. There was not, at the moment, a huge amount of point in them being there, but once they were gone, people would come, because that was what they did.

The flowerbeds were well kept, but it was autumn in the rain and there wasn't an awful lot that could be done to save them on a day like this, and they looked bedraggled and sad. There was a woman walking a dog, another woman with a pram, a woman sitting on a park bench, hunched over, looking at her phone.

The officer on duty watched Buchan's approach. They didn't know each other, and Buchan reached into his pocket for his ID. A moment of wariness at the movement, then Constable Henry read the card, and straightened a little.

'Inspector,' he said.

He wasn't particularly dressed for the weather.

'Constable?'

'Blake Henry, sir.'

'How's it been?'

Something in Buchan's tone, easy-going, no threat, that

made the constable relax.

'It's wet, sir. Not many people about.'

'Anyone stop to speak to you?'

'Four so far. Two asking what it was about, two who knew. They asked how long I was going to be here.'

'You think they were wanting to take a look?'

'Hard to tell. One of them perhaps. Something about her. She seemed amused by my presence. It was like… like it was a competition she knew she'd win, because she would still want to take a look when we'd had to move on. I don't know, maybe I misread it. I reckon she might've been a true crime podcaster, but I didn't want to ask, in case she started telling me about it.'

Buchan couldn't stop the quiet laugh, though he didn't linger over it. The kid had a nice turn of phrase.

'Anyone taking an interest, but not taking the time to speak to you?'

Henry looked away across the park, what they could see of it from there, nodding to himself as he did so.

'I don't know, sir,' he said. 'It is what it is, you know? Pretty much everyone, in answer to your question. I'm an officer standing in the park in the rain, next to a lot of yellow warning tape. People are going to take an interest, and some of them are going to be surreptitious about it, and hardly any of them will actually take the time to come and speak to me, even in Glasgow, where most folk don't know when to shut up.'

Buchan couldn't help smiling. He liked Blake Henry.

'How long have you been on?' asked Buchan.

'Seems a long time now,' he said. 'Maybe a year. I'm off at one.'

Buchan couldn't help the glance at his watch. Eleven-thirty-seven.

'You'll have earned your lunch,' he said.

'Cup of tea I could kill for, sir,' he said.

'You'll have earned that, 'n all,' said Buchan, then he indicated that he was going to take a look at the scene, and Henry nodded, and Buchan dipped below the yellow tape.

*

He stood looking down at the mark on the ground where Markham's body had been left. There was nothing here for anyone now. Not him, not CSI, not the people who came afterwards, looking to carve their names into the stories of the dead.

You could stand here all day, inspector, he thought, and you will feel nothing. And if you did, if something came to you, what would it be? You think you're going to be able to latch on to the last essence of Fin Markham? That she'll speak to you? That you'll magically conjure something from the earth and the air? And if you did, if you felt anything at all, it would mean nothing, because it would be you who'd created it.

'That's not why I'm here,' he muttered to the woods, to himself.

He looked around, following the path through the trees where the body had been dragged. Speaking to Randall may ultimately have been a little disappointing, but it was at least a piece to fit into the narrative. They already had the place, and now they had the approximate time, assuming Markham had been grabbed in the park as she walked through.

The man Randall had described was of interest of course, and while they had only the most basic description, and this person could have been as innocent a player in the drama as Randall, they would at least be able to get what little they had out to the public. Ninety-nine-point-nine percent of them would ignore it, but it just took that one person with something to say to give them a breakthrough.

He let out a long sigh, he took another look around the crime scene, he felt the rain drip through the trees onto his head, and then he finally turned away.

*

'I realise this might ruin the cup of tea you'll get when you get home, but thought it might keep you going, son,' said Buchan, holding out the cup towards Constable Henry.

The constable looked surprised, then he smiled and took the tea.

'No, that's brilliant, sir, thanks. I drink about eight cups a day.'

'You need sugar?'

'Nope, we're good.'

Buchan nodded, had no desire to stand there basking in a fleeting moment of benevolence.

'How long have you been in?' he asked.

'The force?'

Buchan nodded.

'Just over two years.'

'You thought of the detective branch?'

He looked a little taken aback to be even having the conversation, then said, 'Told myself to give it three years, see where I was, see how it was going, and then start planning for what was next.'

'Smart kid,' said Buchan, then he handed him his card. A simple affair. Name, rank, telephone number. 'Give me a call if you ever decide to make the jump.'

Buchan nodded, and turned quickly away.

'Thank you, sir,' came behind him, the surprise still evident in his voice, and Buchan, his back turned, lifted a hand and waved an acknowledgement.

19

Donoghue was at her desk, in her small office along the corridor from the examination room. Buchan knocked, entered, found her staring out of the window, right index finger tapping softly on the arm of her chair.

'Hey,' he said. 'You got time for a chat?'

'Come on in, inspector,' she said. 'I'm not working today, so I've got as long as you need.'

He asked the question with a look, and she said, 'I wanted to be on top of the Markham file, but... well, I've done all I can today, and so I'm sitting here pondering whether to stop off at the Vue on my way home and watch *Megalopolis*, which is either magnificently awful, or just plain awful awful, depending on who you talk to.'

'That's a movie?' said Buchan with familiar gormlessness.

'Yes, inspector, glad to see you're keeping up with the modern arts. How's the investigation coming?'

'About where we'd except to be at this stage of the game. We've got a sighting of Fin Markham entering the park pinned to a few minutes before midnight. How does that tie in with time of death?'

'Liable to be pretty much bang on, I'd say, though obviously I can't be quite that specific. Was the perpetrator seen?'

'Someone was seen, but nothing to indicate he was the perpetrator, and the witness didn't have a description of him in any case.'

'That would've been just too big a break to get in the first two days,' she said, and Buchan nodded ruefully.

'So, have you got anything for us?' he asked.

'Yes, I do.'

She said it quite definitely, and then looked at him, her face expressionless, and Buchan immediately felt his heart sink, an invisible hand reaching in to squeeze his internal organs.

'Go on,' he said.

'As was indicated yesterday morning,' she said, 'there was

semen in the girl.'

'Yes. You were sure she'd been raped.'

'I was. The specimen was prioritised, and we have a partial report in already.'

'Unusually quick, but I appreciate it.'

'Wait until you hear,' she said, and Buchan made a small gesture for her to continue. 'I believe Markham was sexually assaulted with, perhaps, a sex toy, and if not a sex toy, I suppose any similar object. Repeatedly and forcefully thrust into her. Something that would've been much too large, even if she'd been in a position to enjoy it. So, not only would she have had terror, and horror, and helplessness, and shame at what was being done to her, it would've hurt.'

'So, how d'you know she wasn't raped?'

She swallowed, she pursed her lips, she held him there for a short moment, then, 'The semen wasn't human.'

One second, another, then Buchan, his stomach crawling, said, 'Tell me.'

'A jackal.'

'No.'

'Yes. The lab, naturally, called me up asking what the *fuck* was going on. I collected the sample, I packaged the sample, I sent the sample off. Unless it was molested en route, and really I don't know why or at what point that was happening, it arrived at the lab in Alloa, and those guys did their job. When I assured them that as far as I was concerned they had what I'd collected, they got back to work, they confirmed their initial findings, they dug deep, they established that this is the semen of the golden jackal.'

'Jesus, where did they get that?'

'I'll leave that to you. There are five zoos in the UK with jackals, so you might want to start there. It should be noted, and I will concede I had no idea, that jackals are spreading through Europe as the climate warms, and have been seen as far north as the Netherlands, and even Norway. It would appear being an island, as ever, is the only thing stopping them from coming to us. For now. Getting the semen of a jackal might be tricky, but getting hold of the jackal itself... perhaps not so much.'

'Is there any possibility it was the jackal...?' and he left the question, which he'd felt had to be asked, at that.

'There's no evidence of the woman being taken by a jackal. What we have here is someone, and we can no longer be quite so sure it was a man, getting hold of animal semen and squirting it, by some means, into the victim.'

'Why a jackal?'

'I don't know. A roundabout reference to *The Omen*, maybe?'

Buchan looked at her a little helplessly and said, 'What does that mean?'

'You really are a popular culture black hole, aren't you, inspector?'

'I like *Lord of the Rings*,' he said, and she lifted her eyes.

'The movie, *The Omen*?'

'No.'

'It's about the birth of the anti-Christ. The kid's adoptive father goes in search of the grave of the birth mother, and finds out it was a jackal. Far as I know Satan being born of a jackal isn't in the Bible, but again, you might want to check.'

'Jesus. That's what we need, bringing bloody religion into it.'

'Thought your man was already claiming omnipotence?' said Donoghue, and she couldn't help the small, dark smile.

'Perhaps, but there'd been no mention of religion.'

'You'd been hoping for a Thanos-type omnipotent being, then. All powerful, but not expecting to be worshiped?'

Buchan stared at her, once again not getting the reference, a little annoyed at her for making it, feeling she was mocking him.

'What I'm really hoping for is a plain, old, good-time psychopath. I can deal with that. I prefer it when they don't bring religion to the table.'

'I apologise, inspector, I have been unnecessarily flippant,' she said, picking up on his annoyance. 'I sent the report over ten minutes before you came in, so it'll be waiting for you back at the office. The main takeaway, regardless of what kind of semen the perpetrator used, was that we thought he was being bullish and carefree with his DNA, like he thought himself uncatchable, but that turns out not to be the case. He, or she, was likely just as careful as they needed to be.'

'So it seems,' said Buchan. A moment, then, 'Dammit,' crossed his lips, and he turned away, looking out of the window at the damp, near-empty carpark.

'And now, if you don't mind, I'm leaving,' said Donoghue. 'I'll be on the other end of a phone if there are further developments and you need me. And should I hear anything from my end, I'll give you a call.'

'Thanks, Mary.'

He was about to turn away, and then he remembered to try to be human before getting on with his day.

'How's the rest of your weekend looking?' he said. 'Right, the awful movie.'

'Yes, the awful movie. I'm going to pull the trigger and go there now. And then... I think I might start planning a train journey.'

'Yeah?' said Buchan as he walked to the door. 'I hear there's plenty of space on the 17:54 to Lanark most nights.'

Donoghue smiled, and made a gesture towards the door.

'You've got work to do, inspector. Give me a call if you need anything further.'

And Buchan was gone.

20

The rain had stopped, and Buchan hadn't felt like sitting in the office. Kane had joined him across the river, though not without objecting, and they were sitting on a bench beneath La Pasionaria, the statue to the International Brigade volunteers from Great Britain who'd fought in the Spanish Civil War.

'Why are we here again?' said Kane, aware she was sitting on a bench that was still damp.

'Just needed some air.'

'We have air,' said Kane, indicating their building across the water. 'Lots of air.'

'I needed fresh air,' said Buchan, and Kane started to say something about the air in the office being perfectly fresh, then decided not to bother.

'You heard from Ruth?' he asked, passing Kane a large sausage roll.

'Same as last time, I'm afraid. Our god is meticulous in not giving anything of himself away.'

She took a bite of sausage roll, she lifted her tea, she took a drink, she laid it down, she said, 'I thought you said this was coffee,' and Buchan said, 'No, tea, I thought that would be better with a sausage roll,' and Kane said, 'Oh,' and Buchan said, 'Would you have preferred coffee, sorry?' and she said, 'No, it's fine, it's just a bit weird when your brain's expecting something, and it gets something else,' and Buchan nodded, as he took his first bite.

'We're not getting the killer's DNA from Markham's corpse, by the way,' he said casually.

'Why? I thought…'

'The semen had been injected by some other means. Whatever she was raped by, penetrated by, it wasn't a penis.'

'Dammit. Did they get *anything* useful from the semen?'

'It was from a jackal.'

Kane had been about to take a bite of sausage roll, her mouth open, the pastry at her lips. She closed her mouth, she swallowed, she lowered the pastry without taking a bite.

'I would say you're making that up, but you wouldn't, would you?'

'No.'

'Jesus. That is grade-A *Omen* bullshit.' She took a breath, stared into the river, her gaze lost in the low waves, then said, 'God, I absolutely hate these assholes. Bad enough they want to kill someone. Bad enough they want to do it so brutally. But when they start adding in this kind of look-at-me, self-aggrandising bullshit. Oh my God.'

Her head twitched, she lifted the pastry, she took an angry bite.

'You got this at the Stand Alone?' she said through the mouthful, and he nodded, and she said, 'It's good. What are we doing with this?'

'There are five zoos in the UK with jackals. We need to call them, establish whether they've had any break-ins, or seeming break-outs of animals. Then there's also the possibility there's a market in jackal semen, as there's a market in everything, in which case we need to follow that route. We can hope that's how he got it, as that might allow us a way in, but let's not get too carried away. So far, and it's early days, he seems to have been meticulous. And there's also the possibility, however remote, that he just plain got hold of a jackal.'

'In Britain?'

'They've been seen as far north as the Netherlands. Hardly out of the question one, or more, found their way across. Or that someone brought one across out of badness or stupidity. And though there've been no sightings, most folk seeing a jackal in the wild are liable just to think it's an odd-looking fox, or in fact, just a regular fox. Nevertheless, since this clown appears to have been making some sort of *Omen*-related statement with this, presumably there was planning involved, rather than him stumbling across a random jackal in his back garden. And since having a jackal, and having jackal semen are hardly two and the same thing, I'm prepared to bet he bought the semen by some means, and since he won't want there to be receipts, it's going to have been on some underground market somewhere.'

'Which seems a lot of trouble to go to just for some dumb joke, or whatever this is.'

'Perhaps.'

'I'll get on it,' she said.

'Thanks,' said Buchan. 'You and Danny split the black

market, I'll get Isobel to get in touch with the zoos.'

'We've got a statement ready to go out on the witness who spoke to the victim, and the guy on Tollcross Road. Just waiting for the chief to confirm.'

'OK, good,' said Buchan.

The river was dark, the waves agitated, the wind starting to pick up. In the air, the feeling of more rain.

'This is nice 'n all,' said Kane, 'but if we're done, I think I'm going to head back to the office.'

'K,' said Buchan.

He could still smell the raw meat of the butchers, he still felt the ugly discomfort of the murder scene, and he still felt the strange fear that had come with Donoghue telling him about the jackal.

'I'm just going to finish this,' he said. 'See you back there.'

*

'Kind of a gut punch, isn't it?' said DCI Gilmour. A few hours later. Buchan nodded. That was exactly what it had been. 'It's another level of madness, it's another level of planning that's gone into it.'

'Yes.'

'You've looked into where he got the semen?'

'There's an underground market in animal semen, because of course there is. It's never crossed our path before, because there isn't an active one in this area. But there are pretty major operations working out of London, and we're speaking to the Met. This is where we run into the problem of it being a Saturday afternoon, and it's not like some guy's racing back to his desk because Scotland gets on the phone.'

'Quite. Well, we know our perp is a fan of the *Omen*, not that that narrows anything down.'

Perp. Oh well, thought Buchan, it was inevitable someone in the office would start using that particular abbreviation someday.

'Wait,' she said, 'I don't know this stuff. Maybe the movie got it from the Bible, in which case…'

'We checked. Jackals are mentioned seventeen times in the Bible, but there's nothing as it relates to that movie. The Bible has them as illustrators of fallen kingdoms, and desolation. The city had become the haunt of jackals, that kind of thing.'

'Of course, in the movie the mother is a jackal impregnated by Satan. Here we have a young woman made to look like she was raped by a jackal. It's…'

'Clumsy,' said Buchan.

'Exactly. So, do you think it means something specific, or do you think he's randomly throwing shit at the wall, and possibly not even caring if any of it sticks?'

'We're going with the latter,' said Buchan, 'but then, I have a very dim view of these people. I will never invest his actions with any intelligence or cunning.' A pause, and then, 'He's a psychotic asshole, and we need to get him before he does any more damage.'

'I agree. Would you say he's not done?'

'He's not done.'

'You think the next victim will be someone from the same community?'

'How d'you mean?'

She looked at him as though unsure he was being serious, long enough for him to feel the need to repeat himself.

'How d'you mean?'

'LGBTQ+,' said Gilmour.

Buchan continued to stare blankly across the desk, and then he shook his head, dragging himself into the conversation.

'I hadn't been going there,' he said.

'Really?'

'I hadn't seen that as a motive.'

'You don't look at the press or social media?'

'No, ma'am, I just do my job.'

She narrowed her eyes a little, then nodded, accepting the answer.

'Probably best. I appreciate that, inspector. Well, there are plenty of people going there. That this was an attack on her community, and they're all talking about it.'

'That'll be a surprise to her parents and her work colleagues, none of whom knew she considered herself non-binary.'

'Well, this is where we are.'

'He states in his note, I wanted to murder for my own satisfaction. We can't trust anything he says, but we're still working on the basis this was a random attack. Social media can say what it damn well pleases.'

'OK, let's see how it plays out. Perhaps, if you find

yourself in the unfortunate position of having a journalist's phone put in your face, you could try not to be so blunt.'

'I will be as bland as I can possibly be,' said Buchan drily.

'Thank you, inspector, as I will too when speaking to the media in… twenty-five minutes.'

'You're not mentioning the jackal?'

'Oh, don't you worry, I'm not going there. We're not giving the perp the pleasure of that just yet. I'm also not mentioning the letters either, but I was wondering about putting something out there, like a public reply to them, so we can speak to the guy. The killer.'

'Yes, we've thought of that. I don't want to reach, though. It has to be bland, just try to establish some sort of communication.'

'Yes, good.'

'We also need to get back onto the deaths he took credit for in his first letter. I still think the guy'll have looked at the news, and created a narrative that suited him, but we can't ignore it now. Last week, a few of the officers in other stations were looking at me like, what are you talking about?'

She was nodding.

'Right,' she said. 'Send me a list of names, and I'll get on it right now. The sooner the better. Once these letters are out there, the press are going to want to know what we did about them.'

'People will make what they can of it, as they always do, but I think we did what we could given the limited information available. There may be the odd constable in the odd station exaggerating just how seriously they took my approach, but let's not get into some stupid turf war.'

'Agreed. Thank you, inspector. Send me the names, keep me posted on anything that comes up,' she said, and she glanced at her watch then added, 'Particularly in the next twenty minutes,' and Buchan shared her rueful smile.

21

They made love slowly at first. Curtains open, lights off, the bedroom as ever illuminated by the lights of the buildings across the river.

Tender kisses across his back, Roth's fingers fluttering over his skin. Across his chest, and then down across his stomach, her fingers stopping for a moment, a gentle massage. He felt the anticipation, and then she moved down, across his pubic hair, and he gasped softly as her fingers touched his erection for the first time, then circled beneath it, and ran along his length until she felt the dampness at the end.

*

They lay in bed, staring at the patterns the lights of night made on the ceiling. It wasn't late. They would get up and eat something light, though they hadn't talked about it.

'You said you'd got another letter,' said Roth, her voice sudden in the quiet of the evening.

Buchan lay in silence for a moment. His mind had been empty, still enjoying the feeling of tired fulfilment.

The letter.

'Yes,' he said.

His mind had been so empty, that starting to think about it felt like winding a crank, forcing his brain to work.

'I wanted to murder for my own satisfaction. That was what he wrote.'

'Damn,' said Roth.

'Hmm.'

Silence returned. The window was open, letting in a little of the evening, so the silence was as usual, the silence of the city on a Saturday night. The low hum of traffic, the occasional car horn, the distant siren. But right outside their window, the river and the well-lit inactivity of Pacific Quay and the Science Museum, all was quiet.

'Dostoyevsky,' said Roth.

Buchan was still having to force himself to focus.

'Dostoyevsky?'

'It's a Dostoyevsky quote,' said Roth.

Buchan's eyes opened properly.

*

'Tell me,' he said.

They had toast, cheese, a few tomatoes, a little salad. A glass of Pouilly left over from the previous evening. Sitting at the small dining table, listening to Bud Powell again. She was reading the letter.

Coming home he'd decided he wouldn't talk about the case. Roth didn't need to know about it, and he would've been happy to let it go. Yet here they were.

'I don't think there's anything else here that relates to *Crime and Punishment*. I'm not familiar enough with any other Dostoyevsky to know if he's referenced them. You should probably run this by an actual literary scholar.'

'I might,' said Buchan, and she smiled at his tone, the implied distaste of literature.

'So, what's the story?' he asked.

'How d'you mean? I really, really like this wine by the way.'

'Yes,' said Buchan.

She lifted the bottle. The label was in French, and she read it as best she could with her standard grade language skills.

'You got this from the vintners?'

'Forty-one pounds,' he said, knowing what she was actually asking.

'Huh. Well, thank you. And far as my French goes, it says on the label, eat with cheese and toast.'

'I'll bet it does. What's *Crime and Punishment* about?'

'Oh, you know. There's a guy with no money, and he knows someone with money who doesn't do anything with it, and he thinks they're underserving, and he supposes to himself that if he kills her and takes the money, then he could do great things with it, thereby justifying the murder. Then he commits the murder, and he has to kill someone else in the process, and he doesn't steal much anyway, then he feels guilty for a thousand pages. It's the usual heavy Russian literature kind of thing. Not a fan. I crawled my way through that one in sixth year, and vowed to never go there again. You want me to look into it?'

'No, it's OK, thanks. I should get it done officially.'

'And properly,' added Roth. 'I don't really have the time to immerse myself in Fyodor.'

Buchan nodded, had nothing else to say on it. Took another drink, cut himself another piece of cheese.

'How's it looking anyway?' asked Roth.

'We don't have to talk about it.'

Buchan ate and drank, his gaze to the side, into the middle of nowhere, somewhere just above the river.

'Hmmm' said Roth. 'There's something about you. Are you thinking of following the doc into the great blue yonder? Hey, you could quit, and come and study something at St Andrews. We could take a term-time residence together.'

He smiled sadly, leant on the table, and rested his chin on his hands. One of those looks, one of those spaces in time that Hemingway would have filled with, 'I do love you so very much, darling,' but which neither Buchan nor Roth felt the need to.

'What is it you would have me study at my age?' said Buchan.

'At your age?' she said, laughing. 'God, you're not a hundred. You should watch *University Challenge*, there are always folk way older than you on.' She laughed again, thinking of something else. 'We were talking about it yesterday in the café, and Annie and Drake were like, you know, Annie says it's OK to pause the show to give yourself time to answer a question, because you're competing against the questions, not the genius kid from Jesus, Oxford, and if you don't pause, there are a tonne of things you don't get to answer because the geek got there first. And Drake's like, he was going crazy, I mean, like he got really mad. It was nuts. He says, if you stop the show you might as well Google the answer. You might as well Shazam the music round. He even used the phrase, if you pause the show, you're breaking the sacred bond between quiz show and viewer.'

Buchan was still at the stage in their relationship where he was happy to just sit and listen to Roth talk, he didn't really care what it was about. Maybe it would last. He had no idea, having never felt it before.

'Who won?'

'Honestly, they were stand up screaming at each other when I left. I mean, I don't care.'

'I've noticed you pause the show when you're watching,' said Buchan.

'I know.'

'You're happy to break the scared bond?' he said with a smile, and Roth laughed.

*

Later, lying in bed again. Past midnight.

'History,' said Roth into the darkness. 'You could study history. You'd be good at that. Analytical.'

Beneath the covers, Buchan reached out and squeezed her fingers. He didn't say anything, but he liked the idea.

22

'Sergeant Holmes, thanks for taking the time.'

'It's all good, inspector. I'd read about your murder up there, so when your call got passed on, I was happy to take it. I didn't get much detail other than what I read on the news. Tell me what's happening.'

Five minutes past nine on Sunday morning, Buchan on a video call with a sergeant at the Mct. Early thirties, Caribbean descent, the accent all London. Both men had coffee, the sergeant was also eating a frosted doughnut.

Buchan and Roth had eaten breakfast at seven, the radio playing, as they had split the online newspapers, and read what was being said about the murder investigation. The press didn't yet have word of the letters that'd been sent to Buchan, so that at least was positive. There was, after all, very rarely anything positive in the media once one of their cases started to get public attention.

The narrative had been decided, and every single news site was running with it. Fin Markham had been murdered because she'd been non-binary. It was an attack, it was being said, on every non-cis person in Scotland, and an illustration of how far Scotland still had to go to relieve itself of gender conformist barbarity. Or words to that effect.

They had shared what they'd read, but hadn't commented on it. They were on the same side, after all, discussion was liable just to get them annoyed. And there was always the possibility the news sites would turn out to be right. 'Stopped clocks and all that,' Roth had said ruefully.

'The victim was brutally sexually assaulted,' said Buchan, as Holmes bit into the doughnut. 'That was on top of having both of her hands cut off, and ultimately her throat slit.' Holmes winced, though that part he would likely already have read about. 'We found semen inside her, and there was an assumption at first she'd been raped. There were all the signs, and she'd been penetrated with thick branches afterwards, as though the killer had tried to despoil the evidence.'

Holmes took a drink, then lips closed, he ran his tongue over his teeth, laying the doughnut to the side, and Buchan recognised that Holmes had just realised he'd picked a bad time to have breakfast.

'Given I do what I do,' said Holmes, 'I presume this is about to get even uglier.'

'The semen of a jackal,' said Buchan.

'Jesus Christ, are you serious?' Holmes shook his head. 'Sorry, inspector, of course you're serious. Semen of a jackal. Tell me.'

'That's all we have. We've done some investigation of where he might've got that from, and as far as they can tell, none of the zoos in the UK which are home to jackals report their jackals having been molested. It would also, really, be pretty hard to molest a jackal without killing, or at least drugging it, and that hasn't happened. They're becoming more prevalent on the European continent, but we're assuming it's more likely he bought the goods.'

'Right, right.'

Holmes stared off to the side for a few moments, returned nodding.

'Top of my head, I can think of three possibilities.'

'Three? Damn, I thought there was one at most. We already checked the legal options in relation to the sale of animal products and came up empty.'

'I was assuming you had,' said Holmes, and he tapped the side of his head. 'I know of three illegal ops. Parlane, he's the big one. Parlane's dead, to be honest, but they keep the name. It may be illegal, but they're just like every other damn company trying to make a buck. Don't want to lose name recognition. Then we have the Albanians and the Ghanaians. The Ghanaians are pretty small. I can check them out for you in a couple of minutes, we've got someone in there. Need to be more careful with Parlane, but I might be able to get an answer. The Albanians are always trickier.'

'Albanians…'

'There are always Albanians. Leave it with me.'

'You're sure?'

'This is why we're here, inspector,' said Holmes with a smile. 'So, we have jackal semen, no more than what would've been seen as a single ejaculation?'

'That's correct.'

'I will get on it, and get back to you as quick as I can.'

'Appreciate it, sergeant.'

Holmes was lifting the doughnut with one hand, as he was leaning into the computer to end the call with the other.

Buchan stared at the picture on his computer screen for a moment, and then closed the laptop and pulled his notepad over, lifting a pen as he did so.

'Got a call, sir,' said Cherry from behind.

He was out of his seat, already reaching for his coat.

Buchan turned and looked at him. He didn't need to ask.

23

Buchan and Donoghue were standing with their backs to the small wood, and the tied-up corpse of Kieran Sledd. His killer had, at least, given him a lovely view to look out on once dawn had broken, although the Lord giveth and the Lord taketh away, so having given him the view, he'd then gouged out his eyes. Not to mention, killing him, of course, which would seriously have impacted his ability to appreciate the view, even if he'd still been in possession of his sight.

They were on the hill above Largs, at the top of a field, off to the right of the Haylie Brae as it sweeps down towards the town. Before them the firth of Clyde, Cumbrae, Bute and Arran layered against a pale blue sky; away to their right the hills of Argyll, the first dusting of snow on top; to their left the sweep of the mainland south, and the channel to the Irish Sea.

'I love it up here,' said Donoghue. 'Usually you just see it in passing, that brief glimpse as you're flying down the road. I think this is the first time I've actually stopped to enjoy it.'

Buchan had nothing to say. He hadn't been down this way often, and the last time he'd been in Largs they'd come along the coast road, through Weymss Bay.

'Then you get down into Largs, and it's just like any old town in Scotland, and the view's lost, and you're looking through the smeary rain at what you can see of Cumbrae, and you're sitting in the ferry queue wondering why it is you're going to Millport again.'

'I don't get that so much,' said Buchan. 'But you're right, it's nice up here. Could be in the Highlands.'

She sighed, she nodded, they shared a glance, an acceptance that there was work to be done, then they turned and looked back at the copse of beech trees directly behind them. Tied to one on the outside, no more than five yards away, Kieran Sledd. Naked. Eyes removed, brutally rather than surgically. A knife had been dragged across his stomach, slicing through the flesh. Gravity had not taken full effect, and neither had the killer taken the time to pull open the wound, and so the viscera were just poking at the gap, stopping short of spilling out. Beneath the wound, the body blood-soaked.

His genitals had been mutilated, though it was so bad it was hard to tell from first glance exactly what had been done to them. There was further bruising around his body.

'Torture,' said Buchan.

'Looks like it.'

Another few moments standing in near silence. The distant sound of cars on the road. A chill wind. The mournful cry of a gull.

'OK,' said Buchan, and he nodded to himself, took a last look at the victim, and then walked along the front of the trees to speak to Kane, who was discussing with a constable from Largs the extent of the perimeter to be established.

'Hey,' said Kane, turning away, the constable leaving her, and starting to call instructions to another couple of officers further up the hill.

Buchan nodded, but didn't say anything, then he couldn't stop himself turning away and looking out over the view.

'The doc have a time of death for us yet?' asked Kane.

'No,' said Buchan, 'she's just taking a look now. Guess it's going to be some time in the middle of the night, for what it's worth. We need to get the guy ID'd.'

'His name's Kieran Sledd,' said Kane. 'I recognise him.'

Buchan glanced curiously at her, then looked along the bank of trees to where Donoghue was now kneeling beside the corpse, masked and gloved, examining the wounds around the groin.

'Wife-beater. Case was high profile. Not sure there was any particular reason for it. Maybe someone at one of the papers knew his wife, and wanted to make something of it. The guy admitted guilt, he didn't really have much option, then he put on a show of remorse, weeping in court. The female judge gave him a two-year suspended sentence and told him to buy his wife flowers every now and again. She then clarified that, as I guess she knew she'd get a bit of kickback, to say she was being metaphorical. Just be kind, Mr Sledd, she said, and we need never see each other again.'

'Right,' said Buchan, nodding. 'That guy. I didn't recognise him.' He let out a long breath 'That opens up a world of possibility. You remember where the guy lived?'

'Ardrossan,' said Kane, nodding along the coast to their

81

left.

'We have our first port of call.'

'I'll get her address,' said Kane, knowing Buchan had been referring to Sledd's wife.

Kane had her phone in hand, but stopped short of making the call in order to have the other important part of the conversation first.

'Two brutal murders in three days,' she said. 'Are we assuming the same killer?'

Buchan had, of course, been thinking about that since the moment the call had come in. It made sense, regardless of the murders being thirty miles apart. It made sense given the country they lived in, where this kind of random brutal killer was a rarity.

'We'll see,' he said, nevertheless. 'There might be a specific reason this man's dead.'

'Nobody's going to be crying for him.'

'Exactly. If it's not his wife behind it, perhaps it's someone who cares about his wife. Someone who cares about all abused women, and decided it was time men were taught a lesson. If the courts aren't going to deal with them, we will. The brutalisation of the genitals certainly points to that. And if that's what it is, then what does that have to do with Fin Markham? She was just a girl going about her life, fringe politics and working in a supermarket.'

'Need to wait and see what the doc comes up with,' said Kane.

'Yep. You know if there were any threats made against Sledd while the trial was on-going, or in its aftermath?'

'Don't know. I'll call Ellie, get her to run a check.'

'K, thanks.'

He looked down over the firth once more, and then turned away and surveyed the scene. The perimeter was being established, although there was no sign of anyone taking an interest anyway, as the fields and the wood were away from the road, with no houses in the immediate vicinity. There was an ambulance and four police vehicles. Somewhere, away to their left, the sound of a helicopter, but he didn't think it was one of theirs.

'Where's the guy who found the body?' asked Buchan, and Kane made a gesture towards a man who was standing on the other side of the trees, leaning on a pole, a dog sitting obediently beside him.

'He looks happy,' said Buchan, and Kane laughed and said, 'I'll leave you to it.'

*

'Mr Hill?'

'I was going to be moving the sheep in here today,' said Hill.

He straightened up, but didn't alter the look on his face.

'We'll be out of your hair as quickly as possible. This area will be closed off for a few days, but once we've finished here today, if you want to move your livestock into the lower part of the field, that won't be an issue.'

Hill looked like he wanted to make some disgruntled comment about that, but then he hadn't been expecting to be able to use his field at all for the foreseeable future, and so he didn't say anything and just nodded grudgingly with his chin.

'You found the body?' said Buchan.

'Spirit found the body,' said Hill, indicating the dog. 'You'd better tell your pathologist he had a lick at the corpse before I got to him. Didn't you, you filthy mutt?'

The dog looked up at Hill, something human in his eyes, thought Buchan. And whatever emotion it was he was showing, it wasn't shame at having licked a fresh corpse.

'Where's the farmhouse?' asked Buchan.

'Farmhouse? Alright, grandad,' said Hill with a laugh. He was at least ten years older than Buchan. 'We live in Kilbirnie, big house just by the golf club. Can't miss it on the way down the road.'

'Who's we?'

'Margaret and me. Couple of the lads, Jamie and Ginger, they live in Largs, they're more hands-on now than me.'

'How come it was you who found the corpse?'

'Ginger's in Spain somewhere, Jamie was working 'til midnight, I said I'd do the sheep this morning. And here I am, not doing the sheep.'

'Was Jamie working near here until midnight?'

'Ha. Nah, not going to be that simple, grandad,' said Hill. 'He was way over by, seeing to the milking herd. Got a sick 'un.'

'There was a vet out?'

83

'There was. Lad said he left about eleven.'

'If you can give me the guy's name…'

'Not sure who it was. You can speak to Jamie.'

'He's working?'

'Got the day off. I gave your sergeant lassie his number already.'

'OK. The corpse aside, anything unusual about the area? Fences down, signs of a car being parked somewhere it shouldn't have been, something lying around that shouldn't have been there?'

Hill was shaking his head long before Buchan had finished talking.

'This place never changes. Just a couple of fields with a wood in the middle of 'em. Ain't nothing different about them this morning.'

'You didn't get the feeling for there being something wrong when you arrived?'

'Nah. Was just coming down here, checking Ginger had done a good job with the fencing before he buggered off to the sun, and then suddenly Spirit's sniffing the wind. I couldn't smell nothing, of course. I'm thinking, probably just someone cooking sausages fifteen miles away, he's a smart 'un, Spirit, and then he's running away to the wood, and he starts barking, and so's I go over there, and here we are, another couple of days behind schedule, just like that.'

24

Laura Sledd was leaning forward, elbow resting on her knee, forehead resting in her hand, her fingers pushing through her hair. There had been no tears.

She'd opened the door wearing large dark glasses. On learning the police were here to inform her of her husband's murder, rather than because someone had reported him for beating her again – despite the judge instructing him to be kind – she'd asked them in, removed the dark glasses, and offered to make them tea. They'd both refused.

'Will I have to come and identify the body?' she asked.

'We'd like you to,' said Kane, 'although we can find someone else to do that if you'd rather not.'

Her swallow was loud in the room. Buchan was standing at the window, his back turned to it and the grim estate outside.

'Yes,' she said. 'I should. I will.' She lifted her head, her face ashen, bar the ugly discolouring around her left eye. 'Only way I'll know he's really dead.'

She didn't say it with any bitterness.

'When was the last time you saw Kieran?'

'Yesterday. Lunchtime. He went to play golf. Then the four of them were going to get something to eat. Sometimes he's home by seven or eight, sometimes they go to the pub, and it's after midnight. I didn't hear from him, just presumed that's what they'd done.'

'He did this a lot?'

'Every Saturday. Golf, food, pub. Or no pub. Just depended what they felt like.'

'When did he do that?' asked Kane, indicating the mark on her face.

She stared at Kane, lips sealed.

'He can't harm you now, Laura,' said Kane.

'Hardly matters, does it?'

'Had there been any threats made against your husband?' asked Buchan, and the cold, grey eyes were turned towards him.

'There was a lot of mouthing off at him after the trial, but you know how these things are. He was the man, I was a woman, the judge was a woman. That stupid bitch and I got a lot more abuse than Kieran did, because that's what men do, right? They go after women. Softer target. Online, in person, hardly seems to matter.'

'He can't hurt you anymore,' said Kane again, and Laura Sledd snorted quietly, head shaking.

'Aye, no need to worry yourself, darlin', because literally every other man alive is a chivalrous cunt.'

'Who else?' asked Buchan harshness instantly in his tone.

'What does it matter?'

'Who else?' asked Kane, the question more gently delivered.

'When he felt like bringing the other three home for dessert he did it. Happy to share. And you think none of them'll be turning up now? None of them's married, they'll probably be thinking, nice house, free sex, decent tits, cook and a cleaner, I might just move in.'

'You don't have children?' said Kane.

What was she basing that on? Little more than that there just didn't seem to be children, that was all.

Laura Sledd shook her head, barely a movement, her eyes lowered.

'What's keeping you here?'

'Where else am I going to go?' she said, harshly, lifting her head.

'You own the house?'

'I'm going to have a mortgage coming out my literal arse, and how am I going to pay that working twenty hours a week at the optician?'

'You're not covered in the event of Kieran's death?'

They could see the idea cross her face. The opposite of the more common occurrence, the shadow passing across the face. This was the shadow being removed.

She looked away, thinking it over. She may have been acting – indeed in other circumstances, Buchan would automatically have assumed she was – but there was nothing about her to indicate deceit. This was her, seeing the light at the end of the tunnel for the first time.

'I don't know,' she said.

'You should look into it,' said Kane. 'And in the meantime, if you're worried any of these friends of Kieran's will come round here, make other arrangements. We can help.'

'What were you doing last night?' asked Buchan, and she lifted her head and looked at him, something in her face to suggest she didn't really understand the question. 'You were here late evening, midnight, early morning?'

The look of curiosity continued, and then broke on a choke that was part laughter part tears, and then again, and then she leaned forward, head shaking, then her head in her hands, and a sob, and when she finally looked up there was a strange, desperate smile on her face.

'Are you serious?'

Buchan didn't answer. He felt Kane's glance.

'OK,' said Laura Sledd, nodding her way out of her reaction. 'OK, you are serious. Shit. I was here. I was here, as I was instructed to be every Saturday. Sometimes Kieran would want sex, sometimes he'd bring them back and they'd all want sex, sometimes Kieran came in and he wouldn't even stick his head into the living room.' She looked at Kane, then back to Buchan, her shoulders straightening a little. 'You'd think those times might've been a bit of a relief, but he managed to make that awkward. Sometimes I'd follow him to bed and he'd be pissed off at me, because he wanted to be alone to fall asleep, and sometimes I wouldn't follow him to bed, and he'd accuse me of all sorts, staying up while he'd gone upstairs. He'd say I was watching porn and masturbating because he wasn't satisfying me, for example. A bit of projection going on there, I think. Or he'd accuse me of getting Ally or Reggie or Jimmy in, or all three of them, once he'd gone to bed.'

She was annoyed by the time she'd finished, albeit, she hadn't finished. Annoyed at her dead husband, annoyed at Buchan for asking the question.

'I was here. I was always here. I won't lie, when he didn't come home last night, I was relieved. I went to bed at midnight and waited. And I fell asleep waiting.'

'D'you know of anyone who might've wished to harm Kieran in retaliation for what he'd done to you?' asked Buchan, and she turned to him, her face with a further air of confusion.

'Who?'

'I don't know, that's why I'm asking.'

'No, I mean, like, who? Who would do that? I don't know anyone. I don't have any friends. He didn't want me having friends. I wasn't *allowed* friends.'

Buchan made the decision to stop asking. Her life had been awful. She'd made one break for freedom previously when the police had become involved thanks to a neighbour, but the fact that she'd been back here, living with the man who had hospitalised her more than once, told the tale. If these three other friends really were just as bad, then she would possibly never escape their orbit.

'Is it possible one of the three friends would have done it? Or all three of them?' asked Kane.

'Why would they?'

'Either in disgust at the way he treated you,' said Kane, then she talked on through the harsh laugh, and added, 'or because they wanted you for themselves.'

Another bitter laugh.

'Aye, sure, look at Jennifer fucking Lawrence over here, the guys are queuing up.' A pause, and then, 'No, I don't think so.'

'Did your husband have any tech we can look at?' asked Buchan, and Sledd turned to him. Suspicion returned.

'You mean steal?'

'A temporary measure while we search for evidence,' said Buchan, his voice as neutral as possible, not wishing to get into an argument with a widow.

'Well, if that's what you call it. Fine, I don't care. There's a laptop in the front room upstairs. He called it his office. There's a small, plain, blue notebook that's got all his passwords in it.'

'He didn't keep them securely online?'

'He liked to call himself old-school,' said Sledd. 'If you want to include treating women like shit, then I suppose he wasn't wrong.'

25

One of Sledd's three golfing buddies was at home, and Buchan and Kane stopped off to see him before splitting up and heading their separate ways. They had left Laura Sledd in the hands of a constable, while she packed a bag. The constable would take her to identify the body, and then help her make other plans. Buchan and Kane didn't discuss it, but neither thought she would stick to them. Her old life would beckon, the call of the familiar, and she would likely be back in her own home before nightfall.

The guy looked angry. No compassion, no despair, certainly no tears. Just annoyance.

'He was in a shit mood all day,' said Jimmy Hardcastle. 'His golf was pish. We were taking the mick. Don't think he had better than a double bogey all round. Then we went to that pizza place opposite the Co-Op, then 'Spoons. We all fucked off about ten.'

'When was the last time you saw him?'

He gave Kane the look he likely gave all women.

'I just said, about ten.'

'Specifically, what was the set up?' she persevered. 'You all went your separate ways? Someone went off with someone else? You walked to a point with Kieran, said goodbye, and he walked off up whatever street? Not the time, the situation,' she tagged on at the end.

'Reggie had already gone. Knackered for some reason. Just a big pussy, more than likely. Ally says I'm heading, man, and Kieran was like, aye, whatever, and I thought I might as well just go home masel' and watch *Match of the Day*. We walk out, I goes to get my car, I says you two want a lift, and that dickhead Ally says, after the amount you've been drinking, ya spanner, I don't think so, and I told him to get to fuck, and Kieran says fuck all, and away the two of them went. Presume they split at the end of Glasgow Street, but you'd have to ask Ally, 'cause I wasnae there.'

'What about Ally?' she said.

'What d'you mean?'

'You've got a tone. You don't like him?'
'Have you met him?'
'No.'
'He's a dickhead.'
'Why?'
'Fuck should I know? Bad parenting?'
He laughed.

'What is it about him that makes him a dickhead?' asked Kane, sticking with the line of questioning.

He let out an ugly sigh with accompanying head shake.

'He's just boring, man. Into every conspiracy theory on the planet. Stolen elections, NASA never went to the moon, the Pope was behind Rangers going out of business... I mean, whatever. Couple of drinks in him, and he's even worse. Had enough of that guy. Kieran liked him for some reason.'

'So, was Kieran usually as sullen as he was yesterday?'
'Naw.'
'You didn't ask him what was wrong?'

Hardcastle burst out laughing, an ugly, grim laugh.

'Fuck me. Seriously, have you met men, darlin'? Some polis officer you must be, eh?' He turned to Buchan and said, 'You're quiet. How shite are you that you leave it all to the bird?'

'Just answer the sergeant's questions, please.'

Eye roll. Head shake.

'No, I did not ask him how he was. Obviously, I'd usually give him a hug, maybe a bit of a back rub, you know what I mean? I'd stroke his forehead while I got him to tell me all his troubles. But yesterday, it didn't seem right, so we just talked about sport and that *Rings of Power* shite on Amazon.'

'You think it's possible,' continued Kane, 'that someone had threatened him, or someone had made an arrangement to see him last night, and it was preying on his mind?'

For the first time Hardcastle looked as though he considered he'd been asked a decent question. A look to the side, a twitch on his lips, a scowl.

Yes, thought Buchan, that made sense.

'What d'you think?' said Kane.

Hardcastle didn't look at her, but he shook his head.

'I don't know, but he was being a bit weird.'

'Had he said anything about needing to be somewhere, there being a time limit on the evening, anything like that?'

'Naw,' said Hardcastle, and they could immediately see the self-correction that happened in his head. 'Reggie said something about going back to Kieran's. We did that sometimes, say hello to Laura. Have a few drinks. She likes us going round there on a Saturday. And Kieran was like, no. That was it, just no. Cut him dead.' A pause, and then, 'Huh, dead. That's ironic.'

It's not really, thought Buchan.

26

Kane went to speak to the other two friends, Buchan headed back to town. First to speak to Donoghue, then back to the office to start marshalling the investigation.

Buchan walked into the morgue, and the silence, Donoghue with her head bowed over the cadaver. There were another two bodies to the far side of the lab, both beneath sheets, one much smaller than the other.

Buchan stood over Sledd's corpse, watching Donoghue at work. She had split the chest cavity open, the long cut coming down to meet the horizontal incision in his abdomen. The body with gouged-out eye sockets was already grotesque, even without the new, massive incision.

She was extracting a sample from the stomach. He watched for a few moments, then the smell became too much, and he turned away.

'Who are these two?' he asked.

'Mother and daughter, murder suicide.'

'You know why?'

'That's your job. Well it won't, obviously, be your job, inspector, it will be for one of your fellows. I just get to establish the precise cause of death, though I'd say the slit wrists probably did for the mum. Can we talk about Mr Sledd?'

Buchan turned back. Donoghue straightened up, turned away from the corpse, clipped a small cap onto a test tube, did the same to another, then she turned back to the corpse, and temporarily pushed the two sides of the chest back together, as though that made all the difference to the macabre sight of the corpse, or the stench of the innards.

'Tell me,' said Buchan.

'I don't have the order yet, that'll take a few more tests. His eyes obviously were cut out. Definitely still alive while that happened. And, at a guess, I'd say that happened first, once we get past the initial capture and trussing of the victim, however that was done. I also don't have that. Obviously he could have blind-folded our man while he went about terrorising him, but you can see the thought process in cutting out the eyes. Blindfold, you might be full of fear, but there's that hope at the back of your head. You'll get out, and, if you're a particular kind of person, you'll get your revenge. But you lose your eyes straight off the bat. That's ugly. That's painful, and there goes your most important sense, just like that. And then you have more pain and unseen terror. Psychologically, very good from your killer here.

'The genitals have been brutalised. The testicles beaten repeatedly. I can't associate, but I imagine that would have been excruciating. Ultimately, they would've been rendered useless, for what it's worth. You can decide if that was a statement of some sort. There's a lot of bruising elsewhere, and your killer knew what he was doing. Kidneys, lung, heart. He picked his spots. Several lacerations, as you can see. There's also a few in the back of his throat, and inside his mouth, where a knife was thrust in. I don't think it's a botched attempt to cut out the tongue, I think it was just done for badness. He was also brutally raped. Anally, obviously. Again, unsure by what. On first glance, I would've said it had been done in the familiar fashion of anal rape, but after yesterday, I think we may find the killer used a variety of other implements. It would've been very painful, and then the branches were used again, although I note they weren't left inserted this time.'

'Semen?'

'Yes. Don't ask. It's already been dispatched. If you're interested in my methods, I went there first just in case, and lo and behold.'

'You think we've got the same killer?'

Donoghue didn't answer immediately. Her head was down, staring at the corpse, and Buchan finally looked at her. She looked beaten, worse even than she had the previous day.

'I hope so,' she said. 'Perish the thought there's more than one psychopath out there acting like this.'

She looked up, and they held the mournful gaze across the cadaver.

'Yes,' said Buchan.

'They'll expedite it, and the first thing they're doing is testing against the other sample, so that should be straightforward. You'll be the first to know after me. Now, leave me, I have a long, long day ahead of me, and it isn't getting any better.'

'What happened to Sophie?' asked Buchan. 'It's not like you're the only one in the entire –'

'I foolishly agreed she could take a holiday, thinking things were pretty quiet around here. She's walking in the Ardennes.'

Another hopeless look, and then she waved Buchan away, and he turned and left.

27

Mid-afternoon, the team assembled in the ops room, going over the case. Doughnuts, burgers, more coffee. The room smelled of frustration and all the food groups.

On the wall, three large whiteboards filled with information. The only thing they had linking the two murders was the jackal semen. Given the initial narrow search window that had been requested, confirmation had come quickly. They had the same killer.

There was also a space on the board, still requiring a lot of detail, for the four people listed in the killer's initial letter, and the now more urgent investigation required of their deaths. Gilmour had done what she promised, and at last the right amount of manpower had been applied.

'If we include the four previous deaths,' said Constable Marks, 'then Sledd's death makes perfect sense. He was accused of something, he may have been found guilty, but he effectively got away with it. In fact, given that his wife returned to him, and he went straight back to treating her like he had done previously, he completely got away with it. It was like it'd never happened, which is where we are with the others. Except Fin Markham. An ordinary young woman, it seems. Unexceptional, unless there's something hidden from those who knew her.'

'She was no stranger to keeping a secret,' said Kane, having already referenced Markham's selectiveness in who she talked to about gender.

'Not a dark secret, though,' said Buchan. 'Not as far as we know. And even if there was one, what is it that connects her to Sledd?'

'They come from such different worlds, such different ends of the spectrum,' said Cherry.

'That applies to the four previous victims,' chipped in Marks.

'But the thing that connects them to Sledd, doesn't apply to Fin Markham,' said Buchan, and he shook his head, and Marks nodded, and said, 'Right, we're going in circles.'

'Yes,' said Buchan.

He blew out a long breath through puffed up cheeks, then lifted his coffee, took a drink, immediately set it back down.

'We can't forget it's early days,' he said. 'The press are going to be screaming, and God forbid this gets any worse –'

'It's going to get worse,' said Kane.

Buchan was about to respond with a glib, well, let's hope it's someone who's got it coming to them, but chose to keep his mouth shut. They could all think it, but vigilantes were no one's friend.

'Yes,' he said. 'Nevertheless, we can't rush headlong into anything, we can't let outside forces, the media, the chief constable, we can't let them control the narrative. It's day three, let's not get our heads down. Ellie, where are we on getting Sledd's phone records? We need to know if there was a reason he was in such a grim mood yesterday.'

'It's in motion,' said Dawkins. 'Sense of urgency or not, it's Sunday afternoon. Hopefully we'll manage to get something tomorrow.'

Buchan nodded, looking through his notes. Still waiting to hear from the Met, but he'd already sent them a message to say they'd had another murder, and once again the jackal semen had been found present.

He glanced at the clock above the door, then turned back to the team.

'One more thing,' he said. 'I'm going to put out a short message in the morning, a statement to the press, but really aimed at the killer. Short, vague, nothing much to it.'

'Interesting,' said Kane. 'What are you going to say?'

'Going to pick him up on his grammar,' said Buchan.

A couple of curious looks.

'The missing question mark?' said Marks.

Buchan nodded.

Kane stared across the desk, thinking about the letter, then she nodded.

'I like it,' she said. 'Taunting.'

'More or less. Let's see if it gets a reaction,' said Buchan. 'So, we all know what we're doing for now? Give it another two hours tops, then go home. No one works beyond five.'

Acknowledgement around the table, chairs were pushed back, the day continued.

28

Sunday evening, Buchan and Roth standing at the window looking out on the river at night. Edelman somewhere else in the apartment.

Dinner had been waiting for Buchan when he got home, the conversation about the case brief. He hadn't particularly wanted to talk about it.

He liked the rhythm of the weeks now, even when he had to work at the weekends. A few days on his own, a few days with Roth around. The best of both worlds, while he adjusted to the new reality of life with a partner. He never thought of the future and how that would look.

'How's Mary?' asked Roth, breaking a long, comfortable silence.

Buchan lifted what was left of his shot of pear schnapps, drained the glass, set it down on the small table behind him, then turned back to the river. Hands in pockets, focussing on trying not to slouch.

'She looks tired. Alienated. Like she's doing something grim and unfamiliar. Normally I'd say she needs a holiday, but she just needs her leaving date to come around. It's going to be a long three months.'

'She needs to play *Here Comes The Sun* on a loop for twelve weeks, see her through the madness.'

'I never said,' said Buchan. 'She stopped playing the Beatles.'

'Wow, really? That was one of the things that defined her. God, she hasn't gone all contemporary, has she? Like she's listening to Megan Thee Stallion or BTS?'

Buchan gave her half a curious glance, then said, 'No, she just said the job was ruining her appreciation of the Beatles.'

'That never happened before.'

'No, it didn't. Shows how awful she's feeling. So, when you go in there now, it's completely silent.' A beat, then he added, 'It's like a morgue,' and Roth gently nudged his ribs.

'She can reclaim the Beatles when she's quit, and she's spending her time doing whatever.'

'What d'you think that'll be?' asked Roth.

'She doesn't know. Just not counting the dead, that's all.'

Roth gave Buchan a quick glance, read something in the tone, but decided not to push it any further. They'd already talked about how he was feeling, and how much he was beginning to share Donoghue's burnout.

'Hey, you know what I hate about the Beatles,' she said.

Buchan smiled, recognising the deliberate change of subject.

'The hair? The moustaches?'

'I mean, I get they were a thing. I get they pushed music in new directions, they were innovative, they changed songwriting and albums, and were at the forefront of the great sweep of the cultural revolution,' she began.

'I'm looking forward to the but,' said Buchan, the smile still on his face.

'It's like the people who're curating their back catalogue, they treat everything they did with awe. It's like this deification. No acknowledgement of the fact that some of it… I mean, some of it's just not that great. It doesn't have to be, you know? You can acknowledge that, for example, *Let It Be* just isn't much of an album, and it's a really lousy movie, without taking away from the fact there's a couple of decent songs on there. And now we're getting these mammoth fiftieth anniversary editions of mundane solo albums from the seventies. They're the *Star Wars* of music.'

He glanced at her, the smile gone, but still enjoying her enthusiasm for the subject, happy to let the case go for the rest of the day.

'What does that mean?'

'They're taking the original product, plundering it for everything they can. At least with *Star Wars* they can make new stuff, even if they're endlessly filling gaps in the story that most people never cared to have filled. But the Beatles? There's no new product, apart from occasional solo records by the two old guys who are left, and no one's actually interested in that, so they focus on selling repackaged product from fifty and sixty years ago.'

'The two old guys who are left,' said Buchan, shaking his head. 'I'll pass your thoughts on to Mary tomorrow, let you know if she has a rebuttal.'

'Good luck with that,' said Roth, and she touched his arm, then they looked at each other, and Roth said, 'Right, inspector, come on, take me to bed or lose me forever.'

29

Buchan wrote the statement to be read on the morning news. Poking the bear. *We received a communication from someone claiming to be the killer of Fin Markham. Investigations are ongoing to establish the veracity of the letter, though doubt has been cast on its authenticity by a mistake in the text.*

*

'I think we got what you need,' said Sgt Holmes of the Metropolitan Police.

Eight-seventeen, Monday. Holmes was sitting at the same desk as the previous day. Today, rather than coffee, he had a huge transparent, plastic cup, a lid and a straw, with what looked like a rich, berry smoothie. At least, thought Buchan, he didn't slurp when he took a drink.

'Tell me,' said Buchan.

'So, look, there's one caveat here. I told you we had three options. We got a confirmed no from our man with the Ghanaians, so we can rule those guys out. We got a yes from Parlane's gang, and I've got something that might be useful for you. The caveat is we have nothing from the Albanians. So it could be the lead we have is the wrong one, and the guy went through the Balkan crowd, that's all.'

'I'll take what you've got,' said Buchan. There was a line about not being able to believe there was more than one person in the west of Scotland looking to purchase jackal semen, but how could you say anything about the modern world with any certainty? People did, and believed, anything and everything.

'So, there was a purchase made a week ago. Semen of a jackal, two hundred millilitres.'

Buchan stared at Holmes's impassive face, trying to visualise how much that would be, but that clearly wasn't how his brain worked.

'I checked for you,' said Holmes. 'You're looking at approximately six or seven individual ejaculation events worth.'

'Six or seven,' repeated Buchan.

'It was purchased through one of Parlane's underground sites, but I don't have those details. I also don't have the method by which it was paid for, but that's never going to get you anywhere anyway. I do have the mailbox to which it was delivered, however.'

Buchan found himself snapping his fingers, his shoulders straightening a little.

'That's good,' he said, and he pulled the notepad a little closer to him, pen already in hand. 'Tell me.'

'All-In Mailboxes, 57 Gordonstoun Road, Glasgow. It was delivered there last Tuesday morning. Signed for at eleven-fifty-seven.'

'Perfect,' said Buchan, writing out the details. 'D'you know if that was all the delivery included?'

'That was it. Plus, there've been no other deliveries made to the same mailbox from Parlane. We went back to the Ghanaians and ran that address by them, and they've never delivered anything there. Strong possibility that that's it for our guy.' He lifted his smoothie, took a long drink, set the cup back down, licked his lips as surreptitiously as he could manage, and added, 'At least in terms of illegal movement of animal products,' and Buchan was already beginning to move towards ending the call.

'Perfect, thanks, sergeant. I'll be in touch if there's anything else.'

The call was ended, and Buchan was up and out of his seat.

*

He put Cherry on the task of getting an emergency warrant to have the mailbox opened, and all the details of the owner of the box revealed to them. Not that they thought there'd be anything waiting in the box, it was the latter piece of information that would be more revealing.

Nevertheless, it wasn't something that was going to get Buchan too optimistic. The killer may well have forgotten a question mark, but otherwise he had been meticulous in not giving himself away. He would have known the police would identify the jackal semen, he would've known they would have a good chance of tracking it down. This was highly unlikely to lead to his door.

'People are regularly more stupid than we expect them to

be,' Cherry had said.

The storefront was no more than a fifteen-minute walk from the office, and as soon as he had the paperwork in hand – everything in relation to this investigation was being expedited – he left the building, and walked quickly along Clyde Street.

A cold, bright day, something of the season in the air again, though less of it than when he'd seen Roth off that morning, on her walk up to Queen Street station.

The All-In Mailboxes storefront was in between a laundrette and a bookies. Not a coffee shop in sight along this small stretch of road, just pubs, and charity shops, and boarded-up windows. He took in the surroundings, got the sure and certain feeling that this lead wasn't going to go anywhere, then he opened the door and entered.

There was a young woman leaning on the counter, looking at her phone. She took a moment, but didn't glance up until the door was closed, and Buchan was standing in front of her.

'Hey,' she said. Her accent was north American, which was unexpected. 'You look official,' she added. Her name badge said Sandy.

Buchan held out his ID and placed the warrant for the opening of the mailbox on the countertop.

Sandy leaned forward, letting out a low whistle, reading through the wording of the warrant. Buchan watched her eyes, deciding that she was in fact reading it, and not just staring blankly, stalling for time.

She got to the bottom of the page, turned it over to the other side, read the single paragraph that wrapped it up, then said, 'The Honourable William Strachan, KC.'

She pronounced Strachan *Straun*. Buchan didn't bother correcting her.

'Would you look at that,' she said, lifting her eyes to Buchan, then held his gaze as though deciding whether or not she could trust him.

'Can you give me the key to mailbox two-three-seven, please?' said Buchan, and she nodded and finally straightened up.

'I guess I can,' then she looked past him out onto the street. 'This seems like a pretty low-key raid, I guess you're not thinking you're going to find five hundred pounds of cocaine in there, right?'

Buchan glanced to the side, and the boxes set against the

wall. There were likely larger boxes located in the rear of the facility, but the ones out front – which included box two-three-seven – were not designed for anything other than a few pieces of mail.

'I think we all know there's not going to be five hundred pounds of cocaine,' he said.

She laughed lightly, then turned away to the key rack behind the counter.

'This set-up seems a little vulnerable,' said Buchan. 'You don't get any hassle along here?'

'Panic button beneath the counter. In fact, two panic buttons beneath the counter, and another beneath the shelf at the back there, another in the back room. Any hassle, the call goes out.'

'Nice to have that much faith in the police,' said Buchan, drily.

'Oh, no one has that much faith in the police. Neighbourhood protection racket basically. Those guys are pretty hot.'

She smiled, Buchan took the key from her, nodding ruefully.

'Thanks,' he said.

'Sure thing.'

He walked to the rows and columns of boxes, box two-three-seven on the far left, near the top. Light conversation aside, this could be the moment, he thought, even though he didn't truly believe. But, as Cherry had observed, people were often far more stupid than you imagined they'd be.

He opened the box. There, in front of him at head height, the long thin space with a single white envelope inside, turned face down.

Buchan studied it for a moment, made sure, insomuch as he could, that there was no boobytrap device attached to it, took out the pair of gloves he always kept in his pocket, slipped them on and then he lifted out the letter and turned it over. On the front, printed in black, the mailbox address, with a name above it.

DI Buchan.

He felt the prickle of fear on his spine. No, not fear. Anticipation.

They'd been worried about this guy being good, about him being perhaps a step or two ahead of the game. This indicated it was a lot more than that.

He thought of slipping the note into his pocket and taking it back to the station, but there was always the possibility he'd want to speak to Sandy again after he'd read it.

'You know when this was delivered?' he asked, as he took the small penknife from his pocket, and ran it along the envelope's edge, careful not to cut what was inside.

'Nah, sorry. I only do two days a week, so I can't really help you.'

'You read the warrant,' he said. 'You have to provide me with any and all materials that might assist in the execution of my duties.'

'Hey, I'm not hiding anything. I really don't know. We don't log customers' box usage. It's part of the deal, you know. So, there's nothing for me to check, and really, we get a lot of folks in and out here, present time excepted obviously, and I'm not keeping track of numbers.'

'What percentage of your customers are criminals, d'you think?' asked Buchan, and she laughed.

'I'm getting paid minimum wage, and no health insurance,' she said.

'This is Scotland, you don't need health insurance.'

'Hey, I've waited for over twenty hours in ER, my friend, and I beg to differ.'

He held her gaze for a moment, then turned back to the letter. Getting into a back and forth with anyone was rarely going to end well for him.

He took the small letter from the envelope.

A single piece of paper, a short, typed message.

I am everywhere.

I am everyone and everything.

All the animals of the earth, all the fishes of the sea.

I am the jackal, I am the butterfly, I am the raven, I am the snake.

I am Lord.

He read it over four times, then refolded the piece of paper, placed it back in the envelope, took an evidence bag from his pocket, envelope inside, and then put the bag back into his coat pocket.

He looked at the girl, wondering whether to say anything further. Whoever had left this letter had clearly thought through how the police would pursue the case, and it had likely been done several days in advance. They would not be back here.

'Can you let me see the details of the keyholder, and a list of names for whom the store will accept mail for this box?'

'Sure thing,' said Laurie. 'Already got it up on the screen, seeing as your official document was asking for it.'

She turned the screen round so that Buchan could take a look.

The information on the keyholder was non-existent. This was a place that really did thrive on confidentiality.

There was one name listed to receive mail to this address, and as he read it, she smiled at him.

'Seems like someone knew you were coming,' she said.

'Can you see if my name's been there since this box was established, or if there've been any changes recently?'

She moved the screen away from him again, her fingers flying rapidly, but briefly across the keyboard.

'The box was sold on a three-month lease five weeks ago. It was set up to receive mail to a single name, that was Baylock. No other name. Like, no title, no first name, just Baylock. Then five days ago that name was removed and replaced with the name Buchan. Again, just Buchan. I presume that's you, right?'

She looked up, a small teasing smile on her face. Having no idea what this was about, she was kind of enjoying herself, recognising in Buchan that he wasn't about to start berating her, or to take the warrant and attempt to far exceed the authority it had granted him.

'That name mean anything to you?' he asked.

'Baylock? Nah. Weird name, though, huh?'

'Can you make a note that I should be notified if any further mail arrives, please?' he asked, and he placed his card with his phone number on the counter.

She looked at him, she looked at the warrant which still lay where they'd left it on the counter, she started to read it again, quickly growing bored on the back of not really caring, and then said, 'Sure, no problem.'

Again she typed quickly, and then she decisively pressed the return key, and she looked at Buchan.

'All done.'

'Thanks,' he said. Then, acting on something Kane had said to him more than once about engaging with people, he said, 'What brings you to Glasgow?'

'Golf,' she says. 'Hoping to make the tour next year. Got the qualifying event in Florida next month. My coach says, spend a few months in Scotland. Play in the wind and the rain and on those courses. You'll get back here, and the greens'll take a little getting used to again, but boy, it'll feel like heaven. I wasn't convinced, but I thought I'd give it a go, then my sponsors pulled out and so I have to do this shit just to be able to eat, but you know, I love the golf. I mean, I love it. Florida ain't going to feel like heaven after this, not when I'm already here.'

Buchan turned and looked at the street outside. Cars parked, not much traffic. Away to their left the urgent tantrum of a car horn. Across the street, a boarded-up shop front next to a small key-cutting stall, and a bookies. In the doorway of the boarded-up shop a figure covered in damp newspapers and black plastic bags.

He turned back. She laughed.

'This afternoon I've got an invite down to Loch Lomond club, and the sun's going to be shining, at least for some of it. I'll take the wins. As for this… you should see whole areas of LA, my friend.'

'I'll give that a miss,' said Buchan. 'Thanks for your help.'

'You're welcome.'

He turned away, and walked back out into the only Glasgow he really knew.

30

Buchan had made copies of the letter and they were all sitting around the table in the ops room reading it for the first time. Kane and Dawkins on one side, Cherry and Marks on the other. Kane was reading it aloud to herself, her voice low, the words barely sitting on the edge of her lips. 'I am the jackal, I am the butterfly, I am the raven, I am the snake…'

No one commented. They read through it again, and a third time, Kane now silent.

'So he knew you were coming,' she said eventually. 'Which means he knew we'd identify the semen, we'd track down where it had come from, we'd get the mailbox address.'

'Logical rather than genius,' said Marks.

She had a formal way of putting things. Buchan nodded in agreement.

'So, is there anything specific to link these? Jackal, butterfly, raven, snake,' said Dawkins.

'I had a quick look on my phone as I walked back from there,' said Buchan, 'but couldn't see anything. Best guess is that he's just taken four animals, creatures, whatever, that can be seen as ominous in some way, or have become that through popular culture. Well, apart from the butterfly, I don't know what's going on there.'

'He may be pretty smart,' said Kane, 'but ultimately, he's just making shit up on a whim, throwing it at the wall, saying, look at me, look at my otherworldly, creepy-assed bullshit. I *hate* this guy.'

'Can you look into it, Ellie, please? These four creatures, see if there's anything specific, if they've ever all been used in the same context, in the arts, in history, or whatever. You may have to dig pretty deep.'

'On it,' she said.

'Oh, there was another thing,' said Buchan. 'The name he was using to receive mail to the box was Baylock. Mean anything to anyone?'

Blank faces around the table, Kane immediately shaking

her head. Cherry started tapping the desk, his right forefinger rapid-fire, brain working. Eyes closed, trying to pluck the reference out of the air. Tapping increasing in intensity, and then he snapped his fingers.

'Got it,' he said, eyes opening. '*The Omen* again. Billie Whitelaw, the demonic nanny character. Mrs Baylock.'

Kane was nodding, added, 'Good spot.'

'OK, I don't know it,' said Buchan, 'but we're getting a pattern here, then.'

'And the raven,' said Cherry. 'That's a general theme of the series. The ominous raven.'

Buchan was nodding.

'All right,' he said, 'that's decent. That's decent.' A moment, and then, 'Dammit, we're going to have to watch this movie, right?'

There were a couple of smiles, then Dawkins said, 'We could do it this afternoon, set up a screening in-house.'

'Nice try,' said Buchan.

'I'm not so sure,' said Cherry. 'I know that movie pretty well. No snakes, no butterflies. The methods of murder we've seen here, the desecration of the bodies, that's not taken from the movie. The butterfly could be *Silence of the Lambs*, maybe. I mean, that was a moth, but the imagery, the concept, is similar.'

'What are you thinking?'

'I think he's just hoovering up symbolism and motifs from popular culture, perhaps ancient culture, anything goes, and spewing it out there. Perhaps he's creating his own mythology.'

'I like that,' said Marks.

'Me too,' said Dawkins. 'In its way, you know, it's like *Harry Potter* or *Lord of the Rings*. Rowling didn't create giant spiders and wizards and centaurs and wands and magic and the rest, but she took popular themes, wove them together, and created her own magical world. Same with Tolkien and elves and dwarves and objects of power. Used popular myths, made them his own. Maybe this clown is doing the same thing. Picking and choosing what he sees as the best bits, creating his own mythology, as Danny says, and thinking it ultimately transcends popular culture.'

Buchan was nodding.

Kane and Marks started speaking at the same time, they both stopped, they both deferred, Kane said, 'On you go.'

'I was just going to say that it's not just popular culture, because Christianity's done exactly the same thing, whether it's the concept of resurrection from Osiris, or the timing of Christmas from the pagans. Throughout the last two millennia, they've taken popular themes, things that people would be familiar with. This guy absolutely wants us to fear, and so he does this. He brings snakes and jackals and ravens into play, and the butterfly of course is not on the face of it so sinister, but it's open to all sorts of interpretation.' She paused then added, 'I'm not sure we really need to watch *The Omen*, because I think he might be lifting from every cultural reference out there, but…'

'At least one of us should,' said Buchan, and he looked at Cherry.

'Monday night is movie night at my place,' said Cherry, smiling. 'I'll get the pizza in. You know, if anyone wants to come over.'

'I'm in,' said Dawkins, and Marks more tentatively nodded.

'What were you going to say?' said Buchan to Kane.

'I like this. Trying to understand our quarry is a step we have to take, but I don't think this guy is giving us anything. We might think he is, but if he's just hoovering up cultural references from all over the place, then part of that is making sure we have no idea what he's going to do next.'

'I agree,' said Buchan, 'but this sounds like he's used *The Omen* twice already, so let's at least take a look at it.'

'All this omnipotence crap,' said Cherry, 'you think the use of the movie is him pointing to a belief he's the anti-Christ?'

'Oh my God,' said Kane, shaking her head.

'Let's hope not,' said Buchan, 'though I'm not sure how it could make it any worse.'

He tapped the table, pushed the chair back, got to his feet.

'Right, back to what we were doing. I'll run this letter by the usual suspects, and we'll meet back here for the daily brief at three, emergencies notwithstanding.'

'Boss,' came a muttering or two, and they were on their way.

Walking back to the open-plan, Buchan checked his phone. A text from Roth.

Got as far as Edinburgh. Message arrived cancelling today's lecture/seminar with Dr Cairns. Thought I might as well come home. Let me know if you want dinner! x

Buchan felt that familiar lifting of his heart, which still seemed vaguely ridiculous, as though the very notion of him feeling affection for another human was absurd, then he typed back **Lobster thermidor please x** because it was the first thing he could think of, even though he didn't know what the thermidor part of lobster thermidor actually represented.

31

'Maybe we could do a Robin Hood kind of a thing.'

Buchan had gone to stand at the window while DCI Gilmour read the brief, and the letter which had been left for them at the mailbox. He'd been by the window for a minute or so before he recognised that it hadn't taken him long to do the thing he didn't think he was comfortable doing.

Just a regular day out on the river. A slow-moving barge going against the tide, the only traffic. Cars across the road, the sounds of the city distant behind double glazing. Someone sitting on the bench beneath the Pasionaria, cup of coffee in one hand, phone in the other.

I'm no different to all these people, he thought. Little more than a symbol of our times, as much, or as little a part of it as sociopaths creating their own mythology.

He turned quickly, dragged from his morose self-reflection. Stared at her for a moment while he tried work out what she'd said, but couldn't find it. He'd been too far buried in himself.

'Sorry, wasn't focussed,' he said.

'You're not just mocking my idea with silence?'

'Genuinely didn't hear you.'

'Maybe we could do a Robin Hood kind of a thing,' she said.

He stared again for a moment, and then smiled.

'Hearing you didn't really help. How d'you mean?'

'This man – and I take it we're still just assuming it's a man, rather than knowing for definite…'

'We think so, but usual caveats apply, so you know…'

'Taking nothing for granted, good. So, I accept the premise here, that the guy is throwing the curtains wide, letting everything into the room. Perhaps he has a very definite idea of how this mythology he's creating will look, perhaps he sees it as an experiment. Let the people pick and choose what's important to them. He can then undermine that if he doesn't like it, or play to it, as his legend grows.'

'A symbiotic relationship between living myth and devoted

and curious public.'

'Yes. Nevertheless, I find the repeated use of *The Omen* reference interesting,' she said, then she stopped, when she saw the reservation flash across Buchan's face, and she said, 'Go on.'

'Could be that the jackal or Baylock or both of them actually come from elsewhere. He could have a reference we don't know about. We could be barking up the wrong tree. Could be he's not using *any* cultural references, he's never seen *The Omen*, and he just thought, semen of a jackal, that sounds weird, I'll do that.'

'You're right, of course. But by this means we can talk ourselves out of every idea we think of. We have to choose what sounds right to us, what fits the narrative we're constructing, and run with it. You and your team are here in this job because you're good at what you do. And in police work, that means you have good instincts.'

'So what's the Robin Hood plan?' asked Buchan, to move the conversation along from how good a detective he was. He rarely had moments of considering himself a good detective.

'We get the Filmhouse, or some such, to put on a special showing of *The Omen*.'

Buchan gave it a moment, running the idea through the matrix.

'What makes it special?' he said.

'We'll have to gameplan that.'

'And we hope our guy shows up because we think he's a huge *Omen* fan.'

'Yes.'

'Let's say there are a hundred people in the audience, how do we know?'

'We don't, but then we have a hundred people to investigate, which may be a lot, but it's less than we have at the moment, which is somewhere in the region of the entire population of Scotland.'

They stared at each other while they thought through the mechanics.

'I'm not sure it works,' said Buchan. 'Cinemas are usually going to telegraph that kind of thing by at least a couple of weeks, if not more. And since our guy has obviously given some thought as to how we're going to conduct ourselves, not out of the question he sees through it.'

'But,' said Gilmour, 'Robin Hood saw through the golden arrow competition. That was almost the point of it. He goes along there just to see how it plays out, fully confident they won't catch him. I'd say this guy is going to have exactly the same kind of bravado.'

'Hmm,' said Buchan.

'I like it. I believe we can be as bold as we choose to be. We can announce a showing of the movie in two days. Give it some kind of a hook, and then get last minute ads in the press and online. He's playing a game, he might well respect us playing a game, even if it's not the same one.'

Buchan ran his hands across his face, then let out a long sigh.

'Maybe,' he said. 'I'll get the team on it, see what everyone thinks. We may just be talking ourselves into something that's completely preposterous.'

'Maybe,' she said.

She looked at her desk, mind whirring, and Buchan recognised exactly what she was thinking.

'You want to look into it, set up a plan?' he asked, and she shook her head.

'That's OK, I don't want to interfere.'

'You're not interfering,' said Buchan. 'This is a massive, all-hands investigation. We need everyone we can get. And the chances are there will be more death before we stop this clown.'

She held his gaze while she thought it over, but Buchan was happy to play out the pretence that he was asking her for help.

'In fact, I think it might be best if as few of us knew about it as possible,' he said. 'Obviously I trust the team, but we're in an open-plan with another team, and word gets around. The press would not be forgiving of this kind of thing. I mean, it's on one level utterly ridiculous. Also, it might work, so maybe it's worth trying. Test the guy out, let's see just how confident he actually is. And, if he really does think of himself as omnipotent, he's going to be confident enough to show.'

'If it's as relevant as we think it is,' she added.

'Yes. You'll take it on?'

She nodded.

'Thank you, inspector, yes.' She looked around the desk, she glanced at her computer. 'Paperwork can be fascinating obviously, and I'm not complaining about the money, but I do miss getting my hands dirty.'

'OK, sounds good. You turn your hand to that, the team and I will keep working with what we've currently got on.'

'I'll speak to a couple of people, put something together, get back to you by tomorrow morning at the latest,' she said. 'Thanks, inspector,' and the conversation was over.

32

Buchan sat in traffic on the way to the Queen Elizabeth. He could obviously have settled with reading Donoghue's report, or he could have video-called if there was something he'd wanted to clarify. But he didn't like spending too much time at the office, and so he was out now, with people to speak to.

He needed to return to the Fin Markham murder. They'd been in this position before, of course. The multiple murders, where you got caught up in the process and the mind-set of the killer, and your focus was all on them, and not on the victims, and sometimes the detail eluded you.

What was it about Markham? The four previous victims the killer had spoken of in the letter, whether they were his victims or not, were all linked by public knowledge of their wrongdoing. They were people the system hadn't dealt with. Kieran Sledd slotted exactly into that category. Naturally they'd spent the previous twenty-four hours focussing on his death, and what it was beginning to say about the killer. And there'd been the second letter, and the communication sent to the mailbox. Consequently, there'd been a lot to distract them from Fin Markham's murder.

Markham remained the outlier. She hadn't escaped justice because of defence lawyers, or weakness in the system. Hers had unquestionably been the same killer – the jackal semen proved it beyond doubt – but the motive remained shrouded in mystery.

And so he had left Kane at the helm, and was out for the day.

*

'You didn't need to come,' said Donoghue, though there was tiredness in her voice, rather than the more familiar irascibility.

'Out and about,' said Buchan. 'Going to speak to Fin Markham's boyfriend again.'

'Regular follow-up, or do you have your suspicions?'

'Oh, the former. We know why Kieran Sledd was

murdered, we don't know the story with Fin Markham.'

Donoghue was working on the corpse of a young man, mid-twenties perhaps. A regular examination, nothing about his person to indicate cause of death. She had yet to split open the abdomen, if that was something she intended to do in this instance.

'What's the story?' asked Buchan, indicating the cadaver.

'Ketamine overdose, far as we know. Just got to confirm that, and check for any sign of coercion.'

'It might've been murder?'

'Manslaughter at worst, I believe, but we'll see. It's McKenna's case.'

'Right,' said Buchan nodding. 'I shan't ask any more in case she thinks I've an ulterior motive,' and Donoghue smiled grimly. There were office politics everywhere.

'I sent the Sledd report over this morning,' she said. 'You didn't see it?'

'I read it,' said Buchan. 'Just out and about, like I said.'

She finally raised her eyes, letting go of the victim's jaw, straightening her shoulders a little.

'You think I might've had a brilliant idea, and decided not to bother including it in the report? Because, to be honest, I don't usually do that.'

'Come on, Mary,' he said, 'you know how I work.'

'Yes, all right,' she said, and then once more leaned over the deceased's head.

'So, it begins with a classic GHB injection to incapacitate him,' said Buchan.

'It's going to work every time. Well, ninety-five percent of the time, and when it doesn't immediately induce unconsciousness, it's going to leave the victim very vulnerable. So Mr Sledd, even if it didn't knock him out, and allowing for the fact he was known to be aggressive and combative, would have been in no position to resist attack. The killer knows about doses of GHB. Enough to bring them to their knees, not enough to kill them, not enough to put them to sleep for hour upon end.'

'And I take it that's the kind of information you can learn from the Internet easily enough?'

'*Everything* is the kind of information you can learn from the Internet,' said Donoghue drily. 'OK, I know what you mean. There's a certain level, a feel for it, that with some things you're going to need the experience. This, though, all experience is going to tell you is that everyone's different. The strongest, fittest guy can be more susceptible to the drug than the puniest wimp at the pool. It's like alcohol. You just never know until you're in the moment.'

'Can you tell how close he was to getting it spot on here?'

'Impossible. Look, he didn't gag him which might imply the guy was unconscious, but then, they were in the middle of nowhere, with a wind blowing up the hill from the sea. From the marks on his body, I'd say that some of that torture was him telling Sledd to keep his mouth shut, and then gently reminding him with the massive blow to the testicles when he disobeyed.

'Sledd is going to have been awake and aware for his final breath, and that surely must be part of this guy's schtick He's killing them for a reason, and he's going to want them to know what that is.'

'Hmm,' said Buchan.

He's killing them for a reason.

'Mistaken identity,' he said out loud, his voice quiet.

Donoghue stopped what she was doing, and lifted her eyes.

'Not this guy. You mean Fin Markham?'

'Must be possible.'

'Well, I don't think so. That wasn't a random drive-by, it wasn't a hit, wasn't a bullet popped in someone's head from a hundred yards. That was as intimate and personal an attack as could've been done on someone. He knew who he was killing.'

Buchan nodded. He lifted his eyes, looking at the time. Whatever comfort was to be had from standing over a corpse idly chatting with the pathologist, had run its course.

'Thanks,' he said. 'I'll see you soon enough, I expect,' and Donoghue let out an audible sigh.

33

Fin Markham's boyfriend was sitting at his kitchen table, a laptop open in front of him. He hadn't closed it upon Buchan's arrival, but he had at least stopped writing. He was, nevertheless, glancing at it often enough to illustrate how distracted he was.

'I really don't know,' he said. 'I mean, like I said before. Like I've said about, I don't know, a hundred times since Friday to you people. They were just Fin, you know. They were nice.'

'Have you read about yesterday's murder down at the coast?' asked Buchan.

Alan Conway's continued glances at the screen were beginning to annoy him.

'Sure. I saw they thought it might be the same killer, but…' He waved away the thought, stared around the room as though searching for something to pluck out of the air, then continued, 'I don't care. The guy who killed Fin, he can kill another hundred people. A thousand. He can be Harold Shipman multiplied by Fred West. I don't care. Fin's dead, they're not coming back. That's all that there is.'

'There's no might about it,' said Buchan. He felt there was something affected in Conway's tone, as he had done the previous time they'd talked. 'Yesterday's victim was killed by the same man who killed Fin. The reason why Kieran Sledd was killed is evident. He was a bad man, he'd been convicted of his crimes, and the judge had been lenient. This was the killer taking vengeance. Now, there's potential he did the same with several previous deaths around Scotland in the past few weeks. People in the public eye who had not suffered for their crimes.'

'Fuck them, then,' said Conway. He glanced at the screen, he looked away, he shrugged. 'I don't care,' he added.

Buchan gave him a moment to see if he was going to ask himself the question, understand where he was being led without Buchan having to say it, but it wasn't happening. Conway looked at his screen again.

'You watching something?' asked Buchan.

'No, it's my work.'
'What d'you do?'
'Really?'
'What do you do?'
'Do I have to tell you that?'

'No, of course not. I might start wondering why you don't tell me, but it won't play into the investigation.' Probably won't, he thought. 'But I wouldn't mind if you just closed the thing and concentrated. It'll only be a few minutes.'

Conway let out a low curse.

'Romantic fiction,' he said. 'You know, like little romantic stories.'

Buchan stared curiously at him. Well, this is the police, he thought, nothing new under the sun 'n all that.

'You have a publisher?'

'Of course. I'm not going to waste my time writing this crap if I don't.'

'What medium is it published in?'

Conway pressed a couple of buttons, logged himself out of the computer and closed the lid.

'Just knew it, by the way. You're here to question me for Fin's murder. You people are absolutely clueless, you always are, and you can't see past the end of your nose. So here I am, sitting in front of you, and you're like, must be you. You were close to them, you must've had a motive. And wait what, you write romantic dramas? Well, that's weird for a bloke. Seals it. Un-fucking-believable.'

'Are you finished?'

'I'm here all day, but I wouldn't mind if you went elsewhere. I have nothing else to tell you.'

'I need you to help me out here,' said Buchan.

'Fine, my work is published in comic books, you happy? Why is there a market for romantic comic books?' he said, talking through Buchan's look of disdain. 'I have no idea, but there it is. Maybe people, even the ones who read crappy romance novels, are getting too stupid, or too impatient, to read entire novels. I'm just here to make a living out of it. We all good? Now, if you don't mind…'

'I need you to help me out with Fin, because this man kills for a reason, and I don't know how Fin fits into his narrative.'

'What are you saying about them?'

'I'm not saying anything about them. I need to know what

the killer would say. Fin was killed for a reason, and we don't know what that is. Can you think of anything?'

'Hello! They were non-binary!'

'Kieran Sledd was not from that community. None of the other victims in the deaths we're investigating were from that community. This killer is not targeting that community. Can you think of another reason why someone might have gone after Fin?'

His bottom lip dropped a little. The look said it all. He was pissed off that Buchan had even asked, and if there was going to be something useful, buried somewhere in the deep recesses of his memory, he wasn't about to go searching for it. Buchan was the messenger, and if he could shoot the messenger, he would do. He certainly wasn't about to put his mind to giving the messenger any help.

'No.'

'How long had you and Fin been together?'

'Really?'

'Yes.'

'I gave a statement to someone, like a sergeant or something.'

'I know. I read the statement. How long had you and Fin been together?'

Conway laughed, head shaking. He looked to the side, at an imaginary camera perhaps, then came back to the conversation, his hands spread to the side.

'I don't get it.'

'How long had you and Fin been together?'

Another head shake, a laugh, and then a grim smile.

'As they say in the court case dramas, I refer the right honourable gentleman to my previous answer.'

34

He was back at the butchers to speak to Rachel Randall, the last person to see Fin Markham as she'd entered the park. When he'd arrived Randall had been operating the sausage machine, she'd looked annoyed at his return, had said, 'I've got to do this,' and she'd indicated the blue protective foot and headwear, and Buchan had said he needed to put photographs in front of her, it would be five minutes, and he was going to stand there until she agreed, and she'd given him a head shake, made some cheap comment about police brutality, and now there were in the small back office, a bleak, airless affair, grey in every regard, with a Playboy calendar on the wall behind the desk, as though it was 1974.

'So, let's get this straight,' said Randall. 'I spoke to you like three days ago or whatever, I literally said I have no idea what this person looked like, like I said the guy existed and that was about the extent of my knowledge, and you're back with photographs? Seriously? Have you got photographs of the back of someone's head in the dark from a hundred yards?'

'You're the only witness we have, and we have to try. Five minutes of your time. If there's nothing, we all move on.'

Buchan had a brown envelope with blown-up photographs of all the men who'd fallen into the scope of the investigation, and he took them out one at a time, placing them on the desk.

He started with Alan Conway.

'I can't believe you're serious,' she said.

'There have been two murders,' he replied, coldly.

'I knew you'd turn out to be an asshole.'

He held her look, the photograph of Alan Conway in between.

'What does that mean?'

'What d'you mean, what does that mean?'

'*I knew you'd turn out to be an asshole,*' said Buchan.

'Saw you on TV last year sometime. All that Poundshop Al Pacino bullshit when those two gangs were going at it. And you were in amongst it, not preventing much death the way I remember it. Then you showed up the other night, and I thought, how do I know this guy? Then I remembered. Off the tele. Police officer of the month.'

She laughed humourlessly.

Something different about her this time, thought Buchan. She'd been gallus the first time they'd spoken.

Nothing unusual in that, he thought. Just life. It'll do it to you, on a whim.

'I don't know him,' she said, as the picture of Conway was still lying in between them.

Next photograph out of the envelope was Ally Nairn. He, Buchan had thought, might be the best match, because of his height. She played the game this time at least, then shook her head.

'Nope.'

'He's tall,' said Buchan, annoyed at himself for having to lead the witness, and she looked up at him with a bit of a smirk.

'He's *tall*?'

'You said the man you saw following Fin along the road was tall.'

'Yeah, whatever, because there's pretty much only the one tall guy in all the land. Must be him.'

'You don't recognise him?'

'No! And you know, I never said he was following Fin, just that he was walking in the same direction.'

That, thought Buchan, was a fair rebuke.

Next he placed a picture of Jimmy Hardcastle on top of the two others.

She studied it for a moment, she shook her head, she made a small, hopeless gesture.

'I'm sorry, boss,' she said, 'but this is a waste of time. I mean, I want to help 'n all, but this is… I just didn't see the guy's face, that's all.'

She held his gaze for a moment, Buchan wanted to read something in her eyes, aware he was reaching, then he persevered, pulled the next photograph from the envelope, and set it down on top of the others.

'Do you recognise this man?' he asked.

35

He drove back down to the coast, back to the spot where Kieran Sledd's body had been discovered the previous morning.

Looking down over the firth of Clyde was different today. Mid-afternoon, low, grey cloud, the light dull. No beauty in the view. Just the west of Scotland in its natural, dreary state.

The area remained closed off, but there was nothing to see, nothing to find, nothing of use that could be plundered, and so, unlike the first crime scene in the heart of a populated area, there was no lingering police presence.

There was dampness in the air, a feeling that rain would soon be falling. The sound of traffic coming up from the Haylie Brae, the wind in the trees, and no one within sight.

Buchan looked at the tree where Sledd had been bound and murdered, letting his thoughts run over the scene, and the scene of the corpse lying on the pathologist's slab, and then he turned away and looked over the sweep of the hill down to the sea, the island of Cumbrae sitting in the near distance.

His phone rang. Sgt Kane.

'Sam,' he said.

'We might have the creature connection, for what it's worth,' said Kane.

'The creature connection?'

'The creatures our deity compares himself to in the note. The jackal, butterfly, raven and snake.'

Buchan let out a low whistle. He hadn't excepted them to find anything.

'There was nothing online. Ellie phoned around some people, spreading a wide net. Literary and historical scholars, see if there was anything. She came up with an idea, she called someone at the Heraldry Society, and there's potential there. The creatures have all been known to be used in heraldry, although the jackal might usually be some other canine, the snake more familiarly a serpent.'

'You think we might be able to find a clan name, or a family?' said Buchan. 'Seems like a bit of an obvious clue to leave.'

'If the thread is really obscure, he might have taken a risk. Planting a clue that maybe, just maybe, we might be able to pin down, if we're good enough. It's a test. Might not go anywhere, or it might be an intentional dead end, or… maybe he's raising the stakes for himself.'

'Living on the edge?'

'Why not? The guy seems fairly contemptuous of us. Maybe it amuses him to leave something that might lead us to him, but which he expects us not to be able to follow through on. That would fit his narrative of disdain.'

'How does that tie in with him knowing we'd find the mailbox?'

'Pretty well, I think. Maybe he's peppered the playing field with clues. We find some, we don't find others. Perhaps he's ranked all the clues in order of difficulty, and he thinks, well they got to this level, that's how good they are. Oh, damn, they got to this level, they're better than I thought. Whatever. He's toying with us, and why wouldn't he enjoy putting a little danger for himself into the game?'

'Yeah, I see that,' said Buchan. 'Can you ask Ellie to keep at it, please? If there are strands, and she can easily split the work without two of them getting in each other's way, then she can bring Isobel into the mix. I like this lead.'

'Will do. You near the coast?'

'Quality of the sound?'

'Yep.'

'At the murder scene. Just getting the feel for it again. About to go and put the squeeze on Ally Nairn.'

'Right,' said Kane. 'Let us know when you'll be back.'

'You OK to lead the three o'clock?'

'Yes, chef.'

She hung up. Buchan stared at the phone. He hadn't put it back in his pocket when the text came through from Kane. **Don't know where that came from. Yes, boss.**

36

Ally Nairn worked in a small builders' yard on the coast, a space that at one time would have been a boatyard, and had been repurposed. Buchan found him outside the walls of the yard, sitting on the rocks, looking across the water. Cumbrae, Little Cumbrae, Bute, and beyond to Arran. Cold down here on the shore, but Nairn was sitting in a dark blue, Marvel T-shirt. He had a homemade sandwich – ham and cheese on plain white – in one hand, a can of full-fat Coke, on the rocks between his legs.

He watched Buchan approach, and then glanced at the ID card before turning away.

'Mr Nairn?' said Buchan.

'I spoke to your lot already. Yesterday afternoon. Some bird.'

'I know, I read the report,' said Buchan.

'The fuck are you doing here, then?'

He asked the question while looking out across the water. Buchan didn't answer, and eventually Nairn was forced to look round again.

'What?'

'I'm trying to find out who killed Kieran Sledd.'

'The fuck's that got to do with me? You think I killed him?'

'No. But my sergeant spoke to all three of Kieran's golfing partners, you all said he'd been in a peculiar mood on Saturday, and she thought you were the only one who was hiding something.'

Nairn barked out a laugh, looked at Buchan a little longer, and then turned away with a complacent smile.

'Aye, whatever.'

'So, what was the story?'

'What story?'

'Why was Kieran a bit off? No jokes, no banter, snapping at you, disinterested in the golf, then uncomfortable company at dinner?'

He was shaking his head a little, still looking away from

Buchan, out over the water, but at least he didn't just bat the question away this time.

Buchan followed his gaze into the shallows. Pale rocks and seaweed, barnacles, a few mussels, some cockles. No sign of any fish. A short stretch, the water quickly deepening, the rocks disappearing from view into the darkness.

'One of the others said you weren't happy either.'

'The fuck said that?' snapped Nairn, heading whipping round.

As it was, neither of them had said it, but Buchan had picked up the inference from Kane's report.

'Doesn't matter. Tell me what was going on.'

Another scoff, then he lifted his sandwich and crammed what was left of it into his mouth, so that his cheeks bulged a little, then he indicated his mouth, and shrugged at the pointlessness of him trying to talk.

'So, what's happening here, what happened with Kieran and has possibly happened with others, is that there's a vigilante killer at large,' said Buchan. 'Popular with some people, no doubt, but ultimately we can't really have a vigilante roaming the streets. If he gets away with it, someone else will think they can get away with it, and before you know it, chaos.'

Nairn was looking at him, his mouth open a little, the masticated sandwich visible between his lips.

'Kieran had been found guilty of domestic violence, and had avoided prison thanks to the leniency of the judge.' Nairn scowled, Buchan talked through it. 'This is why he's now dead. Why Kieran out of all the similar cases in Scotland? We don't know yet, but we do know that whoever did it, whoever killed Kieran, very possibly also knows his friends. Neither of the other two, Reggie Coleman, Jimmy Hardcastle, neither of those guys has ever been charged with a crime. You, on the other hand… five accounts of assault, three of rape, another three of sexual assault…'

'Oh, fuck off.'

'Between them, four convictions, and all that adds up to no jail time. Never reached the threshold, according to the judge. So, would you look at that. It was Kieran who got killed, but it could quite easily have been you.'

Can of Coke to his lips, a loud slurp of a drink, face turned away, staring at the sea, seeing nothing.

'So we think Kieran received some warning or other. A

threat maybe. I doubt he was scared by it, more irritated. It got under his skin in some way. And I think he told you about it. Of the three golf partners, you were his closest friend. So I think you knew he'd been threatened, and yet you never said to the sergeant. Why would that be? Is it because you also got the threat? Because whoever knows about Kieran, very likely knows about you.'

Nairn drained the can of Coke, head titled back, can at his lips, then crushed it in his right hand and tossed it into the sea.

'Fuck's sake,' he said.

Buchan, understanding the rhythm of the interview, knew he was about to crack, and all he needed was the gentle prodding of judgemental silence.

'Fine,' said Nairn, a few moments later. 'Kieran got a phone call. Saturday morning, on his mobile. Said it was creepy as fuck. Like… the voice was an AI horror movie voice. That was what he said. And I… Anyway, whatever, he said it was saying something, some bullshit about being everywhere, about being like, fuck, I don't know, a snake and a fish and a butterfly and a something else…'

'A jackal, a butterfly, a raven and a snake,' said Buchan.

Nairn looked at him, wary now, the look on his face suspicious.

'The fuck you know that?'

'We've come across it before,'

'Aye, well there was something about fish 'n all.'

'All the animals of the earth, all the fishes of the sea.'

'Ha. You get the same call, did you?'

'No. Did he get the number the call had come from?'

'What d'you think, ya spanner? Of course no'.'

'Why'd he answer it?'

'Said he got a feeling. Like… like he knew he should. Fucking weird, man, by the way.'

'How'd they know his number?'

'Exactly,' said Nairn, by way of an answer.

'And that scared him.'

A sharp look, another scowl.

'No one was scared. He wasn't scared. It pissed him off, that's all. If they had his number, then it was someone he knew, and he wanted to know who it was.'

'Who did he think?'

'No idea. Presumed it was some friend of Laura's.'

'Laura says she doesn't have any friends.'

'Ha.'

Nothing else.

'Laura says she doesn't have any friends.'

'Whatever. She used to have friends, she pushed them all away because she was so into Kieran. She's friends wi' us lot.'

'Maybe Kieran thought it was one of you three who made the threat?'

He laughed this time, looking round at Buchan.

'Aye, right. The butterfly and the fish? I mean, fuck off with that gay pish. Which one of us lot was calling ourselves that?'

'If Kieran was as dismissive of it as you, then why did he give this thing any credence? You're mocking it, so why wouldn't he have done?'

He was still staring at Buchan, angry, twitching, spit gathering on his lips. He jabbed the side of his head.

'Because he wasn't an idiot. I saw gay pish, but aye, Kieran, Kieran knew stuff. He knew people. He recognised the threat. And look, he was fucking right, wasn't he?'

'So when did you get yours?'

Nairn's jaw was tensing, teeth pressing against each other in an angry rhythm.

'When did I get my what?'

'Your phone call.'

'What makes you think I got a phone call?' he asked, and Buchan answered with a look, and Nairn understood Buchan had the better of him, and he scowled again.

Deep breath. A reckoning with the self. Again, Buchan gave him the space, until finally, nodding to himself, head turned away from Buchan, he said, 'This morning.'

'Tell me about the voice.'

'Just like Kieran says. AI, creepy as fuck. Just kind of crawls inside your brain, you know. Fuck me, man.'

'Can you think of a voice in a horror movie it would sound like? It could be that whoever did it programmed the thing to sound like some character or other.'

'I don't watch horror movies.'

'How d'you know it sounds like a horror movie then?'

'Fuck me.'

'Could you do an impersonation of it?' asked Buchan, and Nairn turned to him again, his look contemptuous.

'Naw. Look, am I getting police protection, then?'

Buchan was amused by the question, but managed not to allow that to show on his face.

'Tell me about the last time you saw Kieran.'

'Really? We've been here before. I told your sergeant.'

'You got to the crossroads at Glasgow Road, he went right, you went left, that about it?'

'Aye, sure, that's about it.'

'Did you look over your shoulder at him after you'd gone off?'

'What? The fuck would I have done that for?'

'Was there anyone around, anyone else in the street?'

He stared harshly at Buchan, but was at least giving this some thought.

'Suppose there were a couple of people about. It was gone ten, but, you know, maybe a couple of guys had left the pub. Maybe there was a lassie walking home alone, but she was in front of me going in the opposite direction from Kieran, so that's no use to you.'

'Anything odd? Any movement in the shadows you think you saw?'

'The shadows?' Another head shake. 'Fuck me, man.'

Buchan really wanted Nairn to take his time, to recreate the scene in his head, but it wasn't happening. All Nairn wanted was for this to be over.

'Naw,' he said, when Buchan was obviously still looking for an answer, then he looked at his watch, grunted, and turned back to Buchan.

'Like I said, what about police protection?'

'Sure,' said Buchan, 'we have procedures we can put in place. And you're right, they're probably appropriate.'

'You think I'm next?'

'We have no idea how many people have received this call, so impossible to say. We can wire you up, give you a panic button, set up an alarm system around the doors and windows of your house, stick a guy outside your door.'

'That it?'

'Seriously?'

'What about a close protection team?'

'I think maybe you're confusing yourself with someone people are going to care about,' said Buchan, bluntly.

'Funny guy. I want a close protection team. You know, like

Charlie's Angels, something like that. A few fit birds.' He laughed.

'I'll get someone to give you a call, they can meet you at your house after work, see what we can sort out. It might be a day or two before it's all in place, so you might want to go somewhere else if you think this person has your address.'

'The fuck do I know if they have my address?'

'They have your phone number, so it wouldn't be out of the question.'

'Aye, fine, whatever,' he said, then he looked at the time again, muttered, 'Fuck's sake,' then forced himself to his feet, groaning and creaking as he went.

*

Buchan sat, a little uncomfortably, in the seat in which Kane had been sitting the previous day. Laura Sledd was wearing the same large sunglasses she'd worn before. Cup of tea in hand, leaning forward, elbows on her knees. She'd offered Buchan tea, and he'd said yes, as some sort of way to ease into the interview. The tea was too weak, and was destined to cool undrunk.

'You're still here,' said Buchan.

She was ready for that, and had been since Buchan had called to establish if she remained at home.

'Like I said yesterday, nowhere else to go.'

'Has anyone been round?'

She took a drink, the movement slow, calculated. Giving herself time, a familiar trope.

'Ally was here last night. Came about nine, something like that.'

She bobbed her head to the side, and Buchan followed the gesture to the low cabinet against the wall, the top of which was a clutter of magazines and keys and glasses and small ornaments lost in the bourach, and in the middle of it a vase of fresh flowers.

'He picked them up for two-ninety-nine in Tesco. Reduced, because they hit their sell-by date.' A pause, and then, 'How thoughtful.'

'How was he?'

'What does that mean?'

'Was he upset? Was he sympathetic?' Buchan paused this time, then added the more cutting, 'Was he here to play a hand?'

Another slurp of tea, and then the small, bitter laugh on the back of it.

'Let's see. Upset? I don't know. He's a bloke. He doesn't do upset. Impossible to tell. Sympathetic? Definitely. Very, very sympathetic. You look like you need a cuddle, darlin'. A sympathy cuddle. Then that became, what would you say, a sympathy shag? Is that a thing? I mean, I don't think I needed that amount of sympathy. To be honest, I didn't need any sympathy, but Ally was keen to give me it. Right there, on the couch, where you're sitting.' She stared blankly at Buchan, although of course he couldn't see what her eyes were doing. 'Don't worry, I cleaned it up this morning.'

37

Buchan stood on the doorstep of the house he'd called at no more than two and a half hours previously. He was not going to be well received.

Darkness had crept in upon the land as he'd driven back up towards the city, and the evening's chill had come with it. Buchan turned and looked along the short road. One in three streetlights were faulty, a couple which were stutter-stepping their way through the night, flashing intermittently and irregularly.

The door opened, and Buchan was greeted by the exact face of Alan Conway he'd been anticipating. Contempt.

'Like a virus,' said Conway. 'You keep on coming back.'

'One more question,' said Buchan.

'Oh, you go right ahead,' said Conway, standing his ground in the doorway, imagining Buchan was about to try to push past him.

'Did Fin receive a threatening or strange phone call prior to their murder?'

He stared blankly at him, for long enough that Buchan wondered if this was his thinking face.

'Did Fin receive a phone call?' Buchan repeated.

'How would I know?'

'Because if it was the same phone call yesterday's victim received, they might well have mentioned it to you.'

'What did that dickhead get?'

'A call from an AI-generated voice. Something unsettling about it, about the tone, even though the words themselves might not have been threatening.'

Conway's face was blank. Buchan sensed something in him, but he was shutting down so much it was hard to tell. Avoidance? Shock? Perhaps she'd told him about it, and he'd dismissed it as trivial.

'What'd it say?' he asked.

'I am everywhere, I am everyone and everything, all the animals of the earth, all the fishes of the sea, I am the jackal, I am the butterfly, I am the raven, I am the snake, I am Lord.'

Buchan recited it quickly in a dull monotone, not attempting to lend it any of the poetic cadence with which the writer perhaps felt it ought to be delivered.

Conway shook his head.

'No,' he said.

'Really?'

'I said no. Why don't you believe me? I'm not a suspect, am I?'

'Not at the moment. You look like you've heard that before.'

'I haven't.'

'You didn't write it, did you?'

'What? Of course I didn't fucking write it. Jesus.'

'But you've heard it.'

'No, officer, and this is the last damned time, I haven't.'

'Maybe it's taken from something. A book you know, a comic book you know, a movie, a play, a …'

He slammed the door shut. Buchan stood staring at it for a moment, contemplated knocking again, but felt that he had enough, and turned away.

38

Dark by the time Buchan returned to the office, troubled and agitated. There had been a murder on the Thursday evening, then one on the Saturday. Two was hardly enough for them to be able to call it a pattern, yet it wasn't stopping that ugly feeling in his gut.

'What about you?' said Kane, in response to Buchan saying he'd set someone up to go and speak to Ally Nairn about protection.

'What about me?'

'Are you going to do anything about your protection?'

'Why?'

'It might not have been a phone call, but you got the exact same message sent to you that Kieran Sledd received.'

'I don't think so,' he said.

'You did, sir,' said Cherry.

They were sitting around the table in the ops room. Buchan, Kane, Cherry, Dawkins and Marks. Usual positions, in the air the familiar aroma of coffee, the door open, the corridor beyond silent.

'The messages to Sledd and Nairn were to their personal phone numbers. There's implicit threat in that,' said Buchan. 'The one I received was to a mailbox on the off-chance I'd discover it. That's not a threat, that's a game. There's been nothing threatening in the letters he's sent to me here. He's enjoying himself, he's enjoying the game, and I'm part of it. I've been threatened before, I know what it's like, and this isn't it. I appreciate the concern, and you know, we may not have two hoots to give about Mr Nairn, given who he is, but this is our job. To protect the guy, and at the moment, he needs it more than me.'

He looked from Kane to Cherry. Neither of them said anything, though he recognised their acceptance.

'I stopped in to see Conway again,' said Buchan, picking up. 'Asked him if Markham had had this phone call, and I told him the substance. He said no, but I don't trust him. He was lying about something. He either knows, and doesn't want to admit it, or he recognises the prose in some way. Or, perhaps, the amalgam of animals listed therein. Isobel, can you do a much, much deeper dive on this guy, please. I want to know everything about him.'

'Sir.'

'But not now. No one's doing anything now, other than going home. But if you could get on it tomorrow morning. If you need to go and speak to Conway, go for it. He works at home, says he writes romantic stories.'

'Yep,' said Marks, 'he does. I don't know how he makes a living from it, because he hasn't written many, but he seems to get by.'

'Well, we've been to his house, and the man ain't living in luxury,' said Buchan. 'How's it going with this family coat of arms thing, Ellie?'

'Good, I think. I've got an heraldic guy in Perth to speak to, and I said you probably wouldn't have the time to go up there and I mentioned Zoom or whatever, and he said he hates Zoom, and that he's more than happy to come to the city in the morning. You've got a nine-thirty.'

'That's great, thanks. What's his name?'

'Fforbes McAdam. Two f's in Fforbes. I mean, I know. The guy is straight out a novel. In fact, he's straight out of *On Her Majesty's Secret Service*. Don't be surprised if he turns up in a kilt.'

There were a couple of smiles.

'We see all human life,' said Buchan, which was the kind of thing he usually said in reference to much darker characters than Fforbes McAdam was likely to turn out to be.

He blew out a long sigh, then sat back as he looked through his notes.

A knock at the door, and Constable Rutledge entered at a pace, likely more in his desire to keep the interruption to a minimum, rather than due to a sense of urgency. A letter in hand.

'This was in the late afternoon mail drop, inspector,' he said, and he handed the envelope to Buchan, nodded at the table in general, a slight awkwardness about him, and then he left.

Buchan tapped the envelope on the table a couple of times, then Kane said, 'You're not opening it?' and Buchan said, 'I was thinking about getting the gloves, and now I'm thinking, dammit, I might as well just get on with it, as we're well aware our guy isn't giving anything of himself,' and he glanced at her, and as he did so he worked his finger into the fold, crudely opened it, and then took out the letter and placed it, opened out, on the table.

They all leaned in, to read it from various angles.

Such an implication in your gormless message, that I'd forgotten an essential part of my own story. And yet, what was this mistake that casts doubt on the "veracity" of my letter? A missing question mark.

I knew the question mark should be there, of course. I'd spotted it. I thought it hardly mattered.

What is grammar anyway? Who uses grammar anymore? Newspapers don't proof read, they don't copy edit, and the bulk of the writing you'll find online is badly-written nonsense aimed at the under-5s. But, sure, now Police Scotland – Police Scotland of all people! – have become the actual grammar police.

You bore me. Frankly, I wonder if it all bores me. This omnipotence thing. What is the point, if everything can just be as you would wish it? What is life without the trial? Without the quest? Without purpose? Because, ultimately, isn't that what omnipotence brings? With it, there is no purpose.

For now I remain a vengeful god, delivering retribution upon the deserving.

You will hear from me again, though I tire of the game.

39

Roth had kept dinner simple. Chicken sautéed in butter and white wine, a small bowl of rice, a trio of steamed vegetables. She had announced it as a trio of steam vegetables, as though reading off a menu.

Oscar Peterson was playing. On the comfortable chair by the window, Edelman sat upright, looking out on what he could see of the river, through the reflection of the room.

They were eating in what would normally have been a comfortable silence, listening to the music, sort of watching Edelman, wondering what was drawing his attention.

'Must be something going on out there,' said Buchan, unexpectedly finding words.

'I think maybe he's a bit on the scale,' said Roth 'He's already in the rhythm of me being away on a Monday, so he's sitting there like, uh-oh, something's amiss.'

'That'll be it,' said Buchan, and Roth decided to force the conversation.

'What's up?' she said. 'You're a little on edge.'

'I am,' said Buchan.

'You worried the guy's going to find you?'

'No, not at all. I'm not worried about us. We've been there before, we've been through that. I honestly don't think that's what's happening this time.'

'OK, good, because neither do I. But you know, it's a classic romantic movie narrative.'

'Is it?'

'Sure. The couple find each other after a year or two of skirting round the issue, and then, boom, bad shit happens just as things seem to be going OK.'

'Well, we've had a good six or seven months already, so maybe we've got past the classic romantic movie narrative hump, and we can relax.'

'You can never relax in a romantic movie narrative.'

'We all die in the end?' said Buchan, and she smiled, and said, 'OK, so what's up?'

'Waiting for the phone to ring,' he said. 'Just got that uncomfortable feeling. This obviously isn't close to being over, there have been at least two, and quite possibly six murders, this guy is unleashed, and we have no idea who it is. We're still at the point of trying to identify if some of the murders were actually murders, and we have to go into all of them in case somewhere in there is the vital clue to this *fucking* guy's identity.'

'DI Buchan never usually swears at home,' said Roth, reviving the old nineteen-seventies gag.

'No, he doesn't,' said Buchan. 'And the trouble with this is… I got Alan, you remember Constable Rutledge?' and Roth laughed and said, 'Of course!' and Buchan continued, 'I got Alan to do a scan online, see what's going on with public opinion, and there's a good eighty-to-twenty in favour of this guy. The killer doing the police's job for them. We can argue, of course, that the police did their job with each of these victims – Markham aside, as we don't yet know why she's a victim – and it was the courts who let them off, but we see the tide of public opinion. There's so much political crap in Scotland now, the police embroiled with the government, either in league with them or plotting against them, and all the shit about male sexual predators suddenly deciding they're women, and us having to pander to them, and…'

He waved away the monologue, boring even himself. Only with Roth would he allow himself to talk like this, but often enough he didn't like the sound of his own voice.

'Well, you're right' she said, 'and then some guy comes along and starts cleaning up the streets, and the public are like, well, thank God someone's doing it. Go this guy.'

'Right up to the point of mistaken identity, or he thinks it's worth killing someone because they didn't pay their TV licence.'

'But then all those people who are happy about the vigilante fellow will point to miscarriages of justice and say, well the police messed *that* up, or the courts messed it up, so why can't we allow Batman a mistake or two?'

'This guy ain't Batman,' said Buchan.

'Batman, Jack Reacher, whoever, it's a trope in fiction, that's for sure. I read a crime novel that was exactly this. Can't remember what it was now. It was a bit all over the place, but basically it was a deranged nutjob killing people he deemed to have deserved it, though he sent them letters as a warning, rather than making phone calls.'

'Completely different then,' said Buchan, drily. 'Our guy's not been influenced by it, you don't think? What was the books' murder method?'

Roth pursed her lips, looked off to the side, then took a mouthful of food while she thought it over.

'Oh, yeah, that was the gross one. He slit open the victims' stomach, made sure not to kill them, then got various animals to eat them alive. Like rats and crows and puppies and huntsmen spiders.'

Buchan stared across the table, then did a comedy look down at his dinner.

'Hey, at least we're not having haggis,' said Roth with a smile.

'I have no idea why people read crime novels,' said Buchan.

'That's just 'cause you have to live it. Humans need a little darkness in their lives, it's who we are.'

'Well, if this case starts to resemble the one you're talking about in the book, let me know. Maybe we could get the writer in, he can tell us what's going to happen next.'

'I'll keep him on speed dial,' said Roth.

They smiled, they ate, they drank. Oscar Peterson played on, *Cleveland Blues*, and on the comfy chair, Edelman accepted that the drama was over for the night, wandered around in a circle for a while, and then finally settled into a curled ball in the middle of the seat.

∗

Buchan awoke with the ringing of the phone at one-twenty-nine. He'd been asleep for seventeen minutes.

40

When Buchan arrived at the end terrace house in Barlanark, Kane was already there. There were three squad cars, no ambulances.

Two-storey terraced houses the length of the street, the community awake, and alive with interest. Lights on in all the surrounding houses, people watching from windows. The woman next door was standing with a cup of tea and a cigarette, in her dressing gown, leaning on the doorframe.

Buchan stood for a moment, looking around the scene, and then he approached Kane, having got the measure of the area and the people who lived here. He hadn't been on this street before, but he knew this part of town well enough.

'Double murder?' he said. He wondered if the message had become garbled in the telling.

'Yes,' said Kane. 'Two dead, unquestionably murdered. Bound, gagged, beaten to death. Pretty straightforward this one. There's a bloody baseball bat left at the scene. Looks like the killer broke in, subdued them in some way which is not immediately apparent, tied them up, and did for them.'

'We know who they are?'

'Oh, yes,' she said.

'I don't like the sound of that.'

'Devon and Jill Craigie.'

Buchan stared at her, dead-eyed, while he processed the names, and then he nodded.

'Killed the kid.'

'Yep. And ultimately the defence did a good job.'

'Remind me. I didn't really pay attention to it. Weren't they found guilty of manslaughter?'

'Yes.'

'Not so sure about the defence, then.'

'But they'd planted the seed, so that when it came to sentencing, the judge had all these great reasons to spare them jail time. The kid had issues, they had issues. Their upbringing, mental health, of course. I mean, I don't think anyone was really buying it, but like I say, the defence played a pretty decent game. The judge went for it, he was soft, howls of protest from all round, none of it made any difference, and Bob's your builder, they never had to spend a night away from their salubrious home here.'

'Tale as old as time,' said Buchan, drily. 'Who called it in?'

Kane turned, found the woman in the dressing gown standing on her doorstep, and nodded in her direction. She was watching them.

'Mrs Miller.'

'Mrs Miller,' said Buchan. 'I'll go and talk to her in a minute.'

'Guess our killer isn't quite as bored of being an omnipotent vigilante as he made out in his last letter.'

Buchan nodded ruefully.

'No one's surprised.' An exhaled breath, a last look around, then he said, 'Suppose I'd better take a look at the corpses,' and Kane ushered him towards the front door, following behind.

The hallway was a clutter of coats and umbrellas and children's toys and boots and shoes. A worn carpet, three doormats jumbled on top of each other at the entrance.

'There's another kid in the house?'

'No. Looks like they just haven't tidied in the eleven months since he died,' said Kane, and she thought she heard a mutter from Buchan in response.

Into the sitting room, the other side of the house from the connecting wall to next door. With the door closed, and the noise kept low, no one outside the house would've been able to pick up anything.

An ugly scene, though not one with which Buchan or Kane were unfamiliar. Death by blunt force trauma was the second most common method of murder in Glasgow behind the still-popular knifing. They were fortunate guns had never taken off, and despite the constant influx of terrible new ideas from the US, Buchan wasn't sure they ever would. Still, it may have been more old-fashioned, but blunt force trauma did not make for a pleasant crime scene.

'Jesus,' he said, after looking over the dead for a minute or so.

They had been bound together, naked, sitting upright on the sofa. Legs tied, tape around their waists and shoulders. Ropes from the small legs of the sofa to their ankles, another rope snaked through their arms, and then tied tightly around the back of the sofa. Trapped.

The bonds had worked, and the two bodies had not parted, nor come loose from the sofa, despite the heavy number of blows that had rained down upon them.

The faces were pulpy, bloody, bruised. The husband, the man who had killed his own stepson, had been beaten on the top of the head until the skull caved. The woman did not have the same trauma, or the same bruising around the body, but had obviously been killed by a couple of blows to the head.

There was a splay of blood around the room. Brain matter had sprayed from the bludgeoned head of Devon Craigie. Draped over the edge of the sofa was a blue surgical gown, gloves, slippers, mask and headwear. The killer had carried out the beating appropriately dressed, and then had removed the soiled clothing and left it behind. There would be nothing to hide, nothing discarded in a bin, nothing stuffed in the back of a wardrobe.

Buchan and Kane looked at the corpses from a distance of a couple of yards away. There wasn't much else they needed to see from here, and getting from their position by the door to the sofa would've meant walking through blood and tissue. Sgt Meyers and the SOCO team were yet to arrive, but little annoyed her more than a crime scene over which officers had trampled.

'How long d'you think?' said Buchan.

'I haven't been over there to feel the skin,' she said. 'Couple of hours maybe.'

Silence again, bar the buzz of activity outside the house, and in the far distance, a police siren heading in their direction.

'Given the reason behind the couples' renown,' said Kane, 'can we be pretty sure it's our guy again?'

'Presumably,' said Buchan, 'unless it's something worse.'

'Worse?'

'It's catching. One vigilante spawns another, then another, and before you know it…'

'You've got the Justice League.'

Buchan continued staring at the corpses for a while, before finally turning to Kane.

'That's a popular culture reference, is it?'

'Yes, boss. And you're not wrong, but we can hope for now we've just got the one lunatic who thinks he has omnipotent powers.'

142

'That would be best.'

There was a noise behind them, and they turned to be greeted by Dr Donoghue and Sgt Meyers arriving in tandem. Buchan and Kane stood to the side, to let them get proper access to the room and the bloody tumult, and they both stopped in roughly the same positions in which the detectives had been standing.

'No one's walked over there through all this?' said Meyers.

Buchan glanced at Kane, who shook her head.

'The first constable in attendance at least had that level of wits about him.'

'It'd be a bloody idiot who thought they had to check for a pulse,' said Meyers, then she made a random gesture to the air. 'If you don't mind, detectives, you're welcome to go about your business. My team can get photographs taken, sweep the area up to the corpse, and then get down to work. You good with that, doc?' and Donoghue nodded, and then Buchan and Donoghue shared a look, Buchan's eyes asking if she was OK, being answered with a look that he read as bleak hopelessness, and then he and Kane were walking back out into the fresh air, and in the couple of minutes they'd been inside, it seemed the police presence outside had more than doubled.

41

'Why did you call when you did?'

The neighbour was drinking another cup of tea, smoking another cigarette. She was on her couch, the TV was playing with the volume off. A jewellery channel. There was a kid standing just outside in the hallway, poking his head round the door, perhaps imagining the adults didn't know he was there.

'Because I didn't call earlier.'

'Why?' said Kane.

'What?'

'Why was it you thought you had to call in the first place?'

She sniffed, took a draw of the cigarette, took a noisy drink of the tea. If it hadn't been for the fact they'd seen the woman make the tea, Buchan would have thought it likely to be alcohol in the mug.

'You two know about them?'

'Yes,' said Kane.

'You know about the wee boy?'

'Yes.'

'You have anything to do with that?'

'It wasn't one of ours.'

'Piece of nonsense. We all knew, every one of us along here, we all knew something bad was going to happen to that poor wee thing. Mind you but, I say that, he'd've grown up like his stepdad. His dad wasn't so bad, but he buggered off. Think maybe he found out he wasn't the dad after all, that's why he left. But they were always... they were always going to end up harming that wee boy. They're just bastards, the pair of them. Evil bastards. And see that fucking judge.'

She glanced at the door, and the kid retreated an inch or two.

'So, what happened tonight?'

'Started off no different. You know, every night it was the same. Screaming, shouting, crying, whatever. Over and over. Same arguments, same crap. I'm trying to bring the wee man up in a stable environment and he has to listen to that shite every night. What's that teaching him? I keep asking the council to move, and they're like, where is it you think you're going? One of they council estates in Newlands? Aye, that'll be right. I mean, the cunt was basically saying you're as bad as they clowns next door. So I managed to find someone else to talk to, and she's like, aye, we'll help you. And how much help has she been? Aye, well, we all know the answer to that, right?'

'What happened tonight?' asked Kane, her voice steady, patient. They would get there in the end.

'It was the usual thing, and then… you know, there was a weird silence out of nowhere. I mean, don't get me wrong, it wasn't like constant, twenty-four-seven shouting. There was silence. But you know how it is, there's a rhythm to these things, and this wasn't that. Then I heard Devon shouting, who the fuck are you, or something, and then like a crash, and then nothing. And I thought, ha, bastard's got his comeuppance. Was expecting more shouting, more everything to be honest, at least a door or two slamming shut, but… nothing. Like, nothing.'

'The rest of the night?'

'Nothing.'

'What time was that?'

'Seven minutes past ten. I looked at my phone, didn't I, Charlie?'

She glanced at the door, and the kid retreated another inch or two. The woman had a small smile on her face, at odds with the situation and her general demeanour.

'Why did you then call the police three hours later?'

'See that pair, they never do nothin'. I mean, like, they never go out. They're in every night, never go anywhere. It's no' like I hear everything that's going on, you know, but see when my TV's off and the whatever, I can hear them take a piss.'

'Seems odd you didn't hear them being murdered then?'

'Depends how they were murdered, doesn't it?'

'Yes, it does,' said Buchan.

'Depends, to be fair, where it was done. See if it was on the far side of the house, I don't hear that. Never heard their TV, especially when we're watching one of our horror movies, that no' right, Charlie?'

This time she didn't look at the kid.

'So, you didn't hear anything…?'

'Aye, so I start thinking, maybe that was something more than the usual, you know, the shouting at the guy or the whoever. And then I thought, maybe I just picked it up wrong, and he was shouting at his missus, you know? Who the fuck are you, like, you know, who are you to do whatever, or say the next thing. You know what I'm talking about?'

'What made you call the police in the end?' asked Kane.

'I couldn't sleep.'

They looked at her. Her shoulders straightened.

'What?' she said.

'You couldn't sleep?'

'Aye, I was lying there thinking, maybe some shit or other's happened. So I called the polis.'

'Did you try ringing the bell next door first?'

'After midnight? Are you kidding?' She laughed humourlessly. 'The only reason that bastard never beat the shite out of me was 'cause I kept as far away from him as possible.'

'How did you get the local police to gain entry to the property?' asked Buchan, curious.

'They all know him. Every cunt knows him. Soon as I said there was some weird shit or other, they were happy to stick their noses in. They were probably hoping they'd find the guy, greetin' like a wean, sitting over his dead missus, a fuckin' cudgel in his hand. But that, see that, both of them dead? That's like winning the World Cup. See in the mornin', the entire street's gonnae be dancing up and down singing *ding-dong, the witch is dead*. It's like fucking Thatcher dyin' all over again.'

'So, let's talk about this moment, the last thing you heard, Devon Craigie shouting *who the fuck are you*? The crash definitely came after that?'

'Aye.'

'Then nothing?'

'Aye.'

'Did you get a feel for what was going on? Anything that came into your head, which you perhaps don't want to mention because it seems speculative?'

She was staring at Kane, her head tilted slightly to the side.

'Did I get a feel for what was going on? Like I'm a fucking Jedi now?'

Kane didn't bother following up with words.

'Naw,' said the neighbour eventually, 'I didn't get a feel.'

'At any point in the evening, had you looked outside, seen anything suspicious?'

'Naw,' she said, as though tiring of the obviousness of the

questions.

'And there was nothing about any of the noise going on next door to indicate who it might have been, or exactly what was going on?'

'Naw.'

'Is the house next door a mirror of yours?'

She thought about it, lifted her eyes, seemed to give this question more of her attention than any of the others, then said, 'Used to be. Then they got like a conservatory built at the back. I wonder who paid for that, eh? Ha, nah, I don't wonder. The fucking government, because of course they bastards are so flush wi' cash they can just hand it out to scrubbers like they two. Ha, fuck it. Dead now.'

'So,' continued Kane, once the political commentary was done, 'if the killer had gained entry at the rear of the property, through the conservatory, they could've been into the kitchen, then into the hallway, and the Craigies would still have been unaware of their presence.'

The neighbour stared for a moment, until accepting that Kane was endeavouring to have a two-way conversation, then said, 'Aye. It's just like here. I always said this should be open-plan through to the kitchen. Would be if it was made now, I suppose. But you's've got to go out of the kitchen, all the way up the hall, and in here, when you's're bringing your dinner through.'

'The killer opens the door, Craigie shouts who the fuck are you, there's a loud crash, nothing.'

'Aye.'

'Why d'you suppose you heard the shout when you don't normally hear the TV?' asked Buchan.

The neighbour shrugged.

'Door to the sitting room was open, because the glorious fucker who's put us all out of our misery had just opened it, hadn't he? Anyway, the way I hear it, Janice up the road said, they never watched that much tele, they played like *Call of Duty* 'n that. *Assassin's Creed*, shite like that. Like, all the time. Headphones in, you know. Like they had all the gear. Again, government funded of course, 'cause basically that was where a' their money came fi'.'

Kane held her look for a moment, and then turned to Buchan, opening the floor. Buchan replied with a blank look. No further questions.

*

'I didn't know anything about Craigie,' said Buchan, 'but having seen his blood-spattered corpse, he looked strong. The first two victims, they made sense. Markham assaulted in the park, easily overcome. Then Sledd, he could've crept up behind him, stabbed him in the arm with the GHB, and the killer's got a twenty-minute pass to get him bound and into position. That doesn't happen here.'

'Definitely not,' said Kane. 'So either he's powerful, but then why bother with the GHB for Sledd, or else he has a tranquilizer gun.'

'Got to be the latter,' said Buchan. 'Doesn't mean he's not strong, of course, but hard to see how there wouldn't have been a pretty massive fight, and the spray of blood aside, there doesn't appear to have been much of an altercation. He steps into the room, presumes they're both going to be there, gun in hand,' and he made the gun gesture with his fingers and fired an imaginary couple of shots. 'Craigie's getting to his feet as he's hit by the tranquilizer, and boom, he falls, and we get the crash.'

'He's going to have to have nailed the dosage, to incapacitate the victim on the spot, while not killing him,' said Kane.

'He knew who he was going after,' said Buchan, 'so he'd've been able to have a stab at their weight. But yes, you're right.'

Buchan nodded as he turned away and looked around. Back outside, the crime scene still heavily policed, the chill growing in the cloudless early morning. From nowhere a great yawn took him, and he rubbed his hand across his face.

'God, don't,' said Kane, forced into the same.

'We should get some sleep. Let's make sure everyone here who needs to work tomorrow gets home first for a couple of hours, and those staying through the night are going home at the end of it.'

'Boss,' said Kane.

And they moved off together, into the midst of the throng of law enforcement.

*

He crawled into the cold half of the bed at four-thirty-seven. Roth had her back turned, but woke with the movement, and put her hand towards him to draw him close, and he pressed himself against her, looping his arm around her and feeling the warmth of her body against his.

42

Eight-twenty-seven, Buchan standing in a musical instrument shop, guitars lining all the walls, a drum kit in the window, a small back room of electronic keyboards, a single banjo, a single mandolin, a couple of £10 ukuleles in amongst the guitars.

The shop didn't open until nine, but the light had been on, and Buchan had pressed his ID against the window until he'd been allowed in.

There hadn't been a lot of progression since, David McKay greeting the news of his ex-wife's murder with a look of deadpan disinterest. A lugubrious looking man, a tangle of dark hair, tattoos covering the length of one arm. He was wearing a black T-shirt, with the image of a shark, and a quote from Robert Shaw's character in *Jaws*.

'You know who done it?' he finally asked.

There was something in his voice that Buchan hadn't been expecting. A softness laced through the thick accent.

'No. They'd been dead a couple of hours by the time the murder was discovered. This is us just getting the investigation underway.'

McKay was sitting on a stool, an acoustic guitar resting on his knee, calloused fingers lightly picking at the strings, the sound barely audible.

'You wondering if maybe I did it because of what they did to wee Aiden?'

Buchan nodded.

'I guess. I won't say… I mean, the way they treated him, that was just horrible. If someone murdered them,' and he looked at Buchan and shook his head. 'To be honest, I'd vouch for the killer. Doing a public service.'

'What were you doing last night?' asked Buchan.

McKay nodded along, accepting the line of questioning, nothing, apparently, to hide.

'You know Turin Brakes?'

'No.'

'They were playing Òran Mór. Went with Malky and Two

Feet. What time was that? We had pizza about six, went to the gig, started at eight, we were out by ten. Then we went to Razzies. Left at half-midnight, went back to Malky's place, smoked a couple of spliffs, listened to *The Optimist* for the gazillionth time, crashed on the sofa. Still wearing the same shit I was last night.'

He dug into his pocket for his phone, opened the photos, turned it round to show Buchan a picture taken the previous evening, in the middle of the concert, the band in the background, McKay in the middle of three guys near the front of the stage.

'Put that on Insta, if that's any use to you.'

'The photo doesn't help with the time, but if you were with your friends after midnight, that'll do it. If you could give me their numbers.'

'Sure.'

'The boy who died, Aiden, he was your son?'

'Presumed he was at first, when Jill got up the duff, but nah. She let me think it for long enough, but see when Aiden was like one or something, we were arguing all the time by then. I never argue with anyone, but Jill really brought it out of you. And one night we're having a big fight about her always sticking the kid in front of the tele, and never reading to him, and whatever, and she's like, it's none of your business, he's not even yours. And on that bombshell, as Clarkson likes to say, the marriage ended.'

'How'd you know she was telling the truth?'

'When she got pregnant, she said one of the condoms had burst, but she hadn't wanted to say at the time. I was like that, aye there was one time she whipped the condom off us, and I was just like aye whatever. It made sense when I found out it had burst, and she says she was trying not to worry us. Ha. Turned out she'd got blind drunk at Big Nora's hen night and had basically been gangbanged by like ten guys. Said she wasn't the only one. She had literally no idea who Aiden's father was. I'm like that, I am out of here. And she was pissed off, but I made sure we got a paternity test done, because I felt bad abandoning the wee guy, but I was going to fight for him if he was mine to fight for. And he wasn't.'

He shrugged, and strummed an E minor major 9th.

'Closing chord of the Bond theme,' he said. 'Some people hate it, but I think it really hits the mark.'

'Did you try to see Aiden? You must have had affection for him regardless.'

'I did for a little while, but… she was making it really hard, and then that *fucking* guy came on the scene, and that was that.'

'How did you feel when you heard about what happened?'

He looked sadly at Buchan, then his head lowered as he spoke.

'Hated myself for walking out on the kid. Drank myself into oblivion for a couple of months. Mum made me get counselling. Took a while, you know…' A pause, and then, 'Still working on it. I just hope…' He stopped, he took a deep breath, he choked back a tear. 'I just hope, wherever the wee man is now, it's not where those bloody people ended up last night.'

43

A young man, good-looking, casually dressed, a backpack draped over his right shoulder, entered the open-plan, and stood for a moment, looking around the sea of faces. Between Buchan's section, admin, and DI Brannen's section in the bottom half, there were seventeen people. All of them working, idle chit-chat already over for the morning.

Cherry, Dawkins and Marks had watched *The Omen* the night before, and had had little to report. Discussion on horror movies, and the difference in feel and quality between now and then, had ensued. There was nothing, however, that spoke of the current murder investigation beyond what they already knew. The jackal, the raven, Baylock. Certainly, no obvious pointers as to what might come next.

The young man didn't look uncomfortable, but there was something about him that said he could stand there all day before he'd actually ask for assistance, or announce why he was there.

'Hey,' said Cherry, whose desk was the closest. He was just off the phone to the police in Dundee – another call about the drug dealer's death three weeks' previously – and lifted his head above the partition, wondering why they'd let the kid into the building.

'Looking for a Detective Inspector Buchan,' he said.

'Who's asking?'

Buchan turned away from the endless scribble of his notes, two adjacent sides of A4, lines and boxes and names and exclamation marks all over, and looked at the kid.

'Dr McAdam,' said the kid.

Not so much of a kid, thought Cherry.

'Right, the heraldic guy,' and McAdam smiled a little at the description, and turned as Buchan pushed his chair back and got to his feet.

'Inspector Buchan,' he said, approaching, hand outstretched.

'Fforbes McAdam.'

They shook hands, Buchan ushered him in the direction of the door, noticing McAdam's glance at the coffee machine as they passed.

'Let's go to the canteen,' said Buchan.

'Oh, that'd be great.'

When they were gone, and the door was closed, Cherry looked round at the others, eyebrows raised at the youthfulness of the doctor. Dawkins was smiling, holding the collar of her shirt away from her neck, letting out a low whistle.

'Oh my God,' she said. 'He looks like that, *and* he's a doctor.'

'But what of?' said Cherry, laughing.

'I don't care.'

'Well, you've already got his phone number.'

'I'm not sure we can let him out the building without a strip search,' she said, and Cherry laughed again.

*

'Thanks for coming down,' said Buchan.

'No problem.'

Buchan had a coffee and a raspberry Danish, McAdam had ordered a full Scottish breakfast, but had then excluded the beans, tomatoes, haggis and tattie scone from the order.

'You look young,' said Buchan, thinking he might as well get that part of the conversation out of the way while McAdam was still adjusting to his meal. He looked like the kind of person who had to get his head round something, before he could think about the next thing.

'Got 'A' levels when I was fifteen, graduated at eighteen, PhD at twenty-two,' he said, then he laughed a little self-consciously. 'My dad was pissed off when I ditched it.'

'What did you ditch?'

'Politics, philosophy and economics. Mum and dad had me down as squeezing in ahead of Pitt the Younger in the Prime Minister stakes.'

'What happened?' asked Buchan.

The lad was eating the breakfast like it was the first food he'd had in weeks, stopping only to butter toast, take a drink of tea.

'Politics happened. You know, I'd always been so interested in it, and invested in it, like, I know it was weird, from like the age of eight or nine. I was way ahead in maths and English, then history, Latin, the classics, and I really got into politics. I loved reading about Nixon, and Watergate. That's what got me into it. Political history, economics, the world today. I loved the news. And then, I don't know, something turned. It wasn't Boris, it wasn't Trump or Farage, it wasn't Putin or MBS... it just happened, and by the time I was presenting my thesis, I was sick of it. Sick of them all. Every party in Scotland, every party in the UK, every murderous dictator around the globe. And the squalid, unthinking, deluded level of student politics in Scotland, you wouldn't believe.'

'I live here,' said Buchan.

'Right? So, I don't know what I'll do. Took this job at the society a few months ago. Just something to keep me going until a brilliant idea falls from the sky.'

'That's the trouble with genius, son,' said Buchan. 'Deciding what to do with it.'

'That's what dad says.'

'Well, I appreciate you coming to help us.'

McAdam speared the rest of a sausage, ran it through egg yolk, and put it into his mouth.

Buchan took a copy of the note that had been left for him at the mailbox, and placed it on the table.

'Did Constable Dawkins read this to you?'

'She did. I noted it down, so it's OK, you don't need to show it to me.'

Buchan left it there for a moment, but McAdam looked like he found its presence uncomfortable for some reason, and so Buchan lifted the piece of paper, folded it, and put it back in his pocket. Then he waited, while McAdam focused on eating for a couple of forkfuls, then he took a bite of toast, a quick drink of tea, and then he reached down to the backpack, undid the zip, and pulled out a single piece of paper, which he placed on the table in the same spot from which Buchan had just lifted the copy of the note.

It was an extract from an old book, an image blown up, so that the quality was a little grainy, the small-print writing around it blurred into unreadability.

The image was of an old family crest. A shield with crossed swords. In the four corners, a butterfly, a raven, a jackal and a snake. Buchan studied it, couldn't stop himself running his fingers over the image, then he tapped it.

'Where'd you find this? The constable never found it online.'

'Despite everything, there remains much in paper form, tucked away in the deep, dark places of the world. This was in a book of heraldry from seventeen-fifty-seven. Produced in the wake of the forty-five rebellion.'

'Friends and enemies of the state?'

'More or less, yes. There's a lot of detail, there's a lot of history which has been lost. There are names here that would never have been a clan name, or indeed even associated with a clan. Forgotten names. And this is one of them.'

'What's the name?'

'McTarbet. I've checked, and there are currently no McTarbets remaining in Scotland, so I'm not sure why you're checking this, but there's potential it's a dead end.'

'Have you identified the specific McTarbets who possessed this coat of arms in the eighteenth century?'

'The family is noted in this book, along with their accomplishments at the time. A very minor landowner in Angus, the son fought with the British at Culloden and claimed fifty-seven kills.'

'Was that normal?'

'Cumberland's forces numbered roughly nine thousand. There were between a thousand and fifteen hundred casualties on the Jacobite side. That one of Cumberland's men should account for fifty-seven of those deaths himself seems unlikely. Not completely out of the question of course, but we're probably in the world of someone claiming far more for themselves than was warranted, a not unfamiliar human foible.'

'What comes next?'

'For the McTarbet family name? So far, nothing. I'd hazard a guess that the man who had the coat of arms created for himself, boasting about his family's triumph, did not live to enjoy it. Perhaps his son did not live to father any children. And so his, and the family's moment of glory, such as it was, was short-lived.'

Buchan stared at the image, then said, 'Tell me. Each of the creatures as motifs, what do they represent?'

'So this would be a serpent, not a snake. I imagine, if the poet here is intending heraldic representation, he used the term snake rather than serpent because it scans better. The serpent represents wisdom and defiance, rather than one of the more dangerous or sinister interpretations you might expect. Equally, the raven represents knowledge and divine providence, rather than the kind of sinister, ominous thing you'd find in the movies.'

'Divine providence,' said Buchan, naturally picking up on it, and McAdam said, 'Everything that happens is God's will,' and Buchan nodded. The raven, then, at least made sense within the context of what was going on. Perhaps the killer thought the serpent's wisdom and defiance also applicable.

'The jackal's interesting, of course, the wolf being far more common in Scottish heraldry. The jackal's a kind of take-your-pick creature here. On the one hand clever, on the other, sly and deceitful. On the one hand courageous, on the other desolate. Like I say, take your pick.'

'And the butterfly?'

'Nominally, peace, life-affirming, which would be no surprise. But here, the combination of the butterfly and this vibrant blue? This blue was used in the herald of Clan McCoulty. They supported the Jacobite cause until… well, they didn't. They turned on them at the last, fought with the British at Falkirk Muir, and then at Culloden. For this specific period then, at this specific time, this blue spoke of treachery, and putting it on the butterfly like this? Naturally it inverts its meaning, so that suddenly the butterfly speaks of war, or at the very least, death.'

Buchan was nodding along by the time he'd finished, as McAdam continued to eat his large breakfast.

'This is related to these grotesque murders that have been on the news?' he asked.

Buchan absent-mindedly took a bite of the pastry, then put the coffee to his lips, took a drink.

'I shouldn't really discuss it,' he said, and he hesitated, as he had every intention of discussing it, then McAdam said, 'Of course, of course,' and Buchan said, 'No, the more information you have, the greater the chance you'll be able to help us.'

Nothing from McAdam, now just waiting to see what Buchan was going to offer up.

'The killer calls his victims, as far as we can tell, and reads this to them as a kind of threat. Toying with them.'

'You got sent this note?'

'I did, though in my case, while he's definitely toying with me, I don't see it as a death threat.'

'Why?'

'Different scenario,' said Buchan.

McAdam continued to eat, racing through his food. Buchan wondered if he was going to want another plateful when he was done.

'I'm not so sure,' said McAdam.

'You don't know all the facts.'

'All I know is what you just told me. The people who died were given this message, and you were also given this message.'

Buchan took a drink, which he recognised in himself was really a gesture with the cup to cut through the conversation, change the subject.

'I'm going to need to follow a line from this coat of arms to someone alive today,' he said.

'And you think this person will be the killer? Wouldn't it be unlikely, if such a trail could be followed, that the killer would leave it for you?'

'Depends how much of a game he's playing,' said Buchan, not wanting to get into the repeat of a conversation he'd already had. 'However it works out, I'm going to need to throw everything at following the ancestral line from here.' He tapped the image.

'I can do that for you, if you like, but you'd be better speaking to someone in this specific field.'

'You're on board already Dr McAdam, and if you know where to look, I'd rather just leave it with you.'

McAdam accepted this, his look matter-of-fact, with an abrupt nod.

'Of course,' he said.

'You can work with Constable Dawkins.'

'Yes.'

Buchan stared at the young man, wondering if there was anything else he needed, then he pushed his chair back, got to his feet, lifted the pastry and the cup of coffee and said, 'If you'll excuse me, I'll leave you to it. I'll send the constable up now, and the two of you can make a plan,' and McAdam said, 'Of course,' again, and Buchan turned away.

*

He stopped in to see Gilmour on his way back to the office.

'We're set for tomorrow evening,' said Gilmour, as he walked in, and he looked at her blankly. He'd come in to give her an update, not to receive one.

'Sorry?'

'The screening of *The Omen* at the Filmhouse.'

He stared curiously at her, and then finally it slotted into place. He'd thought it so unlikely, and so frivolous a plan, that when he'd left it with her, it had been – to him at least – on the understanding that it likely wouldn't happen.

'They're really showing it?' he said.

'Tomorrow evening, ten p.m. Special late night, forty-eighth anniversary, surprise screening.'

'Forty-eighth?'

'It's forty-eight years, what d'you want me to say?' she said.

'Seems a little random.'

'It was never going to be anything else. And this is… what can I say, inspector, these are the days we live in. Everything's random, that's the beauty of it. As we speak, on the Internet, there are ads running for a forty-eighth anniversary special screening of *The Omen*, and literally no one will read that and think, that's odd. Because in this day and age, it's not.'

'It's on at their smaller screen, though right?' said Buchan, already thinking through the logistics of how exactly they were going to go about narrowing down the cast list of customers.

'Yes. One hundred and forty-seven available seats.'

Buchan was still surprised, though incredulity never stayed with him for long. Once you accepted something was happening, then you needed to address it and work through the problems. This is where they were.

'So, how are we tracking these people?' he asked.

'We'll have real-time facial recognition tracking. And that's going to apply to anyone who so much as passes by the cinema, as our perp could of course come along out of curiosity, and then decide maybe it's a trap, it's not worth taking a chance.

'Once in the building, we're looking at a system of, rather than giving out tickets, we do the rock festival idea of a stamp to the rear of the hand.'

'And you attempt to extract DNA from the stamp?' asked Buchan.

'That's the plan. We're still fine-tuning the mechanics.'

'Who with?'

'It's in hand, and they'll be discreet. You asked me to take care of it, and I'm taking care of it.'

'You need some of my people there?' he asked.

'Possibly. I'm not sure of the scenario where we'll need people on the spot. It's not as though we're going to recognise the killer there and then. People will come to the cinema, we poke a nose into their lives, if any require closer inspection, then we go after them, full bore.'

'Who's making the closer inspection call?'

'You and me,' she said, as though surprised he had to ask, then she accepted how the conversation was going. 'I'm not trying to take over the investigation, inspector. I made a suggestion, which I now see you went along with because you didn't think it would actually happen. I'm trying something. Resources are not an issue. If it works, then terrific, if it doesn't, it's just something we tried that didn't come off.'

'Roger that,' said Buchan. 'Keep me up-to-date, let me know how many of my people you'll need.'

'Will do. Otherwise, where are we now? Is there anything from last night's double murder that plays to *The Omen* narrative?'

'Not that we've come across so far. Just about to go and stop in on Mary, see where she's got to. I'm assuming we'll have the same set-up with the jackal semen, but we'll see. That aside, it hasn't added anything to our understanding of the case as yet. The victims had avoided a custodial sentence that for the most part people thought they ought to have been given. The same m.o.'

'It's a tough one to combat. Online at the moment, the Sun is running an approval rating score for the killer, and they're on eighty-three percent. There's not a politician in the galaxy who wouldn't be happy with those numbers.'

'Maybe we'll find it's a politician who's doing it,' said Buchan glibly.

'If that emerges, it might be the only way the killer's approval rating falls again.'

'Well, it'll make a change for us to be popular if we don't catch someone, but I think I'll still give it my best shot,' said Buchan, and Gilmour smiled ruefully.

'You'll have seen the memo on leave,' she said. 'It's all cancelled. We have city-wide all hands. We need a more visible presence, day and night. And we know this is bullshit, we know having an officer walk down one street, means absolutely nothing to the people on the street two blocks away, but we're going to show willing, and we're going to show potential. This perp's popularity aside, we already know the public will be baying for police blood if we don't catch him.'

'Ma'am,' said Buchan.

'How about you, you need to expand your team?'

'I like it the way it is at the moment, and we're expanding it as and when it's required, in any case,' said Buchan, and he nodded at her to indicate Gilmour's part in organising the movie.

'Very well, inspector. I'll be doing the five-thirty with the press, so speak to me at five, please,' and Buchan nodded and turned from the room.

44

The solemnity of the morgue in all its stillness. Buchan and Donoghue standing over the corpse of Devon Craigie.

'I don't think this is helping,' said Buchan after a while standing there in silence.

'What d'you mean?'

'Turning off the music. There was something strange about it, the Beatles always playing in here, but it lifted it, nevertheless. Now it's gone, what are you left with? The silence seems grim.'

'I told you,' she said, 'I don't want it ruined. It means too much to me.'

'There's other music,' said Buchan.

He'd had the thought on the way over, though had decided in the car that he wouldn't say anything.

'I know there's other music.'

'Listen to other music. It's doesn't have to be Eric and Ernie singing *Bring Me Sunshine*.'

She paused what she was doing, and then lifted her eyes. He couldn't see her mouth, but her eyes were smiling at least.

'Perhaps you're right,' she said. 'I'll give that some thought for tomorrow. Thank you, inspector.'

'This is horrible,' said Buchan, indicating Craigie's corpse, suddenly a little discomfited by the fact she hadn't just batted his suggestion aside with a glib comment, as he'd been expecting.

'No less so on closer examination,' said Donoghue, then she straightened a little, and looked along the length of the body. 'There's a small mark in the neck. As you suspected, and the same for his wife. Tranquilizer dart. Damn, that must have been brutal to take him out like that.' She snapped her fingers.

'We're guessing the killer had done their homework, but that was a damned good guess at the required dosage.'

'All of this,' said Donoghue, 'the bruising we see here before we come to the head, was done first. He made him suffer. And you'll note the same attack on the genital area as we saw with Kieran Sledd. There was a lot of pain inflicted.'

'A recurrence of the jackal semen?' he asked, thinking immediately he had worded it poorly, before wondering how else he would have put it.

'Yes, again done early on in the assault, and not done pleasantly. In fact, of the four murders so far, this one has the most severe anal injuries. Very unpleasant. Indeed, he may well have bled to death from those injuries, had not this been done to his head.'

Buchan glanced back at the head, which he'd largely been avoiding looking at.

'What does that tell us?' he asked. 'Did the killer get carried away? Was this his rage, continuing long after death had been administered? In fact, given that the guy was going to bleed out anyway, none of it was actually necessary.'

'No,' she said, 'I don't think so. I don't think this is rage. I think this is cold, calculated murder. I'm not even sure it's made to look like rage. There's probably not a blow here that was misplaced. You want to crush the skull with a baseball bat?' She indicated the area where the skull had been crushed. 'This is the exact point you'd do it. And everything else that was done to Mr Craigie, I think was likely done first. You can decide if this meant the killer wanted to taunt Mrs Craigie, or whether he wanted to see her reaction to her husband being bludgeoned to death before deciding whether to also kill her.

'You'll have noticed last night, she didn't have the same bruising over her body. Her murder, while also being done with a pummelling to the head, was functional. He decided to kill her, and he carried out the execution based on the murder weapon at his disposal.'

'Jackal semen?'

'Yes, but delivered also very functionally. A test tube maybe, semen injected, no other sign of vaginal abuse. Possible, though I haven't made the determination yet, that it was done post mortem.' She thought her next statement over for a second or two, finger tapping lightly on Craigie's bruised leg, then added, 'I'm inclined to think he thought about not killing her. Perhaps he wished to see remorse, perhaps he even considered that he might be doing her a favour, that she'd been living in fear of her husband. Maybe he removed the gag, though one presumes she'd have screamed in that case…'

'We have no report of that.'

'Perhaps he just read it in her eyes. The hate. You hate me

for killing your murderous husband, you are on his side, therefore you deserve the same fate.'

They looked at each other, they looked back down at the corpse.

Every murder gave them a little more to unpack about the killer, but so far, none of it was making his identity any clearer.

'I'll leave you to it,' said Buchan, after a while.

'I'll have the report with you by early afternoon.'

He nodded, he turned away. He stopped for a moment, thinking of a musical suggestion, then decided she was more than capable of deciding that for herself, and probably didn't want to hear anything anyway, and he walked on, out of the room and along the sterile, white corridor, out into the main reception area, and then outside, back into the noise and bustle and the grey light of the city.

45

'How are we doing?' asked Buchan, walking back into the office.

Dawkins and Cherry were on the phone. Cherry acknowledged him but had nothing to say, Dawkins didn't notice his return.

'Progress,' said Kane, indicating Marks as she said it.

'What have we got?' asked Buchan.

'Think I've discovered why Fin Markham was murdered, sir,' said Marks, and Buchan felt the first thrill of getting anywhere in the investigation more or less since they'd started, and he made a gesture for her to continue. 'These romantic stories that Alan Conway was talking about writing. We thought it was curious he made a living out of it, given how infrequently he actually seems to publish. Turns out that's not his main source of revenue. He writes very graphic, and sadistic comic book pornography. Revenge rape, whatever that is, gangbang, abuse, including spousal and child abuse. Nasty, brutal, misogynistic porn.'

'Where's this published?'

'A company called Luxuendo. It used to be dark web, but doesn't have to be anymore. We all get to be who we are now, right? If you're a rape fetishist, then you're a rape fetishist. Go ahead, fill your boots, as long as you just fantasize about it, they can't lock you up. The BBC will probably have you on a human interest segment. What does the cost of living crisis mean for rape fetishists?'

She held up an apologetic hand to stop herself, and Buchan said, 'You're not wrong.'

'Sorry, get carried away sometimes. Anyway… Not only does Alan Conway write this crap, he does it using the name Fin Markham.'

Buchan was rarely surprised by these people, by anything in this job, and yet that one came out of nowhere, and he found himself saying, 'You are kidding?' which wasn't something that usually crossed his lips. 'What is the damned matter with people? Jesus.'

He turned away, angry. Deep breath, thinking it through, then he turned back.

'How do we know?' he said.

'Luxuendo Publishing is on our watch list already. When I'd traced it to them, we were able to track their payments in and out. The payments for the work of Fin Markham were made to Alan Conway. Now, of course, it could be that she wrote them, and he took the money. I haven't been able to get hold of anyone there, unsurprisingly.'

'Are they based in the UK?'

'Payments are made through an account in London, but they're actually based in Guangzhou.'

'Dammit. Right, let's get round there, speak to this bloody man.'

Then he stopped, calming himself down first, thinking it through.

'How did the killer know about Markham though? I mean, to be able to equate this person whose name was on sick pornography, with this girl who worked in a supermarket and was a member of the Democratic Green Party?'

'We don't know,' said Marks.

'Could be the killer just happens to follow this particular cross section of society,' said Kane. 'He's in the Democratic Greens, or at least, he leans that way politically. He reads this kind of porn. We're dealing with a sick individual here. He might well read it, and hate himself for reading it at the same time. He wants it to stop. He sees the name, he already knows someone by that name, he puts them together, he kills her.'

'Dammit,' muttered Buchan, then, 'I'm going to speak to Conway. You OK to stay on this, Isobel, see how far you can get?'

'Of course.'

'Message if anything else comes up while we're out.'

'Sir.'

Buchan nodded at Kane, and she pushed her chair back and followed him from the room.

46

Buchan hated it when they started crying. Perhaps it was because he had no judgement on whether or not they were faking it. He just always assumed they were faking it. Kane had likened it to never believing when a footballer went down injured, which wasn't an analogy that had made a lot of headway with Buchan.

'I remember watching the Brazil World Cup quarter-final in 'fourteen with my dad,' she'd said, 'and Neymar went down injured. Dad's shouting at the tele, get up you cheatin' wee bastard. Turned out he had a fractured vertebra.' She'd smiled at the reminiscence. 'He still maintained Neymar was a cheating wee bastard, and that his own disbelief was a perfect example of footballers crying wolf every time they're on the park.'

'Sorry, I switched off after a while there,' Buchan had said.

For some reason that conversation, from some point a couple of years previously, came into his head. He was at a familiar spot by the window, looking out on a bleak back yard, the back of a row of terraced houses immediately behind. Kane was sitting across the table from the sobbing Conway. In between them, the closed laptop, an empty mug.

'Are your tears genuine?' said Buchan coldly into the room, deciding he'd had enough. He wasn't going to allow the man's crying to take away from the fact he was pissed off at him.

A moment while the question filtered through Conway's apparent torture, and then he sniffed, turned, and stared at Buchan with a look of horror.

'Are your tears genuine?' Buchan repeated.

'What the fuck?' blubbed Conway, through the dampness on his face, the moisture, the mucus in his mouth.

'This is the fourth time I've talked to you,' said Buchan, his voice level and cold. 'Miss Markham is no more dead now than the other three times. You didn't react like this then, and yet you do it now. You do it when the interview is about you. You do it when we come calling with an accusation. You do it when we draw it to your attention that if you were doing something the killer didn't like, and passing it off as Miss Markham's work, then your actions might well have been what got them killed. And while that's news to the sergeant and me, having only just discovered it this morning, you've obviously known about it all along. So, when sitting here facing up to your part in Miss Markham's death, you didn't seem all that troubled. Now though, now that we surprise you with the knowledge of what you were doing, you do this. You weep, having not wept before. I don't believe your tears.'

'How d'you know I haven't wept before?' Conway shouted, rising out of his seat, and then he immediately collapsed back into it, and once again started sobbing, before managing to blurt, 'And they weren't fucking Miss, you asshole,' through the tears.

Buchan and Kane exchanged a glance. Something in her look to say that perhaps it would be best if he left the interview to her, which was of course what he usually did. From nowhere, he thought of Donoghue, standing forlornly in the morgue, not doing anything different than she'd been doing for twenty years. And yet now, from nowhere it had come. The sense of defeat. The sense she'd been there too long. Had seen too much death. And here he was, feeling exactly the same thing. And, he thought, there was something else he could add on top that he didn't think applied to Donoghue.

He didn't care.

He indicated for Kane to follow him, then he walked out into the corridor.

'I'm going to kill this guy,' he said, his voice low. 'You OK to handle it?'

'I think that might be best.'

'K, thanks. I'm happy for you to use me as the bogeyman in my absence.'

Kane smiled and said, 'Oh, I will,' and Buchan nodded, and turned away.

*

He stood still, standing at the end of the short path leading to Conway's house. The street was quiet. The occasional car, a couple of women a hundred yards away chatting. No other sound from close by, but the sounds of the city all around. The low rumble of life, and a plane overhead making its final approach towards the airport.

He stood still, staring directly across the road. Another row of terraced houses, though he was looking at nothing, seeing nothing. In some other timeframe, he would likely have been smoking. In this one, he might have been looking at his phone. But that wasn't Buchan, and his phone stayed in his pocket.

He didn't bother trying to think about the case. He was doing enough of that, had been doing it since he and Roth had parted on Oswald Street just after seven that morning. He needed the pause. Time to reset, and pick it back up again when Kane emerged.

The night before, at dinner, he and Roth had discussed taking a trip. Roth had had all the suggestions. Oman. Japan. Vietnam. Iceland. The Canadian Rockies. Walking in Kyrgyzstan, stopping off in Istanbul on the way back, coming home on the Orient Express. Every one of them sounded exotic and exciting to Buchan, who never thought of going anywhere, and had she forced him to suggest a destination, would likely have said the Alps, because they'd been there before. 'Or we could just go to Millport,' she'd said to round things off.

'The fuck are you doing?'

Buchan focussed. He was staring straight at a woman standing in the doorway across the road. Between them nothing other than six yards of road and pavement. Buchan, in another world, hadn't noticed her.

He stared at her, contemplated replying, then decided not to bother. Shook his head, looked away.

'I'm calling the polis,' she said, already brandishing the phone in her hand.

Buchan sighed.

ID needlessly out of his pocket, as she obviously wasn't going to be able to read it from across the road, and he said, 'DI Buchan. Just waiting for an interview to end.'

She watched him warily for a few moments, and then decided to step into the fray. Phone slipped into the pocket of her dressing gown, and she stepped forward, leaving her door open. She stood in the middle of the road, a couple of yards away, arms folded across her chest.

She was in her mid-twenties maybe. Full make-up, oversized eyelashes, hair tied tightly back. Buchan wondered if she'd found herself distracted from getting ready to go out, or whether she prepped her face every day to sit in her living room looking at her phone.

'Young woman are a mystery to you, aren't they?' Roth had said to him at some point, although they'd both known she hadn't been referring to herself.

'One of you lot in there interviewing that heid-the-ba', are they?' said the woman.

'You know Mr Conway?' asked Buchan.

'Don't speak to him, but I know him. You arresting him for killing the girl?'

'Not as far as I know. Did you know Fin Markham?'

'Seen her about.'

'You ever speak to her?'

She thought about it, her eyes on Buchan as she processed what she knew about Fin Markham, then she said, 'Just that time they had that thing in his house. Pretty cringe to be honest.'

'What thing?'

'It was a party. At least, you know, it was supposed to be a party. They threw out a general invitation. Turned out it was some kind of an open mic night, you know. They had instruments and stuff, anyone who could play could give it a go. Think it was just a chance for heid-the-ba' in there to show off.'

'What'd he play?'

'Alec's like that, the clown knows three chords on the guitar, thinks he's Kurt Cobain. I'm like that, *Smells Like Teen Spirit*'s got five chords, you muppet. It was still shite though.'

'He played this song on the guitar?'

'Aye, that was his wee party piece. And sang. And he had some shitty drum machine track playing along 'n all. *Molto imbarazzante.*'

Buchan gave her a curious look, thought about it, decided he probably knew what that meant, and said, 'What about Fin?'

'She just ran around filling up drinks, producing food, making sure no one threw up on the carpet. Suppose it was an all right evening. I mean, eclectic, I guess. There was a decent guy on the piano, a couple of guys could sing. Oh, wee Tony along the road there, he did a stand-up. Thought that would be all kinds of cringe in itself, but he was pretty funny. Did a routine on spider season. You know it's spider season in September and October?'

'I heard that,' said Buchan.

'But like I say, there was all sorts, so plenty of toe-curling shockers 'n all. A smorgasbord.'

'Nice word.'

'Ha. Don't be so condescending.'

Buchan was about to object, stopped himself, accepted that yes, he had been condescending.

'Did you speak to either Fin or Alan?'

'Spoke to the lassie a bit. She was right into green politics, and the rigging of the system in favour of the petrochemical giants. I was like that, yada, yada, yada. Bit of a nihilist myself. We're all fucked anyway, that's the way I see it. Fast track to destruction, everything dies – including all of us – then the earth can start again. Maybe it'll work out better next time, eh? Going to be hard pushed to be worse than what we've come to now.'

The word smorgasbord sat in Buchan's head. It was, whether one was being condescending or not, a good word. And that, he thought, was where they were with this killer. *The Omen* thing the following evening, he thought, was pointless, because as the team had previously discussed, he was picking his cultural references from a great array of options. Indeed, all the artistic options in the world, from Russian literature to nineteen-seventies horror, and everything in between. And, given that, wasn't it also likely that the butterfly, the raven, the jackal and the snake combination wasn't real life, it wasn't something that could be traced back to an obscure family who disappeared shortly after the battle of Culloden?

Dawkins had set out to throw a wide net, she'd hit upon that link, but as a result, she'd stepped back from the search.

We will have missed something, he thought. Out of nowhere, based on no new information, that seemed to make sense. The McTarbet coat of arms link would turn out to be a red herring.

'What d'you read?' asked Buchan, absent-mindedly. Wanting to talk about this, and picking the only option currently open to him.

'What do I *read*?' She laughed. 'You mean, like at university? I read physics, chemistry and Latin, with a side of Harry Potter.'

'Coats of arms,' said Buchan, turning away from her, thinking out loud. 'They're prevalent in real life, of course, but they must be far more prevalent in fiction. Agnes is always talking about all those fantasy books, the proliferation of them.'

'The fuck's Agnes?'

She was amused by Buchan, aware that his mind was racing

away in some other direction, and that he had no particular interest in taking her with him.

'Dammit,' he said, and he turned back to her, even though his look into her eyes was vague. 'Movie and TV as well. Must be hundreds of these things. Thousands.'

'Fantasy shows?' she said. 'Double that. And I tell you what, you can't watch one without mixing it up with all the others. That's how the entertainment business works, right? Something's a hit, and then boom, it's like that, a million copies come along. That's why I'm reading physics, chemistry and Latin.' She laughed again.

'What does the jackal, the butterfly, the raven and the snake mean to you?' asked Buchan, still talking abstractly, not expecting any answer. When he finally focussed on her face, he saw she was looking at him with amusement.

'Who even are you?'

'That combination of animals doesn't mean anything?'

'Maybe a weird episode of David Attenborough? I love that shit, by the way. See when Attenborough goes, I'm going to be like that…'

Buchan held her look for another moment, nodded, muttered thanks, and then turned away.

'It's peanuts compared to gaming though,' she said to his back.

A moment while the words slowly filtered through, then Buchan cancelled the call he had just made, and turned back.

'Gaming?'

'I mean, all that fantasy crap online. Good luck sorting through that garbage. There you will find the very worst, and most depressingly dull of humanity.'

She smiled, she was getting nothing from Buchan in return, then she laughed to herself, waved him off, and turned away, taking her phone from her pocket as she went.

47

Dawkins was shaking her head.

'Yes, we spent time on it, but I suppose in relation to just how much there's going to be to check, only a small percentage, sorry,' she said. 'To be honest, the heraldic idea occurred to me, I thought I should check the real thing first, found this example, got hold of Dr McAdam, and it seemed like it might be falling into place.'

'And so it might,' said Buchan, 'but I feel we have to at least look at the other thing.'

'And by other thing, you mean, every fictional and online historical movie, show, game or book to see if there's ever been this conflation of creatures?'

Buchan wasn't any more impressed with the idea than Dawkins, but the need to do it seemed inevitable.

'I'm not sure,' said Kane, and Buchan made a small gesture for her to continue.

Early afternoon in the ops room, Buchan, Kane, Dawkins, Cherry and Marks.

'Sounds like a lot of man hours, and then what do we get? This isn't anything we've discovered for ourselves. He's fed it to us, which means he wants us to know it. Should we manage to find the genuine source, and let's say we can trace some similar usage of these four creatures online, and we can pinpoint it to a specific account, which leads us to a specific IP address, which leads us to a house, he's going to know we're capable of all that, and what's going to be there when we arrive? Another note? Something else that'll serve solely to mock us? By chasing all these little clues he's leaving, we're playing his game.'

'I'm not going to argue,' said Buchan. 'However, I'm just not sure what we should be doing otherwise. It's not like we're not going through the usual procedures, but this guy is good. So far there's no DNA left behind, there've been no sightings. The more we can track down, the greater the chance we come across a mistake. We have to follow all these leads on the off-chance he inadvertently left a little of himself behind somewhere. I'm not sure what else it is that we've got.'

Dawkins was tapping her forefinger on the desk, nodding to herself, then she said, 'Yes, yes. I spoke to Fforbes twenty minutes ago, and he's not making much progress. Far as he can tell, that line died out and...' and she ran a finger across her throat.

A couple of the others were nodding in agreement. Kane was tapping a pen on her notes. She didn't like it, but she didn't really have an argument against what Buchan was saying.

'And if we do find something,' Buchan continued, 'it's contingent on us to find a way to use it. That we haven't yet, doesn't mean we won't.'

'I don't believe this guy,' said Marks, who was sitting back, hands resting on the table, a pen in her right hand, tapping slowly on a notebook.

'Go on,' said Buchan.

'Hey, look at me, I'm God, I'm going to kill people who've got it coming? I'm a bit tortured about it, but this is for the public good. What does he think's going to happen? That the thugs and abusers across the land will suddenly think, rats, it'll be me next, I'd better stop hitting my wife, raping my daughter? I don't think so. I don't think that, I'll bet none of us here think it, and there's no way some random guy thinks it either.'

'So, what do you think?' asked Kane, leaning into the discussion, enjoying Marks' certainty.

'I think he wants one of these people dead. I think it's the most ridiculously elaborate set-up. Maybe he killed the first four as well, although I'm not sure. I think, like we've previously discussed, he'll have read the news, and selected his "victims." And all this, the jackal and *The Omen* and the Dostoyevsky, it's all bullshit. I agree with the sergeant, he's throwing us bones, and he's probably pissing himself laughing that we keep running after them.' She tapped her pen, looking around the table. 'We just have to know whether he's already killed his principal intended victim, or whether they're still to come.'

'I like this,' said Kane.

'Yes,' agreed Buchan. 'And if you're right, I think he'll already have taken his victim. If he'd left the main intended victim until later, there's a chance they'd've read about the vigilante and decided to make themselves scarce, or at least would have started to take precautions. He had to get them early, before it became this full-blown, everywhere all at once storyline.'

'Yes,' said Marks. 'I think it's someone invested in one of the victims, and so, not out of the question it's someone we've already spoken to.'

'How'd you get on with Conway?' asked Cherry. 'I mean, that guy's got to be damned high up the list, if not at the top, right?'

'Sergeant,' said Buchan, giving Kane the floor.

'He was feeling sorry for himself,' said Kane. 'We put it to him it was in fact his fault that Markham had been killed, and he collapsed in tearful self-pity. I have no idea how much to believe it, it's not like he wouldn't already have realised by now, particularly after we went round there yesterday and directly put it to him that Markham must have done something someone thought worthy of society's revenge.'

'Self-denial becomes a lot more difficult in the face of the law,' said Dawkins.

'We went easy on him,' said Buchan drily, and then he shared a glance with Kane, who couldn't help the smile.

'Did she know he was using her name?' asked Marks, and Kane shook her head.

'Fin didn't even know he wrote this stuff. No one did. Anyone who asked where he got his money, he just said the romance stories, then we came along and didn't take his word for it.'

'So, why'd he use her name?'

'In his estimation, his own name's too boring for this kind of thing. He started using Fin's name a couple of years ago. He told me through his tears he thought it was sexy he used her name for erotica. Said he always meant to tell her, and that she'd have loved it.'

'She wouldn't have loved it,' said Dawkins.

'No, I don't believe she would, which is why he would never have told her. I put it to him that it was little more than another example of a man exploiting a woman, keeping control over her that she didn't even know he had. And he said…' and she lifted her eyebrows around the table, and Marks said, 'That they weren't a woman, so how could it be misogyny?'

'Bingo.'

'I hate this guy,' said Buchan, 'though I suppose in all the gender thing he's just being true to his partner's wishes. Have you had a look through everything he wrote under the name Fin

Markham?'

Marks nodded to herself as she considered her answer, then she said, 'I have not, to be honest. It was pretty grotesque, and at some stage early on I thought, I've seen enough. Would you like me to?'

'I think you have to. If you need to share it out, maybe you can split it three ways.'

'How hard can reading erotica be?' said Cherry, and Marks scowled and said, 'This is not erotica, regardless of what Conway calls it.'

'Let's split it,' said Dawkins. 'We can compare notes while we're throwing up.'

'Thanks,' said Buchan. A quick glance at his notes, and then, 'How are we doing otherwise?'

'Hey, I don't know if this is a coincidence,' said Cherry, 'but I saw an ad for a showing of *The Omen* tomorrow night at the Filmhouse. The forty-eighth anniversary. I mean, that seems kind of random, doesn't it?'

Buchan was nodding, something in his face that let Cherry know he already knew what was going on.

'It's the boss's plan,' said Buchan. 'And, I might add, it's not to leave this room. No leaks, or she'll be upset.'

'She's sticking her nose in?' said Cherry, curious.

'I wouldn't say that,' said Buchan. 'She's still the boss, and this is getting bigger and bigger, so I'm not going to go trying to get her to stay in her box. She likes the idea our killer is invested in *The Omen*. I think the more we learn, the more we'll see he's taking a scattergun approach to cultural reference points, but *The Omen* is obviously a prominent one. She suggested we do a Robin Hood, golden arrow competition affair. A screening of the movie, with the likelihood our *Omen*-obsessed guy shows up.'

'Really?' said Kane.

'Yes.'

'No, I mean, like, seriously? She thinks *that'll* work?'

'Yes, she does, and she's the senior detective in the building, so there's that. She suggested it, it's not like we have a fecundity of ideas here, so I said if she wanted to run the op, it was all hers. Did I think she'd actually be invested enough in it to even bother trying to overcome the first hurdle she faced? No, I didn't.' He indicated Cherry. 'As Danny already discovered, she overcame the hurdles.'

'Wow,' said Kane. 'How exactly is it we're identifying the

killer on the off-chance he's there? I mean, the guy could be sitting in the front row and we wouldn't know.'

'She's working on the specifics with Greg and Sandra.'

Kane looked surprised at that, and then finally shrugged.

'OK, well at least she's got decent people on it. Are we getting involved?'

'Waiting to hear. If she needs us, we'll be there. And, to be honest, I wouldn't mind if one or two of us were there whether we're needed or not.'

'It's not going to work, though,' said Kane. 'I mean, seriously?'

'Who knows?' said Buchan. 'I'll keep you posted with our required attendance tomorrow evening. And, like I said, not a word. You may think it's dumb, but don't be mentioning it to anyone. You can tell them all how dumb you thought it was on Thursday morning.'

Nods around the room, then Buchan pushed his chair away and got to his feet.

'We have a busy afternoon ahead,' he said. 'Let's get to it,' and he went to the door and led the way back to the office.

48

Late afternoon, darkness had come. Buchan and Kane standing at the window, looking down through their own reflections at the lights cast across the river. Outside, the sound of the city at rush hour.

'Sorry if I sounded too contemptuous of the boss's Robin Hood idea,' said Kane out of nowhere.

'You spoke for all of us,' said Buchan. 'But that's DCI Gilmour's rep, isn't it? She tries things. Sometimes they come off.'

'Those are the ones you get to hear about,' said Kane, and Buchan responded with a smile.

'I don't see how it's a disaster,' he said. 'At worst, it'll just be a waste of everyone's time.'

'Yeah, I guess,' said Kane. 'So I like the idea we already know who this is. That makes sense. It might seem elaborate, but it's the world we live in. There are so many stories, so much drama, and everyone wants to go that little bit extra. Look how *my* murder spree is even more batshit than that last one everyone's talking about.'

'That's exactly who we are as a species,' said Buchan.

'So we work towards identifying someone who wanted one of the victims dead,' said Kane, 'then they would have looked around for other suitable victims.'

'Fin Markham being the exception, because even if we think the reason she was killed was because of comic book revenge porn, it still doesn't really fit the narrative.'

'Feels off,' said Kane.

'It does. You see a name listed as the writer of a comic book, one of many by the sounds of it, they could live literally anywhere on earth, and you somehow know they're from Glasgow.'

'Because the Fin Markham that was on display on social media had nothing whatsoever to do with what was in those comic books. Which means we can possibly disregard it, but then, why else kill her? You might disagree with her politics, but she was on one side of the great political schism of the day, and she was no more vociferous than two million other people. There's nothing in her life that sets her up to be murdered, which is why we end up looking at the comic book thing and thinking, oh, OK, that might make sense.'

'But I'm not sure it does under closer examination,' said Buchan. 'We need more.'

He looked at his watch, unnecessarily glanced over his shoulder at the clock on the wall.

'Let's work up a list, get to it again in the morning,' he said, and Kane nodded, then he glanced over his shoulder and Kane said, 'You want me to get a notebook? Like, we're doing it here, now?'

'Yes.'

She turned, lifted the notebook and a pen from her desk, returned to her position. Turned a page, wrote Fin Markham at the top of the page.

'Are we talking to Conway again?' she asked.

'One hundred percent,' said Buchan, 'but I want something else before we go back to him. Stick him at the bottom of the list, but we won't forget him. Who else have we got?'

'Conway aside, the only two things she appeared to have in her life were work and politics. Oh there was the kid…,' and she tapped the notebook while she thought about it, 'Ben Holloway, bookshop in Ingram Street. He was upset. I mean, people should be able to be upset about someone dying without us thinking they must've murdered them, but this is where we are.'

'Yes,' said Buchan. 'And we need to do a deeper dive on her part in the Green splinter group. That was something we didn't give enough time to.'

'Danny had those guys, and he didn't think there was anything that warranted too much time.'

'We'll give it another look. And I'll speak to the boss at the supermarket again.'

Kane made notes, nodding as she went, then said, 'K. Anyone else?'

'Damn,' said Buchan, his thoughts jumping ahead, 'we should check in on Ally Nairn. It may not be the most popular use of police money, but we need to make sure he doesn't get killed on our watch.'

'Aye, that was a curious one,' said Kane. 'He got the warning, but still lives. What d'you think's going on there?'

'Could be the killer intended taking them both out at the same time, then when it came to it, the opportunity never arose. They went their separate ways earlier than anticipated, and the chance was lost.'

'That makes sense,' said Kane. 'Which might mean one of the other two friends is the killer. Or, of course, that Nairn is the killer and he's lying about receiving the message. If he was the one who sent it in the first place, he's certainly going to know what it said.'

'Right,' said Buchan. 'And tag on Mrs Sledd again, see if she's managed to think of anyone else close to her who might have held a grudge against her husband.'

'K,' said Kane, and she completed the notes on Sledd, then she said, 'And we come to the Craigies.'

'This is the toughest one,' said Buchan. 'It was the most public court case, causing the greatest amount of outrage. There were a lot of people pissed off with them, a lot of people thinking they deserved punishment. And yet…'

'They were so detached. It was like, they didn't take anything to do with anyone, anywhere. Lived on benefits, this closed shop of a couple. No friends, no contact with neighbours. Kind of sad.'

'Sure, that's the word. I'll speak to the ex-husband again. He didn't jump off the page, but he had motive at least, and of course his reaction might've been genuine, but that kind of thing, where you more or less shut down, that's not the hardest thing to fake. And there was something else I thought of after I left, more than likely nothing, but it's the kind of little thing you look for. He made a couple of pop culture references, that was all. Nothing much, but this feels like who we're dealing with here. Someone steeped in everyone else's stories, while trying to create their own. I don't know, probably nothing.'

'He's on the list. Who else have we got?'

'He's it, which bothers me. I'll see if he's got any other names he can think of, he'd more or less shut down by the time I came to that question.'

He checked his watch again, glancing at the notes Kane had been making.

'Anyone else off the top of your head?'

'Think we've got enough to be going on with in the morning.'

'K. Let's split them, you, me and Danny. I'm going to

speak to the station in Ardrossan, see what they've set up for Nairn.'

*

Buchan in the ops room, making the video call. On the other end, Sgt Handsworth, in uniform, sceptical in response to Buchan's question.

'If I can quote, sir,' she said. 'He told us we can fuck off. A lot of fucking good you did Kieran, he said. We pointed out we didn't know a threat had been made against Kieran, while we do know a threat has been made against him, but he wasn't one for logic. You lot are useless, et cetera, et cetera, then he gave us the well-worn line about us spending all our time arresting people for using the wrong pronouns which, I don't know about you, but we get more or less every day now.'

'I too have heard it,' said Buchan, playing along.

Roth had humanised him somewhat, though he rarely thought about it. This was just who he was now.

'Are you keeping an eye on his property in any case?' he asked.

'We were, except, he's not currently there, so there doesn't seem to be a lot of point. He left work at four. We spoke to him about his plans. He was not happy. Told my man to fuck off again. My guy followed him home. Lost him at lights, but wasn't too concerned, and no one's blaming him. This wasn't a blue light, crashing the lights in order to keep up scenario. He got to Nairn's house, no one there. He stayed an hour, I just called him off. There's no point in hanging around.'

She looked like she had something else to say, and then she decided to leave it, and handed over the conversational baton with a *that's where we are* expression.

'Out with it, sergeant,' said Buchan, and she smiled.

'I don't think so, inspector. These things are recorded.'

Buchan nodded. He knew what had been left unsaid in any case. This man was an awful human being. It was bad enough that they felt the need to offer him protection. If he didn't want it, then so be it.

Yes, thought Buchan, let him die.

Unless, of course, he didn't want police protection because he had something to hide.

'Thanks for your time,' said Buchan, and she nodded. 'I

hope we're not speaking again in the next couple of days.'

'I don't think it's over,' she said, 'though perhaps it is down here.'

And the conversation was done, and Buchan ended the call, closed the screen of the laptop, sat back, and stared along the conference table at the blank wall at the far end of the room.

49

Wednesday morning, after a nothing sort of Tuesday evening. Buchan was back in Ardrossan. Another drive down through Beith and Dalry in the Facel, too fast on the country roads.

Another small, depressing front room, the television playing with the sound off. The air smelled sweet, a vape scent like all the others. Jimmy Hardcastle had told them previously he was a joiner. It transpired he was a joiner in between jobs. He'd been laid off some time earlier in the year, hadn't been able to find anything since. 'Probably strike out on my own when I can find the time,' he'd muttered.

Time, Buchan thought, was not really his issue.

'How'd the four of you meet?' asked Buchan.

'Seriously?'

'Yes.'

A bitter laugh.

'Sure, whatever. Primary one. You going to read something in to that? We met in primary fucking one. Maybe Ally and Kieran were at the same nursery 'n all, so they have an extra couple of years on me and Reggie.'

'So, you're all forty-two?'

'Look at the genius head on this guy. Sherlock Holmes multiplied by that bastard Morse. Except Reggie's birthday's on Christmas Day, so that wanker's still forty-one.'

'You're using wanker affectionately there, are you?'

'Ha. Aye. Also accurately,' and he laughed again, this time accompanying it with the appropriate gesture.

'You kept in touch all that time?'

'Why not? Primary school, high school, none of us went to university. Kieran, the posh bastard, went to Ayrshire College, but he dropped out after about a month. Wasn't like he'd moved down to Kilmarnock anyway. Here we all are, still in Ardrossan, all these years later. If only that cunt Springsteen was from Largs and no' New Jersey, he'd'vo written a song about us.'

'What mutual interests have you got?'

'What mutual interests?'

'What kept you friends all these years?'

'Why wouldn't we be friends?'

'What d'you talk about?'

'Fuck me, man. Football, women, shagging, golf, TV. Fine, every now and again we talked about Trump or Boris or the utter shitshow that's the Scottish government, and Ally was always coming out wi' all that government conspiracy crap. Everything's a fucking plot with that guy, you know what I mean? But basically we're four guys fi' Ardrossan, we're not debating the fall of the Roman empire, man.'

'You're the only one not working at the moment?'

'Ally's part-time down at the boatyard. Reggie got some shit thing in construction. I said we were a Springsteen song, didn't I?'

'You see Ally when he's not working?'

'Why would I? Like I say, guy's a dick.'

'What does he do on his days off?'

'Just gaming all the time, man. I tried to get into it, but I'm like that, I don't have the…' and he made a gesture, his thumbs working furiously on an imaginary PlayStation controller. 'No idea how he does it, you know what I mean? You've got to be a Jedi to work one of they things. I'm so far out my depth it's like I'm trying to walk to Arran, man.'

'What's the game?'

'He's on that PlayStation all the time. American football sometimes. Madden, that's what it's called. I don't know anything about that shite, you know? And then there's some fantasy game or other. There's hunners of those things, you know what I mean? I'm like that, how can you even care about this shite? Like *Call of Duty* I sort of get. Kill bad guys. Everyone can get behind that, right? I was still pish at it, but at least it made sense. That fantasy pish though. Finding treasure, and rescuing women, and killing dragons. Get to fuck, man, you know what I mean?'

'What's the fantasy game called?' asked Buchan, trying not to show his level of interest.

'Fucked if I can remember,' said Hardcastle.

'Maybe you can try?'

'That'll help you find Kieran's killer, will it?'

Buchan didn't answer. Hardcastle shook his head, looking away to the side.

'Nope,' he said. 'If that's your big clue that's going to crack

184

the case, chief, you're going to have to get your information elsewhere. I don't know, how about asking Ally? It's him that plays the fucking thing.'

*

Buchan went to the boatyard where Nairn worked, and was told he wasn't in that day. He worked three days a week, usually Monday, Thursday, Friday. Occasionally a Saturday or Sunday was added, as it had been the weekend just gone. He tried asking questions about Nairn, his work attendance, and what kind of character he was, but the yard boss didn't like Buchan being there at all, the interview quickly descending into one-word answers and monosyllabic grunts.

Buchan went to Nairn's house, and found nobody home. He rang the bell of the houses on either side, and spoke to someone across the road, but no one had seen Nairn leave home that day. Or, at least, no one who was willing to talk to the police.

*

When Buchan arrived at the building site, Reggie Coleman was standing in a group of four drinking tea. There didn't seem to be a lot of conversation going on, nor much sign of anyone anywhere on the site doing any work.

Buchan approached the group, ID outstretched.

'Mr Coleman, if I could have a word.'

'You found Kieran's killer?' he asked, detaching himself from the group, and following Buchan to a more isolated spot, by a fence surrounding the site.

North end of town, a new-build estate, three- and four-bedroomed homes, nice view of the Clyde.

'Early days,' said Buchan.

'You lot really think it's related to the other murders?'

'It is definitely related to the other murders.'

Coleman shook his head, steaming mug in one hand, other hand on his hip, staring out over the water.

'Wow,' he said. 'I don't get it. Who even is this guy?'

'That's what we're trying to work out,' said Buchan.

'Aye, right. But I mean, why are they targeting Kieran? You think it was like mistaken identity? I mean, that's a thing, right?'

'You know this, Mr Coleman. Kieran abused his wife, he should have been given, in the estimation of a lot of people, a custodial sentence, and wasn't.'

'Aye, I know, but was it really so bad? I mean, a wee slap now and again.'

'When Laura Sledd finally went to the police, she was examined by three independent doctors. Her body was covered in bruises, she'd been anally and vaginally raped. None of the doctors thought it had been faked. Kieran admitted in court that every single one of the bruises and marks on her body had been as a result of his actions.'

'Aye, OK, fair, but like the judge said, Kieran said he was sorry, you know?' A pause, and then he added, 'He bought her flowers.' Buchan gave him the appropriate, grim look, and Coleman felt the need to add, 'And chocolates.'

'Tell me about Saturday nights?' asked Buchan, ignoring the absurdity of the flowers and chocolates defence.

'What about them?'

'Every Saturday you played golf, you went out for dinner, you went to the pub.'

'Aye.'

'Anything else, or did you all always go your own way after that?'

'More or less.'

'More or less.'

'Aye.'

'What about the times you didn't?'

Coleman knew where this was going, but he had no idea how much Buchan already knew, and he was unnerved. Buchan held a steady gaze, letting him stew in his discomfort.

'Occasionally we went back to Kieran's place. Laura likes it when we go round, you know. Kieran was the only one of us to get hitched, right. Laura was always joking about wanting to come and play golf, and come out for dinner, and come to the pub. She was a bit, you know, there was something of the Yoko Ono about her. Clingy.'

'Did you ever see this behaviour, or was that what Kieran told you?'

This time, Coleman was caught cold by an unexpected question. The comparison between Laura Sledd and Yoko Ono must have been such a solid part of his understanding of the relationship the Sledds shared, he'd never thought about it before.

'Kieran said. He always… you know, he called her Yoko sometimes. Behind her back.'

'How often did you go to Kieran's house on a Saturday?'

He lifted his mug, his expression changed a little as he took a drink, then he glanced at his colleagues, likely in the hope he was about to be summoned back to work.

'I'm here 'til we're done, Mr Coleman,' said Buchan, drily. 'How often did you go to Kieran's house on a Saturday?'

'About once a month,' he said.

'And what did you do there?'

'I don't know, what d'you usually do at a mate's house. Had a few drinks, played cards sometimes, watched *Match of the Day* or *Sportscene* or whatever.'

'Mrs Sledd liked you coming back to her place, so you could all watch football together?'

His eyes were a little wide now. Another glance across the building site. This time he looked like he wanted to say he had to go, but Buchan's presence was intimidating him. He lifted the mug again, then gave up on it long before it reached his mouth, and he tossed the contents away to the side.

'Fine,' he said.

Buchan didn't push him.

'Fine.' Deep breath. 'Look, it was a bit seedy sometimes, you know. Kieran was like, come on, lads, she's all yours, you know. To be honest… you know, felt a bit minging being the fourth one to dip your wick, you know what I mean, but you take what you can get.'

'How was Laura?'

'She was decent. Nice tits.'

Buchan had been looking at him witheringly for some time now. Nevertheless, he managed to make his look even more dismissive.

'What?'

'Was she a willing participant?'

'Aye, she seemed happy enough.'

'Really?'

'Kieran said she was fine.'

'What did she say?' snapped Buchan.

'She never said much, she was just like, aye, whatever.'

'Did it ever occur to you that you were committing rape?'

'The fuck, man? Of course not. Kieran said it was OK.

Jesus.'

For the second day in a row Buchan was ready to lose his temper at an interviewee, which was something he didn't recognise in himself. Usually he had patience for these people, no matter how awful they were. Something was snapping inside him.

This time, however, since there was no one he could pass the interview on to, he took a deep breath, told himself to pull back. This is who Reggie Coleman was, and he wasn't about to alter his entrenched views while standing in the corner of a building site on a chill Wednesday morning in October.

'You must've seen the bruises on Laura's body,' said Buchan.

Coleman shook his head, and Buchan indicated with a small gesture for him to talk.

'She didn't always take her clothes off. You know, if Kieran wasn't that into it, sometimes she was just like, skirt up, knickers pulled to the side, have at it, you know. Sometimes, if Kieran wanted to join in, it was a bit more, you know, intimate. But I never saw bruises.'

'What?' said Buchan his voice harsh again.

'What?'

'There was something in your voice there. Something you're not saying. Tell me.'

He managed to hold Buchan's gaze for a moment, and then turned away, looking out over the water. There was more truth to be told, but not while looking the investigating officer in the eye.

'Ally told me one time that though Kieran liked seeing us lot, you know, fuck her 'n that, when we were gone, and he'd had another couple of drinks, he'd completely lose his shit at her for being a slut. Then he'd, you know… that was when he hit her.'

'And after you found that out you stopped going round there to have sex with her?' said Buchan, although the question was loaded, and of course he already knew the answer.

Coleman didn't reply.

'Did any of the rest of you ever hit her?'

A moment, and then, 'No. No, that wasn't what it was about.'

'What about now?'

'What d'you mean?' he asked, turning back.

188

'Laura's now available. Three single guys. Who gets dibs?'

He looks genuinely shocked at that question, thought Buchan.

'I… I don't know what to say to that. I don't…'

'Have you been to see her?'

'Went round on Monday. She wasn't… she didn't really want to see anyone.'

'Did you kill Kieran so you could have Laura?'

A moment for the question to register, and then, wide-eyed and appalled, he said, 'Fuck off! Really? Course I didn't, what the fuck are you talking about?'

'Do you think either of the others might have done?'

'I don't … I mean, what? That's just…'

'That's just what?' asked Buchan, after it became clear Coleman wasn't going to be able to complete the sentence.

'That's just wrong. None of us would've… he was our best mate. Jesus.'

'OK, good to know the location of your moral compass,' said Buchan. 'Somewhere in the grey area between murdering your best mate, and raping his wife.'

'Man, you're a piece of work.'

'You know what video games Ally Nairn plays?'

Coleman took a moment to stare, adjusting to the abrupt change in the line of questioning.

'Really? Where are you going wi…'

'Do you know?'

'I guess,' he said, and then he turned away again and stared at the sea, nodding to himself as he thought about it. '*Madden, Lost Temple of Arcadia, Call of Duty*. What's that got to do with the price of cheese?'

'Thanks for your help,' said Buchan, abruptly turning away. 'You can go back to work now.'

50

'Do you distinguish between the other three?' asked Buchan.

Laura Sledd was in the same position as she had been the other times he'd spoken to her. Sitting on the sofa, leaning forward, elbows on her knees, holding a cup of cold tea in her hand, a quality to the tea that said it had been cold for a very long time, and she'd picked it up as a prop.

Today she wasn't wearing dark glasses, as the bruising around her eye had begun to fade.

'What does that mean?'

'Kieran's pals. The three of them. You said they'd come round here some Saturday evenings –'

'*Most* Saturday evenings.'

'They'd come here, and they'd treat you with the same contempt Kieran treated you.'

'Yes.'

'When both you and Kieran testified that all the bruises on your body were as a result of his attacks, was that honest?'

She paused before answering, but her eyes never dropped. She could stare through me all day, thought Buchan.

'Kieran didn't want to admit the truth in public, did he?' she said. 'He didn't want to admit he got some weird thrill seeing his mates shag his wife. He didn't want to admit that every time, every single time, he hated himself for it, and of course, I was his punchbag. Hated himself, took it out on the missus.'

'So, did you distinguish between Ally, Reggie and Jimmy? Was there one you preferred? Was there one you felt a little more intimate with, or one of them with whom you had a bit more of a connection? Like you shared an awareness that what they were doing was wrong?'

'No, no, no, and no. And no again, maybe. How many questions did you ask, I lost count?'

'When I asked you yesterday if any of them had been round, you never mentioned Reggie.'

'He tell you that, did he?'

'Yes.'

'Sure, he came round. I didn't want to see him. We stood at the door for about thirty seconds while he attempted to do sadness, then he left.'

'So, how come you didn't ask him in, but you asked Ally Nairn in?'

'I didn't ask Ally Nairn in. He came in. Not the same thing, officer.'

'Nothing today?'

'Just you.'

'Tell me about Ally?'

'What about him?'

'He's got a history of rape, assault, sexual assault.'

'He does, doesn't he?'

'But you never came forward when he was being charged.'

She burst out laughing.

'How remiss of me.'

'Because of Kieran?'

'Check out the big brain on Brett. You're a smart motherfucker…'

'What does that mean?'

'What?'

'Who's Brett?'

'It's a movie line, but if I have to explain it, it doesn't really work, does it?'

'You know any of the women who've been assaulted or raped by Ally? Any other than the ones who were in court?'

'Yes and yes, for what it's worth, and I don't think it's worth much.'

'Will you now make a complaint against Ally?'

'Of course not. He'd be round here faster than a brick through a window.'

'We can protect you.'

Another laugh, longer and louder this time, which ended with a withering look and a, 'Fuck off.' And then, 'Why are you here?'

'You know about Ally playing computer games?'

'What?'

'The others say that he plays computer games a lot.'

'Don't all men? Isn't that one of your things?'

'No.'

She shrugged.

'So, does that mean Kieran played computer games?'

'Of course.'

'Which ones?'

'Seriously? This is about computer games?'

Buchan didn't reply, she shook her head disdainfully, then said, 'FIFA. That's what it's called, in't it? The football one. There was some golf thing, but he was shite at it, so he didn't play it much. And there was some fantasy shite. Ally likes that one 'n all.'

She pretended to yawn.

'Can I see his console, and the games he had?' asked Buchan, aware he was stepping into unknown territory. He knew nothing of computer games.

A shrug, a finger pointed at the TV unit.

'Fill your boots. Don't nick any of them, though, eh, I might have to sell those to pay the heating.'

*

He called it in when he got to the car. He spoke to Dawkins, but asked her to drop everything and get looking at the game. *The Lost Temple of Arcadia* might have come out of nowhere, but it was exactly what they were after, and they'd found it because they'd gone looking for it.

'Feels right,' he said to the empty car, when he'd hung up, and was already accelerating out of town.

51

'I don't think the setting of the game itself is of much interest,' said Dawkins. The five of them were in the ops room. 'A typical fantasy realm, with the usual suspects. Dragons and golems and various monsters, elves and dwarves, majestic castles, dungeons, keeps and holds, and big armies and orcs and the full panoply of fantasy paraphernalia. But there's a character called Lorde. That's, you know, Lorde with an *e* like the singer.' Buchan stared blankly. Marks nodded in recognition. 'Lorde is a demon hunter from the family Anuyron. The etymology of this name doesn't appear to be significant, it's just a creation from within the game. His coat of arms contains, and this is why we're here, the jackal, the raven, the butterfly, the snake. Beyond that, the coat of arms is not referenced within the game, as far as I can see. So, this is pretty obscure. And, I should say, this is an obscure game to start with. It's still there to be downloaded online, but it was a one-off from seven years ago, it obviously bombed, and there were no updates, no reissues, no sequels. This is so arcane, I thought it might be bordering on the coincidence. But then, in there somewhere, there's a character named Baylock, and there are characters named Thorn, Jennings, Damien et cetera. So, rather than the killer being influenced by *The Omen*, it looks like the creators of this game were influenced by *The Omen*.'

'Dammit,' repeated Buchan.

'Enjoy yourself telling Gilmour,' said Kane.

Buchan let out a long sigh.

'I don't know, let's not... I'm going to leave her great Robin Hood plan where it is for the moment.'

'I take it there could've been interaction between players within the game,' said Marks.

'Sure,' said Dawkins, and then she nodded. 'Maybe there's some connection there.'

'We need to get hold of Ally Nairn,' said Buchan, 'and we need to get his games console and all the information on it. Let's put it in motion.'

'You didn't find him at home?'

'No, and he's not due in work 'til tomorrow. Let's flood the town, and let's get into his house. We need to find this guy, and we need to establish whether Markham or the Craigies played this game.'

'We've already got the Craigies' console downstairs,' said Cherry, 'I'll get down there now.'

'I'll go and speak to Alan Conway,' said Buchan, nodding to himself as he spoke. 'Sam, can you speak to David McKay?' and then, at Kane's obvious temporary name blindness, added, 'Jill Craigie's ex. His music shop was an explosion of posters and ads, music and movies and games. All sorts. See if there's anything for *Arcadia* in there.

'Ellie, Isobel, can you both focus on the game, please? Ellie, keep searching, see if there's anything else of note within the game itself. Isobel, focus on who produced it, who created it. Maybe it failed, and the maker took features and details from it, and put them into something completely different.'

'We're focusing on *Arcadia* because that's what Ally Nairn plays, but it could be the same Lorde character crops up elsewhere,' said Marks, and Buchan nodded.

'Exactly. Let's go, people,' and Buchan, unusually, clapped his hands sharply, once, as he got to his feet.

52

If he hadn't been told that Alan Conway stood in front of a small crowd to play the guitar and sing, Buchan would've wondered if he ever left his position at the kitchen table. Perhaps this was the way with all writers.

'Would it be possible,' said Conway, who much to Buchan's relief appeared to have moved on to a grieving phase that didn't involve sobbing, 'that you people could, I don't know, make a shopping list of questions, and ask them all at once? You're like someone who gets home from the shops and thinks, shit, forgot mayonnaise, then you have to go back, then you get home and you're like, damn, forgot Germoloids, and off you go again, you know what I mean? Can't you just *decide*?'

'Investigations evolve, Mr Conway,' said Buchan.

'Whatever. I've got a deadline, and I've got Fin's folks arriving tomorrow morning. This is not a good time for me, and you keep turning up. You're like long Covid, refusing to go away.'

'You know a game called *The Lost Temple of Arcadia*?'

Conway stared blankly across the table, and straight away Buchan knew he had him. He wasn't sure how, or in what way just yet, but the look in the eyes was not one of ignorance. Conway knew exactly the game he was talking about.

'I'm waiting, Mr Conway.'

Conway looked around the table, as though there might be a mug of tea he could lift.

'You see,' said Buchan, 'this is why we have to go back to the shops to get the mayonnaise, because yesterday we had no idea that this game existed, and today, we do.'

'Fine. Yes, the game exists. What has that got to do with Fin, and why they're dead?'

'Let's start with what it's got to do with you.'

'Is this why you exist, just to come here and remind me of all my failures?'

Buchan kept the look of curiosity from his face. At best he'd been thinking that maybe, just maybe, Fin Markham had played the game.

'In what way does *The Lost Temple of Arcadia* represent one of your failures?'

'Ach.' He made a throwaway gesture, and looked genuinely perturbed by having to talk about it. 'Fuck me, man, I sit here all the time. I'm good at this. I write, you know, I can write anything. Crime, romance, erotica, whatever. Nothing works. Then you get some cretin comes along, writes whatever, and suddenly it's a bestseller, and you're like, how the fuck did that happen, then it turns out they're off the TV, or their mum works in publishing, or they're shagging some agent somewhere. Drives you nuts, man. I've done so much cool stuff, I mean, you know, really inventive, original, funny, unique shit, you know. And here I am, sitting in my terraced house, writing revenge porn. And, according to you, I got my imzadi killed.'

Imzadi.

Hmm, thought Buchan, I'll just let that one go.

Conway wasn't the first writer Buchan had come across in the course of his duties. He had, at some point, said to Roth he hoped it would never happen again. 'Few are quite so self-possessed,' he'd said.

'Does that mean you wrote *The Lost Temple of Arcadia*?'

'Yes! I mean, isn't that why you just brought it up?'

'Tell me about it.'

'Man, it was years ago. Like one of the first writing gigs I got. I'll admit, you know, it was pretty naïve, but they were just looking for like a generic fantasy thing.'

'Did you use references from other movies and shows in there?'

Conway laughed suddenly. That heartfelt grief and sobbing from yesterday didn't last so long, thought Buchan.

'It's full of it. It's all references, and not just fantasy, you know what I mean? It's *Lord of the Rings*, it's *Dune*, it's *The Shining*.' He laughed, strangely. 'It's *Iron Man*, it's *Peter Pan*, it's *Avatar*, it's *Labyrinth*, it's *The Thing*, for crying out loud. It's just what I did, you know.'

'The character known as Lorde…?'

'Yeah. So that guy has sort of dominion over things, you know, he's just a guy, but he's kind of omnipotent at the same time. Uses his powers to hunt demons. I like that. I just stuck an *e* on the end there, like the singer. You know, whatever man, it is what it is. All writers, you know, we all do this. Borrow.'

'That character's coat of arms,' said Buchan, not wishing to lead him too much, but he could tell Conway didn't particularly know where this was going, even though Buchan had previously asked him about the conflation of the four creatures.

Conway was, however, enjoying talking about himself and his work. This, thought Buchan, is a true narcissist in action, the reason Buchan was there disregarded.

'Wait a minute, wait a minute, don't tell me.' He laughed, staring at the ceiling, searching the internal database. 'Writers get this all the time. You know, someone's just come across something, or whatever, and they're like, wow, that thing you wrote, and you're sitting there thinking, I have literally no idea what you're talking about, you know how much stuff I've written since then?'

'Lorde's coat of arms?' said Buchan.

'Right.' He stared off to the side this time, fingers of his right hand tapping the table, then he snapped his fingers. 'Right, right. Dolphin, ... no, no, not dolphin, that was, you know, whatshisname. Damn, what was that guy called?'

'Tell me about Lorde.'

'Right. It was a fairly standard crest, yeah, with four creatures around it. You've got the jackal, the butterfly, the raven and the serpent. Ha. I liked that one, that's a pretty cool creature combo.'

Buchan stared at him coldly, and Conway wilted slightly beneath the stare, not understanding.

'What?'

'The jackal, the butterfly, the raven, the snake,' said Buchan, his voice grim.

A moment, then realisation dawned, another second or two and then Conway started nodding, pointing at Buchan.

'See, that's what I'm talking about, right? I write so much, throw so much stuff out there, I don't remember what I did six months ago never mind way back then. So, yeah, yeah, the jackal, the butterfly, the raven, the snake, fine. I remember.'

'What did they represent?'

'You mean, the creatures?'

'Yes. Had you looked at traditional heraldry, and tied that in to make it character specific?'

Another laugh.

'No way, man. Never had the time for that. I was just like, everything at a hundred miles an hour. To be honest, that was one of those where I signed a three-gig deal, you know. The game launched with the intention there'd be at least two further additions to the series. So that's what you do, you throw a tonne of stuff at the wall, plenty of colour, and then there's a whole lot of shit already there when you want to create further back story. So, like that, the coat of arms, that's like, I don't know, the tailor's dummy. That's the canvas. Then, the next time, you put a bit more colour on it. 'Cept, there was no next time.'

He shrugged. He seemed to come off the high of talking about himself and his work.

'Did you reference *The Omen*?'

He looked a little curious, then he snapped his fingers.

'Damn, I'd forgotten about that. I did, just like character names. Thorn, and, what was the priest called? Brennan, that was it. And Baylock, of course. Man, Mrs Baylock,' and he whistled. 'What a bitch.' He laughed.

'And the jackal?' said Buchan.

He looked a little curiously at him, looked off to the side, and then seemed to realise what he was getting at.

'Right, of course. Like, the kid's mum is a jackal, and I put the jackal in the coat of arms. Yeah, no, that wasn't a thing. I mean, that's just something that happened. Jackals are just good crack, you know? I mean, when it comes down to it, they're just what, like a mean-looking bit of a dog. But poetically, you know, they're potent. The jackal, the coyote, the wolf.'

'Is there anything that ties Fin to the game?'

A shadow across his face, at the conversation being brought back to Fin, and her murder.

'I don't know, why? And, in fact, why are we even talking about *Lost Temple*? I mean, that seems kind of weird.'

'Because the killer has referenced this character. Lorde. And it could be coincidence, except the partner of the first victim is the person who created the Lorde character, and who created the game.'

'Fuck.'

Buchan let it play out in Conway's head for a while, happy to wait and see what emerged on the other side.

Conway swallowed. He blinked. He looked around again for something to drink. He turned back to Buchan.

'Yeah, that was… Right… Right…' Another swallow. More self-confirmation. 'Right, right. Fin Markham was the name of the writer of that. Fin Markham. That was who, you know, that was who I had down there as the writer.'

'You did this seven years ago?'

'It came out seven years ago, so I guess I wrote it like eight years ago.'

'But you'd only been going out with Fin three years.'

'Yes.' He made a couple of gestures, another prop on which to hang a few seconds of stalling, then he finally said, 'Right. Yes. So, I do all sorts of writing, all sorts of genres. It's best when you do that to have different names, you know, so that each name has its own vibe, you know what I mean? My name for fantasy game play writing was going to be Fin Markham. Turned out to be one and done. Then I met Fin, and back then they were known as Becky. You know, their birth name. Going to be awkward as fuck tomorrow, by the way, because their mum and dad still thought they were called Becky, you know.'

'The name?'

'Right. So they were called Becky Markham, and we had a bit of a laugh about me having once used Markham as a pseudonym. Then a couple of years ago, when they realised, you know, they realised they were non-binary, and they're looking around for another name, they went for Fin. They thought that was kind of cute.'

'Except, you then also used it for hard core, revenge porn.'

Conway swallowed.

'Had you or Fin had any contact from anyone in the past few weeks about this game?'

Another long stare across the table. Dammit, thought Buchan, they could've been here three days ago, if only they'd known where to look, or if this guy had been prepared to speak to them properly in the first place.

'There was a guy who got in contact with Fin, asking about it. Asking about *Arcadia*, saying he was obsessed with it. Said, you know, said he realised it was linked to everything that was going on in the world. I mean, the guy sounded utterly mental. Mental. Like, Grade A conspiracy theory level shit. Like, he was playing *Arcadia*, and seeing Russia-Ukraine, and Covid, and Trump and, I mean, like Gaza and the Jews. I mean, the Jews? Seriously, I am not touching that stuff with a stick.'

'How did he find Fin from a name on a game's credits? I mean, are the writers of these games given much credit?'

'You can find the name if you try hard enough, but really, I don't get it. It was weird. But you know, it's the modern world, and if you really want to, you can find anything. He had the name, and Fin was on social media of course.'

'What did she say to him?'

'She?'

Buchan didn't play along.

'*They* didn't say anything,' said Conway, 'they were just like to me, this one's all yours. So I replied to him. Guy was nuts.'

'What was his name?'

'Ally.'

'Just Ally?'

'Aye. No second name. Wasn't sure his name was even Ally, to be honest with you.'

He made a lunatic sign at the side of his head.

'What was your last contact?'

'Couple of weeks ago, man. He was, you know… It got creepy.'

'Tell me.'

Conway shuddered, then tried his best to shake it off.

'The guy found out I wrote erotica, and he was like, you're part of it, man. You're part of this descent into hell, man. This is what *Arcadia*'s all about, but you're encouraging it. You're sending messages. This kind of thing is why society's collapsing. This kind of depravity. Then he was like, you've got to stop writing this stuff. You've got to promise me you'll stop writing it.'

'Did he know by now he was writing to you, or did he think he was still writing to Fin?'

Another swallow, another look around the room. This guy really needs a drink, thought Buchan, even if it is just tea.

'Fin,' he said, his voice small. 'Then he started, you know, he said he wanted to meet, and I'm obviously like, no way, man, and then he was just like getting weird, so I blocked him.'

'I'll need to see all those messages.'

'Gone.'

'You deleted them?'

'Gone, gone, gone,' he said. 'Put them in the bin, cleared the bin. That guy was just a freak, man.'

'You can tell me the address he was writing from, though?'

'Yeah, I can get that, but it was like, you know, some site with unhackable, untraceable, triple-locked shit, man, you know what I mean? Good luck with that. Like I say, that guy was some

Grade A conspiracy theorist.'

'You know the name Devon Craigie?'

'Sure, the other guy, the guy who killed the kid, got murdered on like Monday night. What about him?'

'You ever have contact with him about the game?'

He stared across the table, eyes wide. Buchan recognised the interviewee's thinking face. Finally, he shook his head. 'Nah. To be honest, I never had much contact about *Arcadia*. It's pretty niche, man, you know. In gaming terms, it was a total bust. It was weird to find that guy still played it. So weird. Obviously, you know, you get stuff from people every now and again, but for me, it's so rare I tend to remember it happening, you know. That guy means nothing to me. Why?'

'Just piecing things together,' said Buchan. 'I should leave you to it, but before I go, I'm going to need you to find that e-mail address you blocked, and if there's been any other correspondence from anywhere over the past few weeks and months in relation to *Arcadia*, I'd like to see it.'

'Nah, none of that,' he said, opening his laptop. 'But I'll get you the e-mail.'

53

Sitting in the Facel, heading back to the office, on the phone to Kane.

'Danny's been through the Craigie's games console,' she said, 'but no sign of *The Lost Temple of Arcadia*.'

'Rats,' said Buchan.

'Maybe,' said Kane. 'We'll see. We have the link between the game and the killer, and between the game and Sledd. The Craigies' story was well documented, and the killer would have known all about it, and about them, regardless of the game. It's coming together.'

'You're right,' he said, admonishing himself, 'it is coming together. Do we know if the game's manufacturers are still operating?'

'Already spoken to them. They're based in Preston, not a big company, but they survive. The guy said *Arcadia* was their attempt at the fantasy market, it bombed pretty much straight off the bat, and they killed it. Fewer than two thousand copies sold, and far as they know, he said fewer than fifty current players. Fifty is like their base number. If they know there are forty-nine players online, or there are two players, they both register as fewer than fifty.' She paused, then added, 'Actually, he said less than fifty. I'm auto-correcting.'

'So, there are people who play the game against or with each other online?'

'Yes.'

'And the company can tell who they are?'

'He didn't have that information to hand, and didn't sound like he'd be giving it up without us having the necessary paperwork. But as he said, it's very easy to pretend to be someone else when you're signing up to do anything online, and if someone was on there to be nefarious, they're unlikely to be using their real name.'

'Hmm,' said Buchan.

'We need the connection between the game and Fin Markham.'

'Oh, we have that,' said Buchan.

'We do?'

'Alan Conway wrote the narrative of *The Last Temple of Arcadia*.'

'Jesus, there we are,' said Kane.

'And he'd been getting weird messages from someone called Ally in the last few weeks.'

'Ally Nairn?'

'No second name, but it sounds as though very few people still play this game, and we know Ally Nairn does. Furthermore, like the hard core revenge porn, the storyline was credited to Fin Markham.'

'Holy shit. Are you bringing that guy in?'

'I don't think we need to. He could be lying, of course, but for what it's worth, I believe him. Maybe I should say, I currently believe him. I've got an e-mail address for Ally. He'd been writing to Fin Markham, but it was the actual Fin Markham, who he'd found online, that he'd been writing to. Conway took on the job of chatting to him, ultimately blocking him a couple of weeks ago, when the guy was getting freaky.' A pause, and then he added, 'His word,' since the word *freaky* had sounded so uncomfortable crossing his lips.

'Give me the address, I'll get Danny to check it out.'

'I'll be back in five,' said Buchan, 'I'll do it then. The username is a random series of numbers and letters, and the mail host is some server in the US, that's encrypted a mile up its backside.'

'That would be why I wonder if it's really Ally Nairn. If you're taking that much trouble with your contact details, why use your own name?'

'A good point,' said Buchan, 'but, as we know, people are idiots. Anyway, we need to find this person, whoever they are, and we also need to find out what's happened to Ally Nairn. If the two end up being intersected, all the better,' and Kane agreed, then she said, 'Oh, and there's one more thing,' and Buchan said, 'Go on,' and she said, 'The Record have the story of this great police operation to lure out *The Omen* suspect by showing the movie,' and Buchan said, 'Oh, that's terrific,' and, 'I suppose they got that from an anonymous source,' and Kane laughed.

'Dammit,' muttered Buchan.

'You think the boss did it to spike her own plan?' asked

Kane.

'Might all be part of her thinking,' said Buchan. 'Who knows?'

'She's playing chess while the rest of us are playing checkers,' said Kane.

'Aye, something like that,' said Buchan. 'I'll be back in five,' he added, and hung up.

54

Buchan hadn't stayed long at the office before deciding he wanted to take a look at Ally Nairn's house. He could've asked the local police, or sent one of the others, but this was who he was. He preferred to be out driving in the Facel, talking to people, investigating evidence first hand. 'You're not much of a delegator,' Gilmour had already observed to him.

Buchan, with Kane beside him on the phone to Cherry, pulled into the small estate at the back of the town, buried in between roads and trees in the lee of the hills, no outlook on the water.

'The boss's *Omen* screening will remain in place,' said Kane, hanging up the phone.

'Might as well,' said Buchan. 'She hasn't asked for any of us to go, though, has she?'

'Nope. She's also pretty pissed off.'

Buchan smiled grimly.

'I'll bet she is.'

'Danny said we're being mocked online.'

'Police Scotland can handle being mocked,' said Buchan.

'Gilmour won't be able to be so glib when discussing it with the chief constable.'

'Whatever,' said Buchan, 'It'll serve her right for coming up with a dumb idea. At least they'll likely sell more tickets now.'

'Maybe Ally Nairn'll turn up,' said Kane, with a smile, as Buchan parked outside a row of two-up, two-down terraces.

'I don't think that man has an ounce of Robin Hood's romance or curiosity, but you never know.' He glanced at the house, which remained in the dark, then continued, 'But if he did, what does it prove? This is the problem, or one of the problems, with the idea in the first place. In the Robin Hood story, they knew who they were looking for, and they knew he'd identify himself by his ability. Here, we don't know who we're looking for. So, anyone who shows up, can just shrug and say, so I like *The Omen*, everybody likes *The Omen*. Big deal.'

205

'Unless Ally Nairn really has gone on the run, but comes anyway. In which case, we know who we're looking for, and we find him.'

'I remain sceptical,' said Buchan. 'Come on, let's break in.'

*

Buchan was holding the small container in his hand, standing beside the fridge. Marked on the side, *Canis aureus, seminal fluid, – Oct 2024* . Kane read the label, opened her phone, typed the Latin into Google, nodded, and said, 'Golden jackal, right enough. We'd better hope Mr Nairn turns out as gallus as Robin Hood after all, since he doesn't appear to be at home.'

'This is bullshit, isn't it?' said Buchan. 'The label with the Latin, and the typeface, and it's just the work of some squalid crime gang, dealing in whatever it is the black market needs on any particular day.'

'Hey, without squalid crime gangs we'd be out of a job.'

'Wouldn't that be a disaster.'

The house was empty and cold. Nothing to indicate the last time Nairn had been home. There was no mail lying, although it wasn't as though mail turned up at anyone's door in Scotland every day any more.

One empty mug on a kitchen counter, the teabag dumped in the sink. On the kitchen table, a MacBook. It looked old, well-used. Crumbs on the keyboard, a couple of torn stickers and staining on the rim.

The kitchen was basic, not very clean, but not cluttered. The sitting room, the two bedrooms and the bathroom upstairs the same. Ally Nairn did not have a lot of stuff.

'A life lived on his phone, TV and laptop,' Buchan had said, after they'd completed the rounds.

Beneath the TV they'd found an old PlayStation, and scattered on the floor beneath the white TV unit, and crammed in one of the drawers, somewhere between forty and fifty games. Buried in their midst, the empty box for *The Lost Temple of Arcadia*. The disc was in the console.

'You wouldn't want to get that mixed up with your yogurt,' said Kane, as Buchan returned the jackal semen to the fridge. He paused in the movement, but was half-smiling and shaking his head when he turned back and straightened up.

'Thanks for the image,' he said.

'Sorry, that was just out there before I could stop it. You think this might be a set-up?'

Buchan nodded, then took a moment, looking around the drab kitchen. He'd already had the thought. In reality, he always had the thought. When evidence landed in your lap that was this unambiguous, this conclusive, it almost seemed too easy.

'Our killer's been so on top of everything,' said Kane. 'They've been careful, they've been calculating. First of all, I'm not sure Ally Nairn is that guy. He doesn't give off a careful, calculating vibe. He's a thug. And secondly, having this here, keeping this stuff in his fridge... this would've been here, while I interviewed him in the other room. OK, it's a step from officers sitting in your front room, to them asking to look in your fridge. Nevertheless, given the care he's taken so far, I'm not sure I'm buying this.'

'Dammit,' said Buchan. 'I think you might be right, but let's just work with this for the moment. Set-up, or actual damning evidence, it doesn't really matter. It doesn't change what needs to be done right now. We need the house swept, and we need to find Ally Nairn.'

'Aye,' said Kane.

'I'll get Ruth and her team down here, can you step up the search for Nairn? Time to go public.'

'Boss,' said Kane, and they turned their backs to each other as both started making calls.

55

You started with the person who would most benefit from someone being murdered, while someone else was wrongly implicated in that death.

For a fourth time, Buchan was back talking to Laura Sledd. He'd found her in the kitchen, at the table, drinking a glass of cheap white wine, the half-empty bottle on the table, beside an empty packet of Golden Wonder salt 'n vinegar. The washing machine was going. There was a Bluetooth speaker on one of the counters playing music Buchan didn't recognise. Her phone was on the table, to her right, but there was something about the way she was sitting, the look in her eyes, that said she hadn't just been scrolling endlessly through social media before he'd arrived.

He thought of himself, standing at his window, looking out on the river, listening to Thelonious Monk or Bud Powell. It felt better than this, but didn't it just amount to the same thing? Alone with your thoughts, staring into nothingness. And why was Thelonious Monk any better than whatever this was? No piece of music had any more validity than any other. What did the magnificent complexity of Mahler's 5th mean next to the one billion downloads for a three minute RnB song that was written more or less on the hoof?

Don't judge, he thought, that's all. *Don't judge.*

Nevertheless, he was judging.

'When was the last time you heard from Ally Nairn?' he asked.

She'd offered him a glass of wine, he'd refused. From the look in her eyes, he calculated that this was her first bottle, but it was early enough in the evening, that there would possibly be another.

She took another drink, laid the glass down on the table. She wasn't looking at him. Cheeks puffed up, a breath exhaled through pursed lips.

'He texted us this morning,' she said. 'I was sitting here thinking, do I tell you that? Do I say I haven't heard from him since he came round here on Sunday looking for a shag? And last night 'n all, by the way. Don't know what happened on Monday. Maybe on Monday he thought he should, you know, respect the widow's mourning period. What d'you think? Does that sound like Ally to you?'

'What did he say in the text this morning?'

'You know, Ally likes anal, that's who he is. He always wanted that, and Kieran wouldn't let him. Her arse is mine, that's what he'd say. I think he got that line from a Shakespeare sonnet, don't remember the number. I, in case you're making notes, don't like anal sex so much. Or, in fact, at all. I've never had a say in it before, and, as it turns out after last night, I still don't have a say in it. Good to know where you stand going forward, right?'

'What did Ally say this morning?'

'In the text?'

'Yes.'

She sucked her teeth, her eyes drifted down to her phone. She reached towards it, her fingers lightly tapped it, she nodded to herself, she made her decision. She opened the phone, brought up her text message stream with Ally Nairn, and then turned the phone round so that Buchan could read it.

'You're sure?' said Buchan.

'Go right ahead, officer,' she said. 'For all the good it'll do you.'

Buchan pulled the phone a little closer to him. The last message was from 08:17 that morning.

This isn't going to work.

The previous one, at 08:16 read:

Last night was out of order. I shouldn't be like that prick. Hate myself sometimes.

The only messages prior to that were from early the previous evening. **You at home?** he'd asked, and Sledd had replied, **Ye**.

'You'd never messaged each other before last night?' asked Buchan.

'A bit. He was a funny bastard, sometimes. You know, he was like a total thug 'n that, and every now and again... it'd be like he felt guilty. I mean, I always thought, Ally Nairn, feeling guilty? I don't think so.'

'Did he feel guilty about the other women he'd assaulted?'

'God, aye. I mean, when he stood in front of a jury and was

like that, you know, practically greetin', I mean, I know what youse lot are like, you're looking at that kind of thing, and you're thinking, away and shite, you lying bastard. But there was something about him, you know. Like he was a Jekyll and Hyde character.' She paused, she looked curiously at Buchan. 'Everyone says Jekyll and Hyde, but does anyone even know which one of the two of them was the bad guy?'

'Hyde,' said Buchan.

'Huh. Well, that was him. Sometimes he was Hyde, sometimes he was that other cunt.'

'Tell me about last night?'

'What about it?'

'He texted you to ask if you were in at quarter past six. You replied that you were.'

'He was here by half-six. We had sex through there. And he said, I've got to do this, hen, and, you know... shagged my arse.' She smiled at the wince that briefly passed across Buchan's face at the expression. 'Then he sat there and drank beer, and we played *Arcadia*.'

'You remember I was here this morning?' said Buchan, and she laughed.

'Seems so long ago. Don't know why though, it's not like I've done anything all day.'

'Why didn't you tell me any of this then?'

'Because I didn't want to. You didn't specifically ask, so I didn't say. I mean, mister, I'm not broadcasting the fact the guy's had a go at my arse, am I?'

'How did he seem last night before he left? This morning's text implies regret, self-loathing. Did you get that from him last night?'

She laughed, a small, bitter sound.

'Not so much.'

'You mean, not at all?'

'Pretty much, not at all, aye. So little regret, that he grabbed me and fucked me just before he left 'n all. Left my arse alone that time, so that wasn't so bad.'

'Did you say no?'

She laughed again, then, head shaking, she said, 'Fuck off. I mean, really. You going to be a lawyer for the defence? Did you say 'no,' madam? You didn't? Well, that's the same as saying yes, isn't it, even though the reason you don't say no is because you're *absolutely fucking terrified*.'

She snarled the last three words, passion and anger out of nowhere, and then, contemptuous look intact, she lifted her wine glass and took a much longer drink.

'Maybe you could just fuck off now,' she said. She didn't look at him.

'Have you heard from either of the others?'

A glance, a head shake.

'Reggie called. Asked if everything was OK. I said it was shite, but whatever. He asked if I needed anything, I said I didn't. He asked if I wanted him to come round, I said no.'

She shrugged.

'Jimmy Hardcastle?'

'Radio silence. Not unlike Jimmy.'

'We're going to need to search your house.'

The statement came out of nowhere, seemingly detached to what had gone before, and Laura Sledd looked up sharply, eyes narrowed.

'The fuck are you doing that for?'

'We're investigating your husband's murder, and we need to know if there's evidence in the house that would lead to his killer.'

'Am I a suspect now?'

She sounded genuinely incredulous.

'Not yet,' said Buchan, his voice level. 'But it's apparent that you, more than anyone, would benefit from your husband's death.'

She laughed, then glugged some more wine, draining the glass. She lifted the bottle, poured another large one, filling the glass almost to the top.

'Go on,' she said, 'explain it to me. These magical benefits I'm going to get. My husband beat and raped me when he felt like it. And now, now Ally Nairn is going to beat and rape me when he feels like it. *Spot the difference*.'

Buchan had no answer. A moment, and she shook her head.

'Have you considered, what with you being a detective, that maybe someone who hates Ally might be behind this. Because, as we all know, he's no stranger to taking his fist to a woman's face, is he? All those sexual assaults he's been charged with, you think they're the half of it?'

'You know of others?'

She laughed again.

'There are always others.'

'Have you got names, photographs…?'

She pretended to think about it, looking contemplatively off to the side, then she turned back to him.

'Stupid of me, obviously, but I never managed to keep my Women Ally Raped notebook up-to-date. I'll do better.'

A steady look across the table, then finally she snapped the next silence with a laugh, a head shake, a wave of the hand.

'Fuck it, on you go. I don't know whether you lot need a warrant like you do on TV shows, or whether you can just breenge in and do what the fuck you like, but I've got nothing to hide. Feel free, search away.'

Buchan held her gaze for another moment or two, and then got to his feet, walking through to the sitting room before pulling on a pair of gloves.

His phone rang. Quick check, and he answered the call.

'Sam,' he said.

'We've got Ally Nairn,' said Kane. 'Apparent suicide. You should only be twenty-five minutes away.'

Buchan glanced back into the kitchen, and made his decision.

'I'll wait here for now. Can you arrange for someone to get here as quickly as possible, I don't want to leave her on her own.'

'Roger that.'

They hung up, Buchan slipped the phone into his pocket, and then walked back through to the kitchen. She watched him enter, having listened to Buchan's end of the phone call.

'You don't want to leave me on my own?' she said, mockery in her voice. 'How sweet of you, officer. I'm touched.'

56

A couple of hours later, the day zipping along into evening, dark and damp. Buchan and Kane back in formation with Donoghue in the morgue, the police on one side of the corpse, the pathologist on the other. So far, Donoghue had not taken Buchan up on his idea of listening to music other than the Beatles.

Buchan and Kane waited in silence. Beneath them, the corpse of Ally Nairn laid out on the narrow, white table. Naked. Dark bruising where the noose had bitten into the neck. He had a large tattoo on his right shoulder, the figure of death standing over an empty grave. It had not been particularly well executed. Another on the left hand side, just above the hip, a Confederate flag. On his left thigh, a single red rose. There was an arced box beneath it which would once have contained a woman's name, but it had been blacked out. The love of his life had been redacted.

His face was pale and blue and soft in repose, showing none of the aura of brutality he'd given off in life.

Finally Donoghue lifted a hand, indicating the marks around the neck.

'This is all we've got,' she said. 'He hung himself, now he's dead. I've sent his bloods off to toxicology. The more limited testing I've been able to do here doesn't suggest he was drugged, but there's also a lot of alcohol in his system, so perhaps it's being masked. He certainly wasn't shot with a tranquilizer gun, so there's that, but he could have ingested it. But, like I say, there was a tonne of alcohol, which, as we know, has a way of messing with drug analysis.'

The body had been found in a wood just off the Haylie Brae, a few hundred yards from where the body of Kieran Sledd had been left. Being in the midst of the trees, Ally Nairn had not died looking at the view across the water to Cumbrae.

'Time of death?' asked Kane.

'Late morning, more or less. Broad daylight, but then I don't suppose there are many people about in those woods at that time of day. Or ever, in fact. How'd you find him?'

'Classic dogwalker scenario,' said Kane. 'We had the call out. Someone said they saw him leaving Ardrossan at some time after eight-thirty.'

'He sent a text to Kieran Sledd's wife just before,' said Buchan.

'Was it a suicide note?' asked Donoghue, and there was almost a lightness in her tone, as though the idea amused her.

'It was an expression of regret. In light of him being dead, it could have been a suicide note, but it was far from explicit.'

'Well, we can hope,' said Donoghue. 'And you have evidence connecting him to the previous four murders?'

'Yes.'

Donoghue looked between Buchan and Kane, until they returned the gaze.

'Is it possible we can take this as a win, and move on?'

Buchan didn't reply.

'Can't rule that out,' said Kane, 'but it's early days. We're only a few hours on from starting to treat this guy as a suspect, and now there's a huge weight of evidence.'

'Isn't that just because you know where to look?'

Kane nodded.

Buchan checked his watch.

'OK, thanks, Mary,' he said. 'You'll let us know when you've got all the results back?'

'Of course. Pen it in for tomorrow morning some time. But…'

She sighed heavily, the weight of the job still resting obviously and heavily on her shoulders.

'The man killed himself, Alex, what d'you want from me?'

She looked around the room, she made a gesture to indicate the doors behind which other cadavers were currently being held.

'All we have here is death, and please God let it be this guy who caused the other ones, because I've had enough.'

*

They walked silently out into the night, and then stood for a moment beneath the awning at the entrance of the building, watching the rain fall. The more he saw Donoghue, thought Buchan, the more she infected him with her sense of hopelessness.

'She called you Alex,' said Kane, curiosity in her tone. 'That sounded a little weird.'

Buchan glanced at her, didn't necessarily disagree but could think of nothing to say, and then they walked out into the rain.

57

The last note from the omnipotent killer was waiting for them when they returned to the office, Sgt Atholl, already arrived for night duty, stopping Buchan as he walked through the reception area.

'Inspector,' he said, holding aloft the envelope, and Buchan approached, collected it, said, 'Thanks, Tom,' took the letter, then joined Kane in the elevator.

He didn't immediately open it, as the lift began its steady ascent.

'Hmm,' said Kane, sounding dubious.

'Here comes the suicide note,' said Buchan, 'right on cue.'

She nodded.

'In which the killer expresses how wearisome it is to have power over everything,' said Kane, 'and consequently there's only one option open to him.'

'Right,' said Buchan. 'Not a set-up at all.'

The lift continued.

'Of course,' said Kane, as the doors opened and they walked on through to the open-plan, 'this clown Ally Nairn might well have thought he was one of the good guys, might well have thought he was a force for decency in the world, and at some point he realised, dammit, I'm as bad as everyone else.'

Buchan smiled wryly, head shaking.

'We can hope,' he said.

*

'Nice job,' said Gilmour.

Buchan was standing by the window of Gilmour's office, the river at night below him. He turned, hands in pockets.

The letter was on her desk. Short, wistful, talking of ending a quest as though he was finally giving up on a forty-year mission to cure cancer.

I am tired. I do not know why I was afflicted with this curse, but it is the end of me.

I hope I have brought a little light into the world before passing. I hope I have assailed hate and division. With those deaths, the killer Craigie and his wife the facilitator, the abuser Sledd, and Markham, that wretched writer of filth, perhaps at least one small shadow passes from this world. That shadow has, alas, now taken me.

You wore me down, inspector. Victory is yours.

'I'm not so sure we did anything.'

'I think he likely recognised you were closing in. You'd identified this ridiculous game he was so obsessed with, he realised you'd started making connections, he knew the game was up.'

'There's no way he was aware of all the connections we'd started to make.'

'He clearly got a hint of something, and he knew at least that you'd worked out the connection with the game. He likely was as aware as anyone of how few people still played it. He knew his arrest would be forthcoming, he needed to get out, he got out.'

'I'm not convinced he's the kind of guy who commits suicide,' said Buchan.

Gilmour was watching him, leaning forward, forearms resting on the desk.

'His message to Mrs Sledd this morning expresses regret. It sounds like the kind of thing someone would say when they've gone down a path they know they shouldn't have done. When they've lost control.'

'I know,' said Buchan, 'and I don't believe it. I don't believe this is the guy.'

'What's the alternative?'

'The wife's involved. Either she, or perhaps one of the others, is setting him up. The killer has been meticulous, they have been careful, they have been extremely well-organised. This guy had the evidence in his own fridge.'

'Even evil people make dumb mistakes sometimes, inspector.'

Buchan shook his head.

'Not this,' he said. 'The dumb stuff happens when you're in a rush, or something unexpected happens, or you're under pressure. This is very, very basic level planning. Those are the times you don't make dumb mistakes.'

'OK, I'll flip that,' she said. 'Let's say it's all some

wonderful, Machiavellian set-up, then whoever's doing it has, so far, been meticulous and careful and extremely well-organised. In that case, why leave such an obvious, ham-fisted piece of evidence that instantly makes us doubt everything we've been doing?'

'I don't know,' said Buchan.

'Well, exactly, inspector. You've thought it through, you have all that information to hand, and you don't know. I suggest that's because there is no rational explanation. So, either Nairn was careless, or the people who set him up were careless. Why are we pursuing the less obvious, more complicated option? Why can't it be as it appears? This guy lived in a game simulation, he crossed too much of a line between fantasy and reality, his brain couldn't handle it, he snapped.' She snapped her fingers. 'There's one bad guy fewer in the world for us to worry about. I'd take the win if I were you.'

Buchan stared across the short distance of the office, fingers running across his forehead.

'In case you're interested, I haven't cancelled *The Omen* showing this evening, regardless, but I've stood down all our staff. It all seems kind of pointless now, particularly since it's been revealed that it's a secret police plot. That pissed me off, by the way, and I wouldn't mind you finding out who did it.'

'I'll see what I can do, ma'am.'

'The way people are talking about it online, you'd think it was a ruse to trap innocent bystanders in a building and gas them, rather than, you know, catch a multiple murderer – but, whatever, that's how these things go.'

'You don't think it's worth having someone there?' said Buchan.

'Curious, inspector,' she said with a smile, 'given that you didn't seem to think it worth having someone there prior to us identifying the killer, and him committing suicide to avoid capture.'

Buchan nodded.

'I guess so,' he said.

She leaned a little further into the table.

'You can go home now,' she said. 'And make sure your team goes home.'

'I think it's only Isobel left, if she's not already gone.'

'Good. It's been a bad couple of years in this place, inspector, and I think it's left you seeing shadows. We got our man. Disappointing that he denied us the win in the end, but it's over. Go home, relax, come back in the morning and start the job of clearing up the mess.'

Then, when he didn't immediately move, she nodded in the direction of the door.

'Good night, inspector.'

58

Buchan went home and changed, rummaging through the drawers for the kind of clothes that had been sitting at the bottom, unworn for several years.

Jeans, T-shirt, a sweatshirt with a logo for the New England Patriots. Janey had bought it for him maybe twelve years previously, back in the days when they'd done things for each other. She'd bought him sweatshirts he hadn't wanted, and he'd worn them to show willing.

In the drawer beside the bed a pair of glasses with plain lenses, which he hadn't worn as any sort of disguise in several years. He put them on, dug out the maroon beanie he kept in the cupboard in the utility room, and looked at himself in the mirror.

DI Buchan stared back at him, except now he was wearing dark-rimmed glasses and a beanie.

'Bugger it,' he thought, 'it's enough.'

He checked the time, then walked through to the sitting room. Forty-five minutes before the showing of *The Omen* at the Filmhouse, a fifteen-minute walk away.

He went to the kitchen, poured himself a glass of neat gin from the freezer, downed it in one as he looked across the open-plan at Edelman watching him from the sofa, and then he turned away, and walked quickly to the door.

*

Buchan had been dismissive of the Robin Hood idea from the first time Gilmour had mentioned it, and yet, as it had got nearer, he'd begun to think it worthwhile.

He didn't believe for a moment that the writer of the letters, the killer – should he still be alive – would turn up at the showing of *The Omen* because they were so keen to see the movie in the cinema. He did, however, believe the killer would be amused by the idea that the police were trying to trap him. He liked that the Record had used the Robin Hood line when reporting the story. It gave it a frivolity he thought might pique the killer's interest, while giving the police a Keystone Cops air that most people would be happy to believe.

Anyone who actually thought of themselves as omnipotent, or perhaps was just enjoying the idea of pretending to be, might well be lured to a cinema to see what was going on. They would stop short of actually going in – because that would leave them vulnerable to being locked inside – but they would pass by. They might even linger, curious to see the level of police presence.

The fact that there wasn't going to be a police presence was good, thought Buchan. The killer might think the police had been called off because the suspect had committed suicide, but he would still wonder which of the cinema goers, loiterers in the street, and homeless huddled in sleeping bags in doorways, were actually surveillance officers.

The cinema was at the top end of Milsum Street. Buchan approached from the bottom, coming slowly up the hill. The streets were still damp, but the lights of the night no longer picked out raindrops in the air, the evening turning milder than it had been during the day. Now that he was here, approaching the small queue outside the cinema, he had a sense of anticipation which he'd only briefly felt previously as the details of *The Lost Temple of Arcadia* had unfolded.

The cinema had been asked to open the doors not too long before the official start time, so that there'd be a queue building in advance, collecting all the cinemagoers in one place. As he approached, Buchan could see there were also a few people from the press embracing the story, interviewing members of the public, regardless of how the murder investigation had played out that afternoon. Perhaps the fact that the showing hadn't been cancelled was persuading some in the media that the police still had something invested in the evening.

He could see the small billboard stating that the event was sold out, and he wondered how many tickets they'd sold at the last minute based on the possibility of seeing a police manhunt in action.

As well as the cinema queue, there were a few people lingering outside a bar across the street, others approaching from either end of Milsum. Buchan hadn't been sure how he'd handle this when he got here. Standing still would make him obvious, as would walking back and forth past the cinema queue. He'd thought he might be best just to join the queue, however, the bar, and those standing outside, presented him with an opportunity.

Scanning as many faces as he could as he crossed the road, he nipped quickly into the bar. To the left, a vacated table, a couple of drinks left unfinished, and he lifted a near-empty pint glass, then casually stepped outside, as though he was one of the small crowd, gathered to watch events unfold. He was aware as he did so, that whoever he was here to try to identify, might well be doing the same thing.

He stood with the glass in his hand, looking around the crowd. A woman with blond hair, a man in a beanie, a man in a hoodie, a woman in a raincoat. Nameless and faceless characters, everyman and everywoman, passers-by on any street in any city.

He felt obvious, despite standing on the edge of a small group of people more or less doing the same thing as he was, though with curiosity, rather than intent.

He took out his phone as cover. Flicked open the news. Stared blankly at it for a few moments. Glanced up, got eyes on any new faces that had entered the scene from stage left in the previous few moments. Back to his phone. Opened messages, wrote a short text to Roth.

Outside the cinema for The Omen. Killer yet to arrive.

He had a flippancy with Roth that he'd never had before in life. Sometimes it still felt strange to him.

'I've been saying since we were in League Two, man,' said the guy standing next to him. Talking to his friend, not Buchan. 'Got to bring the youth through, it's the only way now, man. The only people we can afford to buy are pish. See our wage bill...'

Buchan tried to tune out.

What was his gut instinct telling him? Did he think he was looking for a man or a woman? It had felt like the work of a man all along, and yet, at some point he'd begun to wonder if Laura Sledd might be the one who'd conceived this elaborate plot in order to get rid of her husband, and if not her, possibly some other woman. Those murdered had been – as far as the killer was aware – the writer of sadistic, misogynistic porn, a wife beater, child killers, and now the suicide of a man guilty of sexual assault. Why wouldn't there be a queue of women thinking these people had got exactly what they deserved?

Sorry to be that guy, but BE CAREFUL!

He smiled.

Isn't your killer dead anyway??

He looked around the crowd. Movement at the door of the

cinema as they prepared to open up. He watched the queue, but remained convinced that if his quarry was here, they wouldn't be going in.

A woman in a dull maroon hoodie walked along the opposite pavement, skirting the crowd, possibly aiming to join the back of the queue. Had he seen that hoodie already? And the scarf pulled over the lower half of the face was noticeable too. It really wasn't that cold.

He typed a quick reply.

I've got a feeling.

He watched the woman in the hoodie for a couple of moments, then looked back through the queue.

'Nothing's going to happen,' said the guy standing next to him.

'Movie's shite anyway,' said the other guy.

In the queue there was a guy with his head down, looking at his phone. Near the front. Buchan hadn't got a good look at the face yet. Another one to keep an eye on, to see if he stepped away at the last minute.

'Want another drink?'

The other guy laughed.

Uh-oh!

'You've been standing here for twenty minutes. You cannae walk off now when something might be about to happen.'

'Nothing's happening!'

'I know! But if it is, it'll be in the next two minutes.'

Not like your gut instinct ever gets you into trouble. Oh wait!

Another glance to the side, to the small crowd outside the pub, watching the cinema queue. A guy with long hair and glasses, head down, looking at his phone. He glanced up, drawn by the feel of someone's eyes upon him, and he and Buchan stared at each other for a second, before he turned away. Buchan hadn't recognised him.

The doors were open, the queue was starting to move.

'Still no sign of the cops,' said the guy next to him.

'Undercover, mate.'

'Like the dickhead in the Celtic top.'

The other guy laughed.

What's happening?

He felt the eyes of the long-haired man on him, and he

223

turned to the side again, just as the man looked back at his phone. A moment, then back to the queue. The man near the front who'd been looking at his phone was gone. Inside, presumably.

He typed a reply.

Nothing yet.

A look to the left and the right. Still too many people loitering, either waiting to join the rear of the queue, or here for the possibility of spectacle.

'Total damp squibaroonie, mate. I'm going to the bar.'

The woman in the maroon hoodie had turned back. The scarf still pulled over her face. In the night, he didn't recognise the eyes, but something inside him clicked.

Take your time. Nothing rushed. Don't let her see you coming.

He looked to his left. The guy with long hair was gone. He scanned the road beyond, glanced back into what he could see of the bar.

Nothing.

Dammit.

'Same again?'

'Aye.'

The queue had diminished quickly, having not been so long in the first place. People were still filing in, the crowd outside the bar starting to thin as some of them crossed the road.

He saw the long-haired guy, just as he entered the cinema.

A look to his right. The woman in the maroon hoodie walking on, not looking back.

This was where his gut instinct was taking him.

The guy next to him turned away, walking back into the bar.

Buchan kept his eyes on the woman, waiting for her to turn. She was walking slowly, taking glances to the left and the right.

'Just like fucking Scotland, eh, man? Just when you think something's going to happen, you get fuck all.'

Buchan turned. The guy was sort of looking at him, but wasn't actually looking for a discussion. Buchan made the appropriate face in agreement.

His phone pinged again.

I'll leave you to it. Let me know how it plays. x

He replied with a thumbs up and put the phone back in his pocket.

He looked up. His eyes fell on the woman in the maroon hoodie. Fifty yards away. Head turned, looking straight at him.

A second. Another.

Then she turned and ran.

59

Buchan thrust the glass into the hands of the nearest customer, and took off in pursuit, aware of the loud laugh and cry of, 'Fuck me!' from behind, followed by, 'Fucking Billy, get out here!'

She was round the top of Milsum Street onto Renfrew Street.

This is why he'd had the trainers all these years, he thought grimly.

He got to the end of the road, round the corner, thinking ahead, where she was likely to go.

Renfrew was quiet, and she was about fifty yards away. Head down, not looking over her shoulder, sprinting full-pelt.

She crossed Cambridge at pace, a car horn blared, then passed in between her and Buchan. He slowed slightly as he reached the junction, then sped up across the road, receiving a loud blare from a car that was still some way away and whose progress he had not impeded at all.

She took a right at Hope Street.

Did she know where she was going? She must. She wouldn't have come here without an escape route.

She flew across the next junction on a green pedestrian light, Buchan now closer, crossing just as the light changed to red.

He felt the stitch arrive, tried to take a deep breath. A cry of, 'Get tae fuck!' from someone she nearly ran into, and then a, 'Jesus,' from the guy as Buchan hared past him.

She glanced over her shoulder, the scarf now fallen from her face. A look that said she hadn't expected Buchan to be so close.

She turned back, nearly ran into a small group, out on to the road to bypass them, but they scattered for Buchan, and he gained another couple of yards.

A red pedestrian light straight ahead. She wasn't slowing. Buchan within fifteen or twenty yards.

She came to the corner, didn't stop. Full pelt across the road.

A dark blue BMW X6 hit her square on, and she flew into the air, her body spiralling up and out of control. A squeal of tyres, a strangled cry, a shout of, 'Fuck!' from somewhere, the car screeching to a halt, the sound mingled with the dull crump of the body thudding brutally into the road.

A SEAT Leon noisily braked behind, its nose stopping a couple of feet from the woman's head.

Buchan, pulling up sharply, still ran into the side of the BMW, then he pushed himself off, and ran over to where the body lay in the road.

Belatedly, running up behind, those who'd followed the chase from Milsum Street.

Buchan bent down beside her, wariness cast aside. She had landed head first. Her skull was crushed on that side. Blood was spreading. Her body, below the neck, lay at a curious angle, her legs lying strangely. Her clothes were starting to dampen, though the red of the blood did not show in the light of the streetlamps.

As a matter of course, Buchan reached out and rested his fingers softly against her neck.

'She dead?' said a voice from above him.

'I called it in, mate,' said another.

'Fuck was that about? She nick your wallet?'

Buchan looked up to the side. There was a woman there, beige coat, face ashen, staring at the scene from several yards away. The driver.

'There's nothing you could've done,' said Buchan.

Only then did he realise he should be out of breath, and suddenly he felt the burn in his lungs, and he stood up, turned away from the corpse, and leant forward, taking great gulps of air.

'You gonnae throw up, man?'

60

Thirty-seven minutes later. Buchan and Kane still at the scene. The body of Rachel Randall, the butcher, had been covered, but was yet to be moved. For once they were at the scene of a death and hadn't had to call Donoghue. This wasn't a crime scene. An accident scene, no more than that.

'Danny should be calling shortly,' said Kane.

Buchan was agitated. People run from the police for all sorts of reasons. It didn't make sense that she would run for any reason other than the one he was presuming – that she'd been behind the *Arcadia* game murders – but sense often enough didn't enter into it. People did what they thought they needed to at any given time, good sense be damned.

'She ran when she saw you, right?' said Kane. 'It wasn't like you went after her, and she panicked and thought, crap, this'll be because I haven't returned my library book.'

'She was staring at me, probably trying to work out if I was who she thought. Then our eyes met, a moment...' He snapped his fingers. 'She ran.'

'She's guilty,' said Kane. 'I mean, I have no idea why she ran instead of just ballsing it out, but I'd guess she knows she's a lousy liar. She can pretend to be something, to play the game, get close to the investigation to see what kinds of questions we were asking, but actually confronted and accused. She'll have thought, he's knows why I'm here, and he's waiting for me.'

'We'll see,' said Buchan.

'Why'd you come, anyway? Did you suspect she'd be here? If you suspected, you should've lined a few more of us up, regardless of what the boss was saying.'

'As we'd talked about, the whole thing with Nairn felt off, that's all. I thought I'd come along. No idea she'd be here.' A moment, he looked around the scene. Still some way short of normality being restored, but they were readying to remove the body, and the BMW had already been moved. 'I thought maybe it would be Laura Sledd. Maybe one of the other two, setting up Nairn, then when the dust had settled, they'd disappear off into the sunset with Laura. Had my money on Reggie.'

'You never said.'

'Didn't have anything to go on.'

Kane's phone rang at the same time as a ping on Buchan's phone, and they turned away from each other.

A text from Roth.

Sure you don't want me to come home?

He typed the quick reply.

It's good. I'll call when I get in. Shouldn't be too long.

Slipped the phone back into his pocket.

Kane was still on the call, but wasn't saying much. The paramedics were moving Randall's body onto the stretcher. There was still a crowd, but much less of one than there would've been earlier in the day. Buchan had been looking around the faces, just as he'd been doing outside the cinema, as though there might be another player in the drama. Someone else to arouse suspicion, who could then run off on being spotted, like he was stuck in a loop of high intensity, unnecessary drama.

'You can relax.'

He turned to Kane, feeling like he'd allowed his thoughts to drift off for a length of time he couldn't quite fathom. Randall's covered body was now on a stretcher, on a trolley, being wheeled towards the ambulance.

Buchan silently asked the question. He didn't feel relaxed.

'Randall's flat is an exhibition of evidence. Bit of a mess, by the sounds of it. But there are blood-stained clothes, yet to be washed, stuck in the machine. There are notebooks which are a basic catalogue of information about the people she killed, and others she'd thought about killing. No jackal semen, but then it does look like she'd given that up as evidence. He said the place is like how we'd've expected Nairn's place to look, if it hadn't just been a set-up. And, naturally, we've got her computer, and once we're in there…'

Buchan looked at his watch, nodding to himself.

'OK, let's get over there. I'm not going to call Ruth's team this evening. We'll check it out, then lock it down for the night.' Another look at his watch. 'We'll all be back in the office in nine hours anyway.'

'K,' said Kane. 'I'll just have a word with…,' and she scanned the crowd, found the officer she was looking for, pointed in her direction, and then walked away from Buchan.

61

One-seventeen in the morning. Sitting at the kitchen table with a glass of gin, Roth lying in bed, on the other end of Facetime.

'Isobel observed that her notebooks were like the ones an author might keep,' said Buchan. 'Apparently. Isobel seems to know about authors.'

'All the best detective constables do,' said Roth.

She'd insisted Buchan call when he got home, though she'd been asleep by the time her phone had rung.

'Randall had planned out the whole game. The deaths around Scotland she'd researched, which she'd clearly had had nothing to do with. She'd obviously studied a lot more than four, but had decided that was enough. Then there were the notes to me, and then victims she chose. We haven't got to her motivation yet, but it'll come.'

'You've got her computer?'

'Yep. At the very least, we know she knew all about Kieran Sledd and his unpleasant band of friends.'

'How did she know about them?'

'Far as we can tell, it was this *Arcadia* game. It all comes through that.'

'You don't see the hand of Alan Conway in it?'

'I don't think we do. As ever, a lot of unravelling to do, but we'll see how it plays out, starting tomorrow. I'll need to get down to Ardrossan and speak to Laura Sledd, take it from there.'

They looked at each other in the night, Buchan realising he felt as tired as Roth looked.

'You recovered from your run yet?' asked Roth, with a small smile.

'I've torn my Achilles, at least one groin muscle, and three or four hamstrings,' said Buchan, to Roth's laughter. 'Think I'm going to miss the rest of the season.'

He lifted the glass, drained it, set it back on the table, and then rested his chin in the palm of his hand.

'I'm home tomorrow evening, remember,' she said.

'Your department's got a thing on Friday,' said Buchan,

and she nodded.

'I'll give you a massage,' she said, and he smiled, then she said, 'You look exhausted.'

'Yes,' said Buchan. 'You too. You've got Renaissance literature at eight-thirty?'

'I do. And I expect you'll be at work long before that.'

He nodded. The need to go to bed, and the good night, and the affection, were exchanged with a look, then Buchan held aloft a hand, Roth blew a silent kiss, and the phone went dead.

62

Buchan rang the doorbell at two minutes past nine. He hadn't called ahead. He stood in silence facing the door, his back turned on the still, grey day and the drab houses of the estate.

He heard movement, the creak of a floorboard, then the door was opened. Laura Sledd, looking tired and sad, wearing a dressing gown over a pair of faded pyjamas, a cup of tea in hand.

'What?' she said.

'I need to ask you some more questions.'

'Ally not dead enough for you?'

'Ally was murdered.'

For a moment, her expression did not change, and then she couldn't stop the small eyeroll, she left the door open, and walked back through the house.

The radio was playing in the kitchen. Classical music, not so loud. Sledd was already sitting at the kitchen table by the time Buchan entered.

'You want tea or coffee or something?'

'I'm OK, thanks.'

'I've got gin.'

Buchan smiled an acknowledgement of her glib delivery, as he pulled a seat out at the table.

'How are you doing?' he asked.

'Best day of my life. What d'you want?'

He reached into his coat pocket and produced the photograph of Rachel Randall, placing it on the table. Sledd was nodding before Buchan had asked the question.

'You recognise this woman?'

'That's Mandy. She came here a couple of times.'

'Mandy?'

'Aye. Never knew her second name.'

'Why was she here?'

'That stupid game, you know? She loved it just as much as Kieran and Ally. That's the trouble with the modern world. All the crazies find each other. They form gangs of crazies, and their craziness is multiplied.'

The music finished, a woman started talking. Buchan, temporarily distracted, listened for a moment, then said, 'Radio 3?' and Sledd said, 'Aye. My dad thought he could better himself by having Radio 3 on in the morning. I grew up listening to this before school. Didn't stop him getting locked up for beating the shit out of mum, but he could tell the difference between Mozart and Handel.'

'She was here?' he asked.

'Mandy?'

'Yes.'

'Aye. Ally brought her along. They'd met 'cause of the game. Went out a couple of times.'

'What happened?'

'He treated her the way he treated all women. She didn't like it. That was that.'

'Did he assault her?'

'Sure.'

'How'd you know?'

'She came to talk to us. She was wondering what to do, you know? She was going to go to the polis – like that makes the slightest difference to anything – then she spoke to me. I told her he'd been tried six times for rape and sexual assault, been found guilty three times, and had done zero prison time. But aye, on you go hen, see what the polis'll do for you.'

'Did you tell her about the way Kieran treated you?'

She stared grimly across the table, then lifted the mug and took a drink. Held the mug at her lips, took another drink. Her eyes had dropped by the time she set the mug down.

'Saw it with her own eyes. One night, might've been a Friday, might've been a Saturday, I don't remember. Think they fancied a bit of an orgy, having two women in one place. That was about as unpleasant a sexual experience as you can imagine.'

'That was the last time you saw her?'

'She came here to talk to us a few weeks later. Ally had started getting brutal, and she said about going to the polis. I laughed at her. Said, aye, good luck with that, hen. She left.'

'But you went to the police.'

'It was a few months later. Nosey cow next door stuck her oar in, the police came to me. The lassie, the police sergeant, she played me like a kipper, and before you know it, I'm telling her everything and Kieran got nicked. My lawyer went looking for Mandy, see if she'd be a witness, but he couldn't find her. He reckoned she didn't want to be found. He presumed she'd made herself scarce so Ally couldn't go giving her hassle. Cannae blame her.'

'Did she ever mention Fin Markham to you?'

'That first lassie to get killed? Nah. I hadn't heard that name before.'

'It was the name of the person who wrote *The Lost Temple of Arcadia*.'

'Oh, OK, well aye, she mentioned her all right. Didn't say the name.' She laughed. Dry, rueful. 'Aye, she hated that bitch. Said she'd loved that *Arcadia* crap so much, she'd gone looking for other things she'd written, and the only thing she'd found was sadistic abuse porn. Basically, men being cunts to women. She hated that, you know? She was like, the fuck are you doing encouraging them? They don't need any encouragement! That was her thing, you know. She hated women who enabled violent men. She hated women standing back and saying, don't upset them it'll make them worse, or you know, they're men, they are who they are, or they're men, they have different rules.'

Buchan decided not to enlighten her about Alan Conway's part in the process or, indeed, Markham's lack of a part.

'What about Devon Craigie?' he asked instead.

A moment, her brain working at not-long-out-of-bed levels, then she nodded. 'Aye, him she mentioned. Think he'd not long been arrested at the time. She was fizzing about that. I remember that, she was like, see if that bastard gets let off... She was a right live wire. She was wee though, so you know, men could take advantage, but she had a temper on her. Good luck to her. You know where she is, by the way? What's she got to do with this pish?'

'Far as we can tell, all this is her doing.'

Sledd looked curiously across the table, her lips slightly parted.

'The fuck?'

'She took her revenge on Kieran and Ally by killing Kieran, framing Ally, then killing him. The story she wove to cover her tracks was elaborate, detailed, well-constructed, and it involved making sure Devon Craigie got what she thought was coming to him as well.'

'Well, would you look at that. Wee Mandy killed Kieran.

I'll have to buy her a pint.' Then she let out a small, dry laugh. 'Typical she also got Craigie's missus, eh? Taking out the handmaiden. It was her kid he killed 'n all. Unbelievable.'

Buchan thought about Rachel Randall, lying dead on the street, her body disfigured, her head crushed by the weight of the fall.

'Think I might come and speak in her defence,' said Sledd, and she laughed.

'She's dead.'

The humourless laugh died on her face, and she looked crestfallen.

'Oh. Well, that's disappointing. Who got her?'

'She was knocked down running away from the police,' said Buchan, the slight disingenuousness of the words sticking in his throat.

'Too bad,' said Sledd. 'Well, at least Reggie and Jimmy can sleep more easily, eh, they must've been wondering if they were next on the list.'

'No,' said Buchan. 'She'd done what she was going to do.'

'How'd you know?'

'Because she faked Ally Nairn's suicide, having planted the evidence he was the killer.'

She nodded, made a small gesture to indicate her own forgetfulness.

'Aye, right.'

They stared at each other across the table, as Sibelius' Karelia Suite played on the radio. Sledd lifted the mug, looked into it, placed it back on the table without taking a drink.

'What now?' she said.

'I'm going to need to take a full statement, start to finish, all your dealings with Rachel Randall.'

'The fuck's Rachel Randall?'

Buchan tapped the photograph.

'Huh, not Mandy, then?'

'She used that name in the game. Likely never told Ally it wasn't her real name.'

'Well, good for her.'

Buchan took his phone from his pocket, and placed it on the table.

'You OK if we record this?'

'Fuck me. Whatever. If we're going to do this, I'm going to need something stronger.'

'Maybe you could wait.'

'I meant coffee,' she said, her voice snarky, and then she went to the kettle, checked the water, and turned it on.

63

Paperwork and interviews, a day like any other. Everything they'd learned confirmed the story, with Rachel Randall's e-mails, phone messages and bank transactions providing all the evidence they needed. The killer was dead, the story was done, all that was left was the dotting of the i's.

'You're a funny bastard,' said DCI Gilmour.

Buchan was in position, standing by the window of her office. Late in the working day, evening having already arrived on this bleak Thursday in October.

'I don't usually get funny,' he said drily.

'You know I mean strange, rather than funny,' she said. 'You hated *The Omen* idea all along, even I'd given up on it, and along you went nevertheless.'

He didn't reply. She had not, after all, asked a question.

'Had you actually liked it all along, or was there something specific that changed your mind?'

'The leaking of the police plan changed the ball game.'

'Why?'

'Because I don't think she would've been interested before that. Having found out the police were behind it, she had the hubris, or at least the insatiable curiosity, to see what was going on. She was never going to actually enter the cinema, but she had to take a look at least.'

Gilmour stared at him, mind working, then she nodded, as she sat back in the chair.

'It was you who leaked it to the press,' she said.

'Yes,' said Buchan.

Another long stare, this time ending with a small head shake.

'Well, you were right not to tell me at the time.'

'I know.'

'What can I say? I was thinking last night, well look at that, my plan came off. But you know, that didn't feel right. It wasn't my plan after all, and I knew there'd be something else. So… well done, inspector.'

There was a *thank you* on his lips, but it never emerged.

'You think you'd have got her if she hadn't turned up last night?'

Good question, thought Buchan.

'Been thinking about that, though not too much. That we got her is really all that matters. But yes, I think we would, eventually. She slipped up with the Nairn suicide. She tried to mask the drug with alcohol, but hadn't quite got her levels right. By this morning, we had the blood results that proved the suicide was faked. Even without last night, we would be looking far more in-depth at Ally Nairn, and who might've wanted to kill him, implicating him in multiple murder along the way. There would've been a lot of candidates, but given that Randall had been to see Laura Sledd, and had been coerced into sex with Kieran Sledd and the rest of them, and of course she played the *Arcadia* game, her name would've come up, and we'd've got an ID soon enough. It was coming.'

She leaned forward now, elbows on the table, hands together.

'How's it going today, you getting everything you need?'

'It's falling into place. Nothing so far to contradict the narrative we've constructed, and there's nothing in Randall's communications and paperwork to suggest she had a partner in crime. She was the lone killer, she tried to set up Ally Nairn, she's dead.'

'There will be plenty who regard her as a hero,' said Gilmour.

'Yes.'

Buchan felt a certain ambivalence about that himself, but that was the kind of thing that had to remain buried while you did the job.

'I won't say it live on television,' said Gilmour, 'but perhaps we got the best result. There'll be no trial, with hordes of protestors outside demanding she be acquitted for having carried out a public service.'

'I don't think that ever applied to Fin Markham, though, did it?' said Buchan.

'Good point, though protestors rarely let nuance get in the way of shouting at authority.' She paused, obviously thought through whether there was anything else that needed to be discussed, then said, 'Right, inspector, Daniel and I have a date this evening in Edinburgh, and I'm leaving. I suggest you do not work much longer. Go home, have a nice evening. That's good work from you and the team, thank you.'

He nodded, he tried to think of something to say, finally, 'Have a nice evening,' came into his head, and then he turned away and left the office.

*

Roth and Edelman were waiting for him when he got home just after eight o'clock. Bottle of white wine opened on the kitchen table, the smell of mushrooms and butter and onions and garlic in the air.

She greeted him, arms around his neck, forehead pressed against his, and then a long kiss. Her lips tasted of wine.

Edelman approached once they'd parted, and Buchan bent to pat the cat's head.

'You're happy now, eh?' he said, and Edelman did not reply.

'Fifteen minutes,' said Roth, and Buchan walked through to the bedroom. He got undressed, splitting the clothes between dumping them on the bed or in the wash basket, and then he walked naked into the bathroom and turned on the shower.

He looked at himself in the mirror, and not for the first time wondered what it was Roth saw in him.

'Yours is not to reason why,' he said quietly to himself, then he stepped into the shower, his head beneath the water, the warmth cascading over his body.

A minute later, the bathroom door opened.

Roth, already undressed. She stepped into the shower, she smiled softly.

'Dinner can wait,' she said.

Printed in Great Britain
by Amazon